BLOOD LURE

A JOHN JORDAN MYSTERY THRILLER BOOK 23

MICHAEL LISTER

ISBN:

Ebook: 978-1-947606-56-2

Paperback: 978-1-947606-54-8

Hardback: 978-1-947606-55-5

Books by Michael Lister

(John Jordan Novels)
Power in the Blood
Blood of the Lamb
Flesh and Blood
(Special Introduction by Margaret Coel)
The Body and the Blood
Double Exposure
Blood Sacrifice
Rivers to Blood
Burnt Offerings
Innocent Blood
(Special Introduction by Michael Connelly)
Separation Anxiety
Blood Money
Blood Moon
Thunder Beach
Blood Cries
A Certain Retribution
Blood Oath
Blood Work
Cold Blood
Blood Betrayal
Blood Shot

Blood Ties
Blood Stone
Blood Trail
Bloodshed
Blue Blood
And the Sea Became Blood
The Blood-Dimmed Tide
Blood and Sand
A John Jordan Christmas

(Jimmy Riley Novels)
The Girl Who Said Goodbye
The Girl in the Grave
The Girl at the End of the Long Dark Night
The Girl Who Cried Blood Tears
The Girl Who Blew Up the World

(Merrick McKnight / Reggie Summers Novels)
Thunder Beach
A Certain Retribution
Blood Oath
Blood Shot

(Remington James Novels)
Double Exposure
(includes intro by Michael Connelly)
Separation Anxiety
Blood Shot

(Sam Michaels / Daniel Davis Novels)
Burnt Offerings
Blood Oath
Cold Blood
Blood Shot

(Love Stories)
Carrie's Gift

(Short Story Collections)

North Florida Noir
Florida Heat Wave
Delta Blues
Another Quiet Night in Desperation

(The Meaning Series)
<u>Meaning Every Moment</u>
<u>The Meaning of Life in Movies</u>

.

For my son, Micah Levi Lister, on the occasion of his 25th birthday.

I'm so very proud of the man you are, so very inspired and challenged by the man you're becoming.

Happy Birthday! I love you!!

THE JOHN JORDAN SERIES ON AUDIOBOOK

The entire John Jordan series is being produced on high quality audiobook. Start listening to these thrilling productions today. For more information and samples go to www. MichaelLister.com

BLOOD LURE

CASE SUMMARY

On Sunday, September 28, 2014, Naomi Newman and Sasha Grande go hiking in the North Florida river swamps close to the Apalachicola River, and are never seen alive again.

The two young women, both in their early twenties, had arrived in the small town of Pottersville on Thursday, September 25, 2014, to volunteer at a wilderness camp for at-risk kids, but had mistakenly arrived a week early.

With little to do and even less to do it with, the two young women filled their days with free or inexpensive activities— most of which were set up by the host family they were staying with.

During the three days before they went missing, Naomi and Sasha accompanied a group of high school girls to a beach volleyball game, attended a backwoods bonfire, kayaked around the Dead Lakes, sang karaoke at the Oasis, rode horses around Cape San Blas, attended a high school football game, and went fishing in the Chipola River.

Though their host family mother, Robbie Gaines, had set up an ecotour for them on Monday, the two young women ventured into the swamp on their own on Sunday with their host family's dog, Biscuit, and only a few supplies.

No one knows exactly why Naomi and Sasha didn't wait until Monday to enter the treacherous swamp with a guide, but most people speculate that their plan had been to go a short way in, take some pictures, and be back before dark.

When Biscuit returned just before dark without the girls, the Gaineses notified the sheriff's department, and a multi-agency search-and-rescue operation began.

The unsuccessful search went on for several days before being halted on Friday, October 3rd because of the landfall of Tropical Storm Fritz, then resumed on Sunday, October 5th.

On Friday, November 21st, Naomi's blue backpack was discovered by an elderly lady fishing with a cane pole from the banks of the Apalachicola River near Potter Landing, some twelve miles from where Naomi and Sasha were last seen. Inside were Naomi's Canon SX270 HS camera and her Samsung Galaxy, Sasha's iPhone, two bathing suit tops, a partially empty bottle of water, a compass, and seventeen dollars—all dry, packed neatly, and in good condition.

The young women's phones showed numerous 911 call attempts from devices that had no service, beginning just hours after they ventured into the swamp and lasting nearly ten days with several intervals of inactivity throughout. The phone data reveals the young women's desperation and despair, but it's the photographs on the camera's memory card that documents their nightmarish descent into darkness and death—and may even reveal a murderer.

A few weeks later, on Wednesday, December 10th, the first of the young women's bones began turning up in various locations. Some of the scattered bones still had flesh on them while others appeared to be almost bleached. A sneaker with a foot still in it was also discovered, which was later identified as belonging to Sasha.

Shifting from a search-and-rescue operation to a suspicious death investigation, Sheriff Jack Jordan worked with several agencies, including the Florida Fish and Wildlife Conservation Commission and the Florida Department of Law Enforcement, but was unable to conclusively determine whether the contradictory evidence pointed to foul play or death by misadventure.

1

"Have you read the case file?" Dad asks.

"Started it," I say.

I'm driving him back from a doctor's appointment. We are in his truck, the Naomi Newman and Sasha Grande case file on the console between us. I had begun looking over it in the waiting room while Dad met with Dr. Brown.

Dr. Raymond Brown, Pottersville's only doctor and our family's GP for decades now, first diagnosed Dad's CLL a few years back and has been overseeing his treatment ever since.

Chronic lymphocytic leukemia, or CLL, is a not uncommon condition for a man in the winter of his life, and Dad had been responding well to treatment—at least until recently when he decided to stop it.

Inexplicably to me, my brother Jake, and Dad's wife Verna, Dad has continued his lifestyle changes of diet and exercise but has stopped undergoing the treatments that seem to be working.

Unwilling to discuss his decision in any detail, he has only said that he has been feeling worse lately and whether it's the

CCL or the side effects of the medication, it comes to the same thing, so he's stopping the meds.

"What'd Doc say?" I ask.

"What he always does—that I seem to be doing okay, but in spite of that I should get back on the meds. What do you make of the case?"

"I'm not far enough in to have formed very many strong opinions," I say. "Always try to resist doing that until I get through the file. But can already see the competing narratives emerging and how either might be true."

He nods. "I went back and forth," he says. "Most of the time I thought it was just a tragic accident, but there was enough that didn't add up that kept me open to the possibility that somebody killed them. That's why I never closed the case. But . . . eventually we reached a point where without somebody comin' forward or the discovery of additional evidence, there was nothing else we could do. Ultimately, I came down on the side of accidental death and just figured we'd never know for sure. All cases have questions that don't get answered. This one just had more than most."

"So what's changed?"

"In some ways nothing," he says. "There's no new evidence or anything like that, but . . ."

He doesn't say anything right away, and I wait.

On either side of the rural North Florida highway we're traveling, like missing teeth in a crooked, decaying smile, huge swaths of muddy fields create gaping holes where once had been pristine planted pine forests.

Resembling an apocalyptic wasteland, jagged stumps and upturned root systems rise out of a seemingly boundaryless bog between enormous piles of rotting timber. On the parcels where there are actually still standing trees, they are mostly saplings leaning in random directions. Remnants and reminders of Hurricane Michael's obliteration of our region.

"Time is running out," he says eventually. "At least for me. There are a handful of cases I was never able to clear or maybe got wrong . . . that I'd like to get some kind of resolution on before I . . . While I still can."

I nod and try not to think of how little time I have left with him.

"There's actually another case I wanted us to look at together before this one, but . . . Now this one has to be first."

"Why's that?"

"It's been getting a lot of attention lately," he said. "Evidently there's a . . . some sort of true crime renaissance is going on."

"Definitely is," I say.

I have been approached by several journalists and producers to be interviewed about cases I've worked over the years.

Though true crime books and TV shows have long enjoyed a certain consistent popularity, the advent of true crime podcasting, beginning with the massively popular hit show *Serial*, has created an explosion of true crime content and interest in it. And it's not just podcasts—more and more books and documentaries, in both TV and feature film format, are being produced. This has led to the advent of citizen sleuths, online communities, groups and forums, infinitely long Reddit threads with an infinite number of rabbit holes to dive into, and, of course, the continuous search for greater and greater amounts of content to meet the demand of insatiable true crime consumers.

"It's been the subject of several shows," he says, "those pod things on your phone."

From what I can tell already, this case has all the elements that true crime podcast listeners love—attractive young women victims, an unsolved case with seemingly contradictory evidence that leads to endless theorizing, plenty that is bizarre and inexplicable, and cellphone and photographic evidence that can be poured over and speculated on for hours on endless end.

"Ben Brooks's book about it came out not too long ago and now Netflix is making a movie based on it. They're already here filming. Everyone is second-guessing everything I did and trying to make me look like a smalltime hick sheriff who couldn't find his own asshole with two hands and a flashlight. It's humiliating and not how I want to go out."

I understand what he's saying and how he feels. He served the people of this county for decades with honor and integrity and doesn't deserve to be belittled or only known for a potentially unsolvable case. But I also know that as much as we would like to, we can't control what people think or believe— even or especially if the truth is on our side.

"They're saying I didn't really search for the girls like I should have, that I didn't adequately investigate their deaths, that my department's work was sloppy and maybe even corrupt, and that at best I'm inept and at worst I'm crooked."

People are going to believe what they want to, but that doesn't mean we leave misinformation out there unchecked and unchallenged. We counter false claims with the truth— even if for the relatively few who are openminded and reasonable.

"They're claiming I closed the case, that I ruled their deaths accidental, that I didn't care, that I didn't do my job. None of that's true. If I missed something, I want us to find it. If the case is solvable, I want us to solve it. And I want us to do it now— before the documentary comes out and while I still can."

2

"I'm scared to leave," Anna says.

I have a certain amount of trepidation about that myself.

We are in our bed in our cool, dim room, the only illumination coming from the nightlight in the bathroom and the LED meters on the baby monitor. The only sounds are those of the box fan in the corner and our breathing—mine and Anna's in the room, Johanna and Taylor's on the monitor.

I'm lying on my back. Anna is partially draped over me, her head on my shoulder.

There's a good reason Anna's imminent departure is causing both of us above-average spoken and unspoken anxiety.

We are still trying to find our footing after an emotionally tumultuous time, and any equilibrium we've found has a fragility and vulnerability that was never there before.

It began as a sudden and sweeping and extreme change in Anna's moods and personality and continued with various health issues—during which time nearly everything Anna directed my way ranged from disgust to contempt. Eventually she was diagnosed with hypothyroidism or underactive thyroid disease disorder. Evidently, it's common in women Anna's age, but hers is an extreme case. Her thyroid gland isn't producing enough thyroid hormone, and though she has been on a daily dose of synthetic thyroid hormone for a while now, she still struggles.

The onset of her condition coincided with the abduction of our daughter, Taylor, which unmoored our family all the more.

"We're just getting back to some semblance of us," she says, "and I'm afraid of losing it again."

"I know," I say. "I am too."

In the morning, Anna leaves for a week-long meditation retreat in Colorado, and unless there is an emergency, we will have no contact during that time. It's something she's wanted to do for quite a while now, and we both believe it will be beneficial, not only for her ongoing spiritual development but in healing from the physical and psychological trauma she has endured recently.

I'm taking the week off from my job as a Gulf County sheriff's investigator to keep Taylor and her big sister Johanna, who is with us because it's her spring break. Being off will also allow me the flexibility and focus I need to assist Dad with the cold case he's reinvestigating.

"Should I not go?" she says.

"No, I think you should," I say.

I believe she is afraid as much of being so far away and so out of touch with the outside world as she is about the precarious nature of our current connection.

"I know the distance and isolation are daunting," I say, "but everything will be fine here. I'm going to take good care of the girls and we'll be here waiting for you, wanting to hear all about it when you get back."

"I've never been away from them for this long," she says. "At least not Taylor."

"She'll be fine," I said. "We all will be. And she'll be safe. I promise."

"I told you I don't blame you for what happened," she says.

She had initially blamed me when Taylor was abducted while I was working a child abduction case, and though it was prior to her diagnosis and treatment and she had attempted to take it back several times since, I still continually felt the need to reassure her of my commitment to keeping the girls safe.

"You really don't need to worry about anything," I say. "Just go and get all you can out of it. Our family is fine—and will be while you're gone and when you get back."

"I think I'll just go another time," she says. "Later when things are better and not so . . ."

"You can do that if you want to," I say, "but there might not be a better time. Everything is already arranged. You're all registered and ready to go. You've got your work taken care of. Your flights are booked. I've taken time off and set everything up with Verna to help with the girls. I think you're just scared and if you push past it you'll be glad you did, but it's totally up to you."

Atypically for her, Anna has on a nightgown and is under the covers, and though I've expressed my admiration and appreciation for her body in countless ways—even more excessively recently—I know she is sensitive and self-conscious about the small weight gain and slight puffiness caused by her malfunctioning thyroid or the medication to treat it or both.

I caress her arm and pull her into me even more and tell her again how much I love her and how beautiful I think she is.

"Love you more," she says. "And you're sweet—because I'm a big fat cow."

"Anna, you're a goddess. You couldn't be more beautiful or desirable."

She squeezes me and we kiss.

A mostly comfortable moment of silence follows, during

which I mostly keep the barking dogs of worry and dread and anxiety at bay.

"Do you think we're going to make it?" she asks.

"You and me?"

Until just recently I would have found the question absurd.

"Yeah."

"I do."

"Really?"

"I'm not going *anywhere*," I say.

Those aren't just words, not just an attempt at reassurance. They are as true as any utterance to ever pass my lips. I am certain of what I am saying. I'm not going anywhere. What I am far less certain of now, what I can no longer know for sure, is if the same is true of her.

"But—"

"Which means I'll be here waiting for you when you get back from your life-changing retreat."

3

"Your dad is a sort of hero to me," Ben Brooks is saying. "I thought he was a god when I was a kid. When I was a stupid teenager, he saved my ass and kept me out of trouble I deserved to be in. And long before there was much to recommend me, he gave me my first job in law enforcement. I have nothing but respect and admiration for him and I'd never do anything to belittle or embarrass him."

Everything about Big Ben Brooks is big—from his size sixteen boots to his bushy dark blond beard. He stands over six and a half feet tall and has enormous arms and thick, meaty hands. Beneath his short, coarse hair and bushy eyebrows, his kind blue eyes and wide mouth are nearly always smiling. And despite his height, muscular arms, and huge frame, there's a softness about him—particularly at his center where his sloping belly presses hard against the buttons of his shirt.

"I know that, Ben," I say, "so it makes me wonder why you're saying it."

We are standing near his FWC truck on a dirt road in early morning, the day fresh, the world still waking up. I was returning from a tearful goodbye with Anna at the airport when Ben called and asked if just the two of us could meet. As we spoke, we realized we weren't far away from one another, so he suggested we pull off the highway onto the old fish hatchery road and talk now.

It's late February, less than five full months since Hurricane Michael decimated the region, and the air is crisp and cool, our noses and cheeks splashed with splotches of red.

Dad and Verna are at our house, where they've been since just before Anna and I left for the airport, listening out for the girls who are still asleep in their beds.

"Have you read the book I wrote about the case?"

About a year ago Ben published a true crime book, *Lost Innocents: the strange disappearance and death of Naomi Newman and Sasha Grande,* with a small independent press out of Jacksonville. As far as I can tell, the book has exceeded both Ben's and the publisher's expectations and has led to numerous interviews of and appearances by Ben in both mainstream and social media since then. And the Netflix docudrama being made about the case is not only based on his book but he's going to be featured prominently in it.

"Not yet," I say. "I just got it. Plan to start it tonight."

"I lay out everything—what we know about Naomi and Sasha, their disappearance, our search for them, and the investigation that followed. I go through all the theories—both for accidental death and foul play—and though I think I am pretty evenhanded, it's fairly clear that I come down on the side of foul play. But even though that goes against the conclusion your dad drew and even though I believe mistakes were made in both the search and the investigation, I am nothing but respectful and I readily acknowledge that we can't know for certain what happened and that I could be wrong."

Referred to as Gentle Ben as often as Big Ben, he is soft spoken and humble—and has a settled, mature wisdom that few young men in their midtwenties do. Because Ben is so big and somewhat oafish and awkward, most people fail to perceive how intelligent he is.

"I'm glad to hear that," I say, "but nothing about it surprises me."

I wonder again what his point in telling me all this is, but don't ask a second time, figuring he'll get to it in his own lumbering bear-like time.

"I'm not an investigator," he says. "Not really."

Ben has been everything from an ecotour guide to a deputy for my dad to a wildlife officer with the Florida Fish and Wildlife Conservation Commission—the position he currently holds.

"But I've devoted nearly every waking non-working hour to this case for years," he continues. "The book and the movie deal have given me some options and opportunities and I'm seriously considering doing this full time. Looking into other cases and writing and maybe podcasting about them. But I love my job, *love* helping take care of our diverse ecosystem and wildlife. And it'd be a big step."

"Which is the only kind you take," I say.

He laughs. "Big, slow steps like a sleepy old bear," he says. "I know what a great investigator you are. I've watched you work and I've read and listened to some of your cases. I'd really like your opinion on my book—and not just the book itself but of my investigation. I'd feel a lot better about taking the leap if you think I have the investigative goods."

"Not sure how useful they'll be, but I'll be happy to give you my thoughts once I finish the book."

"Ah, thanks, man. I'd really appreciate that."

"Is that why you wanted to talk to me alone?" I ask.

"Oh, no. Sorry, man, I got sidetracked. No, I wanted you to know where I was coming from and the approach I took in the book because . . . I get the sense that the filmmakers are taking a different approach. Won't know for sure until it comes out, but . . . from what I can gather I think they're going to come down far more definitively on the side of foul play than I did. Which in itself isn't a big deal, but I'm pretty sure that as a part of doing that they're going to paint your dad and his department as inept or corrupt. I didn't realize this, but when a production company buys the rights to your book, they can do anything they want to with it, change it in any way they see fit. Did you know that? They could just keep the title if they wanted and do something entirely different. Hell, they don't even have to keep the title. It's crazy. They interviewed me extensively for it and they asked for my input and I've told them your dad's not inept or corrupt—but I've been warned that the director goes for the most drama he can manufacture, makes everything as sensational as possible. I didn't know any of this. Hell, I just found out this guy used to be a porn director. I feel horrible about it all. I guess I was just so dang happy to have my book optioned that I didn't ask enough questions."

"Is it too late to back out?" I ask.

He nods. "Way too late. I asked the agent who brokered the deal. Not only can I not take back the book, they've already shot my interview and I can't even stop them from using it. And this is the scary part—they can cut it together however they like. They can take out all the positive things I said about your dad and his department, but even if they don't do that . . . just the way they juxtapose the reenactments or other content with my interview can make a huge difference."

I nod and think about all he's said.

"I'm so sorry man," he says. "I didn't mean for any of this to happen. And it's possible that it won't be as bad as I think. It may all turn out fine, but I don't have a good feeling."

"I appreciate that," I say. "And I really appreciate you telling me, but . . . why're you telling me and not Dad?"

"I plan to," he says, "though the thought of it makes me shudder. I told you first for two reasons really. The first is I hoped you might help me tell your dad or at least be there when I do. But the main reason is . . . I wondered if you might help me reinvestigate it. If we could figure out for sure whether it was misadventure or homicide—or better yet, if it *was* homicide, if we could prove who did it—then the filmmakers would be forced to tell the truth."

4

I find Dad asleep on the couch in our living room, a copy of the case file spread open across his chest.

His eyes open as I sit down in the chair not far from him.

"Must've dozed off," he says.

"Didn't mean to wake you," I say.

"Glad you did," he says, gathering the file and sitting up. "Gives us a chance to talk. Verna took the girls for a walk. What did Ben say?"

I tell him.

"That's good of him," he says. "Bein' reasonable and respectful even in his disagreement."

"He admits he could be wrong," I say. "He's no more certain than you are. Just comes down on the side of foul play and thinks it needs to be investigated further."

"Well, I'm hoping you can tell me what else can be investigated," he says, "'cause I haven't knowingly left any stone unturned."

It's far more likely that a second look at the case will uncover additional information or lead to connections not made during the initial investigation rather than find a line of inquiry ignored or neglected.

"Was just rereading over everything," he is saying. "I defy anyone to say it's cut and dried one way or the other. Every single entry in the file raises more questions."

"Such as?"

"Why'd they go into the swamp alone to begin with? Why not wait for the guide scheduled for the next day—or at least take a local who was familiar with that part of the swamp?"

"What else?"

"What happened to them initially? Did they just get lost or was it something else? Did one or both of them get injured? Did they get attacked—by an animal or a person? We know they tried to reach 911within just a few hours of being out there but didn't have signal. Why? What happened? So much went on for so long after that, but that started it all, and may be the key to understanding everything else."

"I agree."

"Also want to know how they got separated from Biscuit," he says. "The Gaineses say that he's never left anyone in the woods before, so why did he this time?"

I nod and encourage him to continue.

"I want to understand everything done with the phones and camera," he says. "Why they called when they did. Why they stopped for a while. Why they started again. How they got locked out and why they couldn't get back in. Why did they take the pictures they took? Why so many of total darkness? What are the objects in some of them? How did they stay alive so long? Why couldn't the search parties find them? Why was Naomi's backpack found where it was, with the contents it had, in the condition it was in? Why were their remains found where they were? Why did some still have flesh on them while others looked bleached clean? Why did Sasha's appear to have been more scattered than Naomi's?"

The door opens and Verna, Johanna, and Taylor come in talking and laughing.

"That's not even close to all the questions, but ..." Dad says.

"It's enough to get started," I say, "so let's see if we can't find some answers to go with them."

5

J ay and Robbie Gaines live with a pack of untamed foster kids in a cypress house they built themselves on the edge of a section of river swamp known as Cottonmouth Creek. Their unpainted home resembles a found wood gingerbread house still in the process of being completed, though they've been in it for going on twenty years. Their muddy yard is littered with old vehicles, abandoned boats, bee boxes, downed trees and random stacks of firewood, discarded appliances, all sorts of incomplete projects, and the outdoor toys of wild, barefoot boys—bent-frame bicycles dropped in the dirt, netless basketball goals, their rims drooping and backboards missing, rusting go-carts that obviously don't run, and a plethora of small mud-covered plastic toys that were never intended for the outdoors.

The number of foster kids, nearly almost always boys, living with the Gaineses varies. At the moment they have six between the ages of six and seventeen. Besides the boys, the Gaineses have a biological daughter who, though in her early twenties, doesn't attend school or have a job and still lives at home.

Certain people in and around Pottersville have intimated

that they believe the Gaineses only take in foster kids for the money, but over the years I have observed them to exhibit genuine fondness and affection for these lost little boys.

The Gaineses had been the host home for Naomi and Sasha when they disappeared, and I'm here to talk to Robbie, Jay, and the kids about them—and as I do I wonder what the two young women thought when they pulled up in the front yard and saw this place and its occupants.

"They seemed like good girls," Robbie is saying.

Robbie and I are in two weathered wooden rockers on the porch while Jay tinkers with a motor hanging from an oak tree on a chain and four of the six boys run around the yard playing, yelling, and roughhousing.

Robbie is in her midforties but looks much older. Her hair is straight '80s, long and black and teased and sprayed until it stands up like she does for the national anthem—the bumper sticker on her ancient, boxy, big black Cadillac reads "I stand for the flag and kneel at the cross." Her skin is dull and has a grayish pallor and the deep, dark craters beneath her tired eyes seem to be cascading down onto her cheeks like an avalanche of fatigue.

"They were here to volunteer at the wilderness camp—how many young women do something like that? They were sort of wide-eyed and naive, wanting to do good in the world, make a difference. Think that's why Big Ben named his book *Lost Innocents*. They really were. They were young and cute and kind of sassy too. My Meagan worshiped them and my Dylan crushed on them hard."

I start to say something, but she stops me.

"You know, actually, the truth is Naomi was more sweet and naive and Sasha was more sexy and sassy. Naomi was sort of pale and a little homely if I'm being honest, but Sasha . . . she was mixed—had the most beautiful caramel skin. She was a knockout. We've fostered a bunch of mixed kids over the years. They're always the most striking and beautiful. Guess it's God making up for all the other challenges they face."

I think about her perspective, which must be exclusively the rural racists' Deep South.

"There was a mix-up and they arrived about a week early," she says. "Mr. Maurice was sort of mean about it—really surprised me. But I told him and them they were more than welcome to come on and stay here with us early. We were happy to have them. It's our Christian duty to offer anything we can to anyone in need."

I nodded. "That was very good of you."

"It was nothing," she says. "I didn't have their room ready, so they had to bunk in with Meagan, but they didn't seem to mind. They were grateful to have a place to stay. I felt bad for them. They were looking at a week of being stuck in this small town with nothing to do, so I started lining up activities for them. And I'm'a tell you—they were game for anything. 'Course, that shouldn't be a surprise—girls who'll leave the city and come to the swamp to volunteer at a wilderness camp for troubled kids."

Just off the far end of the porch, a yard dog of indeterminate breed contorts to scratch the back of his head just behind his ear with extremely long nails, then nestles back down into the dirt to enjoy the direct sun.

"I was just telling Jay how glad I was that before those poor children met their awful end I was able to give them some incredible experiences. In that short time they really packed a lot in and had a great time."

"You had set up for them to take an ecotour of the swamp and the river on Monday, hadn't you?" I ask.

She nods.

"So why did they go into the swamp on their own on Sunday?"

She frowns and shrugs. "I have no idea," she says. "I was still at church when they left. I wish to God they hadn't have."

"Was anyone here when they left?"

"Technically Meagan and Dylan."

"*Technically*?" I ask.

"When the kids reach a certain age, I don't make them go to church anymore. Meagan and Dylan were here but they were both asleep."

"I understand a dog accompanied them," I say.

She nods at the blondish-buckskin yard dog lying in the sun. "Biscuit did."

"Do you know if they took him—"

"That's what I'm saying," she says. "They—"

"Or if he just followed them?"

"Oh. Well, let's see. No, I don't know for—wait. Yeah. They must've taken him because when he came back without them, he was dragging his leash behind him. No one's ever asked that before. Is that important?"

I shrug. "Have no idea," I say. "Which makes everything important."

Jay joins us on the porch, wiping grease from his hands on a soiled and frayed rag.

"John," he says as he nods to me.

"How's it going, Jay?"

"Oh, can't complain."

He's a small man with a sparse beard and longish, straight, stringy blond hair, most of which is in a ponytail, and, like his wife's hair, it's obvious he cuts it himself.

He sits on the arm of her rocker, continuing to wipe his hands.

"What was your impression of Naomi and Sasha?" I ask.

"They were good girls," he said. "*Good girls*. Broke my damn heart what happened to them. Sorry for the language, Miss Robbie."

"If there's ever a time for it . . ." she says.

"Just keep askin' myself what we could've done differently," he says.

Robbie nods. "Still haunts us. But no matter how much I think about it, I can't really think of anything else we could've done—'cept skip church that day and stay here with them and either told them not to go or gone with them."

"I was just asking Robbie—" I say to Jay. "Do *you* know why they went into the swamp by themselves that day instead of waiting for the guided tour the next day?"

He frowns and shakes his head. "Always figured they just went to take some pictures. Way they were dressed and what they took—no supplies to speak of and all—I don't think they intended to go far. But they went far enough to get turned around or run into some kind of trouble. It's easy as mess to get lost out there. Grown men who grew up going in there and who know it better than anyone still get turned around. At a certain point it all looks the same and you can wander around in circles forever."

I nod, knowing the truth of what he's saying, having experienced it myself on many occasions.

With Jay on the porch with us, the four wild boys in the yard are even louder and more rambunctious than before. They argue and fuss and fight their way from rusted abandoned item to rusted abandoned item like little ADD lost boys on speed. As if normal, accepted behavior, neither Robbie nor Jay ever say anything or even acknowledge them no matter how raucous, violent, or destructive they become.

"You probably know this particular area of the swamp as well as anyone," I say. "I mean, it's your backyard and you spend a lot of time in it, don't you? So when you say they could've run into trouble, what's most likely where they went?"

"Well," he says, narrowing his eyes and rubbing the stubble beneath his beard with his thumbnail, "let's see. Gettin' hurt or injured—the swamp floor is slick as snot on ice. It's real easy to slip and fall, sprain an ankle or even break a bone depending on what you land on. Your feet go out from underneath you and you fall back hard on a cypress knee, give you a concussion if you whack the back of your head, or if it's pointy enough and you hit it on the right spot it can stab you like a spear."

I think about it and encourage him to go on.

Above us the river breeze ripples the four flags on the skinny, leaning pole and causes their rigging to clang softly. The four flags, all frayed and sun-faded, declare who the Gaineses are and what they stand for. From top to bottom, the banners the Gaineses live under are the red, white and blue American flag, the white, blue and red Christian flag, the yellow and black Don't Tread on Me flag, and a red and white Make America Great Again flag.

"They could've been bitten or stung by something poisonous," he is saying. "They don't call it Cottonmouth Creek for nothin'. Swamp's full of 'em. Not to mention all the spiders. It's so easy to walk right into their webs without even seeing them. And lots of times there's a bunch of them in one web. They drop on you and start stinging you . . . doesn't take long. Then there's all the wicked hornets or yellowjacket nests. You get attacked by one of them and . . . you don't even have to be allergic for it to kill you. And I'm not sayin' that even if any of this happened it did kill them, but it could've incapacitated them so they couldn't do what they needed to . . . to get out."

"We've seen it happen," Robbie says. "To more than one of our boys. If Jay hadn't been with them and known what to do . . ."

"Animal coulda got 'em," Jay says. "Wild boar or a bear. A gator. Again, wouldn't have to kill 'em. Just injure them so they couldn't get out. Then there's the swampers. It's easier than you think to run into bad men back in there doin' things they'd kill to keep secret. Drugs a'course, but other stuff too. They come across somebody buryin' a body or raping a—raping someone . . . All that said . . . I don't think that's what happened."

"Yeah," Robbie says, "I know there's certain evidence for it, but the chances of it being murder are just so, so low."

"Low is not zero," I say.

"That's what Ben's always sayin'."

"It's funny," Jay says, "well, not funny, but . . . interesting. I'm makin' the swamp sound so dangerous and it is, but I guarantee it's a million times safer than certain parts of the city they came from."

"No doubt about it," Robbie says. "All the godlessness and debauchery, overrun with Muslims and illegals, crime and drugs."

A generation ago, Jay's and Robbie's parents were probably expressing the same sentiments about the big bad city, only the enemies they were programmed to fear and hate in their "Us versus Them" paradigm had different names and faces.

"I just wish we'd'a started the search the moment ol' Biscuit showed up," Jay says. "Probably wouldn't've made a difference, but it might have and now we'll never know."

"Why didn't you?" I ask.

"Figured they were right behind him," he says. "Called the sheriff's department a little while later when we saw they weren't, but instead of waiting here for everyone to arrive—sheriff, search and rescue, FWC—I shoulda lit out into them woods and seen if I coulda found them myself."

"Easy to second-guess everything now," Robbie says. "That's what all those people on the internet are doin', and I get it. I agree the search should've started that night instead of the next morning. To me that was the biggest mistake of the whole ordeal. But . . . everyone just thought they were lost and we'd find them the next day. Like I said . . . easy to second-guess now. Wouldn't wish this on anyone . . . but sometimes I just wish some of those loudmouths online could be in the position we all were."

"I know you said Meagan and Dylan were asleep when Naomi and Sasha left," I say, "but I understand they spent a lot of time with them in the days before this happened and I'd still like to speak with them."

"We can certainly appreciate that," Robbie says, "but we've gone over it and over it with them and they just don't have anything to add to what we all already know. It's been so traumatic on them as it is, so we're just trying to keep them out of it at this point. Hope as a dad you can understand that."

6

"What'd you make of the Gaineses?"

I'm playing at the park with Johanna and Taylor when Ben stops by.

We are standing not far from each other behind the swings. I'm pushing Taylor and he's pushing Johanna.

"They seem to really care for the girls and feel terrible for what happened to them."

He nods. "I think they're genuinely caring people."

"Higher," Taylor says. "Wanna go higher."

Perhaps overly careful and cautious, I never push her as high as she'd like to go.

"Okay," I say, and act as if I'm pushing her higher.

"I've never suspected them," he says. "There are a lot of people online who do. But most of the people who post online just throw out a theory without even the hint of evidence to suggest that it might be true."

I nod. "I've noticed that. The more outrageous and bizarre the theory, the more people chime in on it. And none of them seem to care that they are talking about real people whose lives can be ruined by their baseless accusations."

"Let's go climb the monkey bars," Johanna says, and jumps out of her swing.

"Yeah," Taylor says, and tries to do what her big sister just did.

I grab the swing with one hand and her arm with the other and help her make a smooth transition to the ground.

I follow them over to the geodome-like jungle gym and Big Ben follows me.

Though neither girl shares both a mom and a dad, I'm always struck at how alike they look—and not just because of their common physical features, big brown eyes and light brown hair, but because of the similarities of their expressions and mannerisms.

"Hold on tight with your hands in case your feet slip," I say to the girls as they climb with more reckless abandon than I'd like.

I move around the rim of the jungle gym trying to stay near them in case they slip or fall—especially Taylor, who is convinced she can do everything her older sister can.

"I never suspected Jay or Robbie," Ben says. "But I can't say the same about Meagan or Dylan."

I turn and look at him, my eyebrows arched.

"Not necessarily of having something to do with Naomi and Sasha's deaths, but of knowing more than they've said. It's not the kind of thing I'd put in my book or post online or even say publicly, but I figured I'd mention it to you."

I nod. "The fact that they were home when Naomi and Sasha left made me want to talk to them," I say.

"Exactly," he says. "I don't buy that they were both still asleep. And I don't buy that the girls would go without them. They had been inseparable before then. And sure, Meagan's their daughter so I'm sure they would never even think to suspect her, but Dylan is a troubled foster kid they adopted. He's been in all kinds of trouble, some of it pretty violent. But none of that means anything and isn't nearly as suspicious as the way Jay and Robbie—especially Robbie—won't let anyone talk to them. I wanted to interview them for my book—and not just about the day they went missing but all the time they spent together before then—and though they initially said I could, they kept making excuses for why they couldn't do it and eventually when I was at my deadline and really pressed them on it, they said they weren't comfortable with it and wanted to protect Meagan and Dylan's privacy. And it wasn't just me and my book. They never let anyone question them. Not the sheriff's investigator. Not the FDLE agent. None of the news shows or reporters. No one. Unless I missed something. You should ask your dad to be sure."

"I will," I say.

"From everything I know of Naomi and Sasha, they wouldn't take someone's pet without permission."

"You think Meagan or Dylan or both went into the swamp with them?" I ask.

"I don't know," he says. "There's nothing to suggest that. But at a minimum I'd be willing to bet at least one of them was awake to give them permission to take Biscuit and knows why they went and what they were planning to do. And not for nothing but every indication is that Dylan had a big ol' crush on Sasha."

My phone vibrates in my pocket and I pull it out to see that Anna is calling.

"Could you step over here a little closer and keep an eye on the girls?" I say to Ben. "I need to take this."

He nods and slides over next to me.

I take a few steps away and answer the call.

"Made it," Anna says.

"Good."

"Miss you so much already," she says.

"Miss you more."

"And the girls," she says. "I don't think I can do this. I'm still at the airport and I'm tempted to get right back on the plane and come home now. What're y'all doing?"

"Playing at the park."

"Oh, my God, that really makes me want to come right back. Is Taylor telling you to push her higher and trying to keep up with Johanna?"

"You know it."

"If I do this," she says, "this will be the last time we talk for a week. I have to give them my phone as soon as I get there. That's too long. I'll go crazy."

"If you think of it that way, of course it will overwhelm you," I say. "Just take each moment and nothing else. And remember that it's voluntary. You can stop at any time. So since you're there, why don't you give it a try and if it gets to be too much, then pull the ripcord and come home?"

"You gettin' tired of talkin' me off all these ledges yet?"

"Not at all," I say. "This is a very difficult and challenging thing you're doing. You're being very brave—so much more than you know. And if I didn't think it would be hugely beneficial, that you'd regret not trying it, I wouldn't be encouraging you to do it. I'd much rather have you here. So much."

7

"And ... *action*," Simien Eggers yells.

The two actresses playing the parts of Naomi Newman and Sasha Grande begin to move about, eyes wide, frantically scanning the area, their lines of dialog coming out in bursts between their labored breathing.

Both actresses had been jumping up and down prior to the director calling *action* so as to be out of breath and frazzled.

"Sasha, we have passed by this way before. I know it. I am telling you. I recognize it. I think we are lost. No, I know we are."

"Nah, Naomi. Girl, I'm tellin' you we are fine. We just got to keep headin' down this direction here and we will be back at the Gaineses' place in time to have dinner with them. See?" She points to the ground. "Paw prints. Biscuit came this way. This is how we get home."

"Sasha, I am pretty sure those are bear tracks, not dog." She whips her head around suddenly. "What was that? Did you hear that? Is someone there?"

The stiff and stilted acting is nearly as bad as the dialog, and I can't believe it doesn't ring false to anyone involved in the production for the girls to keep saying each other's names every time they speak and to use so few contractions.

"And *cut*," Eggers yells. "Okay, not bad for a first take, girls, but let's take it from the top and give me more—more over everything, especially intensity. I want to smell your fear and desperation."

Merrill whispers to me, "I smell *something*. That's for sure."

Merrill Monroe, my closest friend since childhood, is a tall, lean, muscular African-American man who looks more like a former professional athlete—a boxer or baseball player, maybe —than a former correctional officer and current PI and security consultant. He and I are standing about fifty feet away from the set, watching as they shoot a scene from *Lost Innocents*.

Many of the isolated rural roads in the area cut through parts of the river swamps, which means if you're looking out to the side and not down at the road, you'd swear you were deep in the middle of the swamp. The small shoot is taking place off one such road that leads down to the river. This gives them easy access to the site and an open area to set up, while having a flooded cypress swamp in the background. It's odd, even silly looking, but I can see how if it's shot the right way, it could appear as though the young women were lost in the heart of dense jungle-like swamp.

Merrill and I are here because his investigations firm was hired by the mother of Hailee Benson, the actress playing Naomi, to make sure she's okay. Well, that's why Merrill is here. I'm just along for the ride, hoping to get a feel for the production and the slant it's taking. Hailee's mom grew concerned when about a week ago she stopped hearing from her daughter, who prior to that was in daily contact with her.

"Not sure why she stopped communicating with her mom," Merrill whispers, "but it ain't 'cause she missin'. Only things missin' 'round are skill and talent."

We watch as they run the scene again.

If possible, it's even worse than the first take.

Except for the director, the small crew, which only consists of about five people, seem exhausted and unenthusiastic. Based on the low-end prosumer equipment they're using and their youthful, inexperienced appearance, I'd guess this is a micro-budget production with nothing whatsoever to do with Netflix or any other legit content provider.

When the cast and crew takes its next break, Merrill and I walk over to Hailee.

"Nice work," Merrill says.

She lets out a harsh little laugh. "Everybody's a comedian."

"No, I'm serious," he says. "I could really smell the fear on that second take."

"Look," she says, "this shit's humiliating enough without you busting my balls about how bad it is, okay?"

"Just fuckin' with you," he says. "Try to find fun where I can."

"Well, finding it here is at my expense and I don't appreciate it."

"Sorry. Didn't mean any—"

"What do you want?"

"I'm a representative with NUPB," he says, saying it awkwardly as if it's a word instead of an acronym.

Of course, NUPB is no more an actual acronym than it is a word.

"With *what*?"

"The Neglected Parents Bureau," he says, not bothering to find a word to fit the vowel he had randomly thrown in there. "Your mom says she hasn't heard from you in a few days and that's unusual. She's worried about you. Should she be?"

"What?" she asks, shaking her head, a confused expression on her face. "Who're you with?"

"Are you okay?" he asks slowly. "Should your mom be worried?"

"You're with who again?"

"I'm a private investigator," he says, handing her his card. "Your mother hired me to come out and check on you. Are you okay? There a reason you stopped communicating with her?"

Merrill's speech patterns change more often than anyone I know. He can go from straight out of Compton Ebonics to polished professional using standard American English in the same breath—and often does. And often for no other discernible motivation than his own amusement.

"Just been busy," she says. "Being in a shit production is a hell of a lot harder than you'd think."

"But you're okay?" he says. "For real."

"I am."

"You're not being held against your will and forced to be in this—ah, film?"

She lets out a little laugh with more humor and less harshness than before.

"Not bein' blackmailed to be in it?"

"Wish I had an excuse like that."

"Will you call your mom tonight and let her know you're okay?"

"I will," she says. "I can't believe she actually hired someone to come check on me."

"Not just any *someone*," Merrill says. "She spared no expense and hired the very best."

"There a problem?" Simien Eggers says as he walks up to us.

He is a tallish, thin young man with black horned-rimmed glasses and an abundance of curly black hair. He is extremely pale and his face and neck are covered with stubble so black it looks as if he's smeared charcoal on himself.

"There certainly is," Merrill says. "With the state of the cinematic arts in this country today. Am I right?"

Blood Lure   33

"Oh, are you ever right about that," he says. "Y'all reporters? Fans?"

"Just concerned cinephiles," Merrill says.

"There's reason for concern," he says. "Very few of us out here are making art anymore. It's all sequels and super heroes and shit. That's redundant though, isn't it?"

Hailee sighs and rolls her eyes.

"Most certainly is," Merrill says. "And a master of the stature of none other than Mr. Martin Charles Scorsese feels the same way."

"Is it true this is a Netflix production?" I ask.

He turns toward me. "Who told you that? This is an independent production. I'm an independent artist."

Hailee rolls her eyes again.

"We do hope to sell it to Netflix for distribution once it's completed," he continues, "but then and only then. Once my vision is realized and the work can stand on its own."

"Have you sold anything to them before?" I ask.

"I worked on a film that was picked up by Netflix," he says. "I'd say I have a good relationship with them. I understand that they, like a lot of distribution companies out there, are eagerly awaiting my work on this tragic story."

"Doing what?" Merrill says.

"Pardon?" he says, stalling, avoiding the question.

My guess is he was in a very low-level position—more likely a PA than an AD—and no one at Netflix or anywhere else even knows who he is.

"What did you do on the production that Netflix picked up?"

"Hey, wait," he says, looking at me. "I recognize you. You're John Jordan, aren't you? You are. I recognize you from that documentary on the Atlanta Child Murders. I really, really want to get your dad on camera. My audience needs to hear his side of the story. And they need to hear it from him. He won't return my calls. Can you help me get him?"

Hoping to find out more about the production, I neither refuse to help him nor tell him there's absolutely no possibility Dad would ever be a part of this or any other documentary about the case.

"I could certainly talk to him," I say.

"Here's my card," he says. "Call me and let's get together with him to talk about what I'm wanting to do. He'll be glad. I promise. But now we need to get back to work. We're losing light, and me not having light is like a painter not having paint."

8

That night, lying in bed with the girls asleep on either side of me, I read through the case file some more.

Naomi Newman was twenty-one years old and a student in the Research and Experimental Psychology program at the University of North Florida in Jacksonville. A quiet, reserved introvert, she was smart and sensitive and known for her kindness, gentleness, and wickedly dry sense of humor. A star on her high school track and cross country teams, she had the trim, tight build of a runner.

Sasha Grande was a twenty-one-year-old student at the University of North Florida in Jacksonville working toward a degree in Communication. She was a charismatic extravert always in search of fun. She had a dark, striking beauty that often garnered her unwanted attention.

The young women were assigned as roommates by the college and, though nearly opposites in every way, became the unlikeliest of besties.

Naomi had found the wilderness camp volunteering opportunity and immediately signed up. It would not only give her the chance to make a difference, something her parents had instilled in her from an early age, but would give her much-needed volunteer hours for her scholarship program that she couldn't get during the semester because of her class and work load.

Sasha, who had recently been arrested for drunk and disorderly for a bar fight she had been in, only decided to join Naomi at the camp when she realized it would provide her with the community service hours she needed to meet her sentencing requirement.

Neither of the young women ever had any extra money, and so took the bus from Jacksonville to Tallahassee where they were picked up by Robbie Gaines and driven over to Pottersville. Though their positions at the wilderness camp didn't pay anything, the girls saw it as a free camping vacation and an opportunity to explore the wild, beautiful, and brutal environs of untamed North Florida river swamps.

Once Naomi and Sasha were back at the Gaineses' residence, Naomi reached out to Maurice Marcus, the retired extension agent and 4-H director heading up the wilderness camp they were going to be volunteering at.

She had been informed, rather rudely according to her journal entry, that they were a week early and there was nothing for them to do.

Originally, Naomi and Sasha were only supposed to spend a night or two with the Gaineses before relocating to their cabin at Chipola Campgrounds for the wilderness camp, but when Robbie heard what had happened, she not only told the young women they were more than welcome to stay but that she would find them plenty of fun actives to keep them occupied and entertained.

9

"Felt bad for them girls, I surely did," Maurice Marcus is saying, "but wasn't nothin' I could do. Had no place to put them. Couldn't have them staying out in the swamp by themselves—see what happened?"

Maurice Marcus is an enormous older black man who stands over six-six and weighs well over three hundred pounds. He has thick, meaty dark skin and huge hands perpetually wrapped around a shovel or plant.

Merrill and I have found him in the middle of town weeding and replanting the area beneath the armed forces monument between the circle of flagpoles holding the American and Florida flags and one for each branch of the service.

As usual, his huge head holds a papyrus-brim sun hat that shades his hooded eyes and sweat is streaming down his temples.

"Heard reports that says I was rude to them, that I hurt the feelings of the young woman who called," he says, "and I'm'a 'gret that to my grave. I didn't mean to be . . . to give offense. I just get frustrated sometimes 'cause kids don't listen anymore."

"They never did," I say, "even when *they* were us."

"You probably right," he says with a deep frown that seems to fold under the entire bottom of his thick face. "Probably just gittin' cantankerous in my old age."

"What can you tell me about them?" I ask.

"Exactly nothin'," he says. "Never even met 'em."

"Any ideas on what happened to them?" Merrill says.

"Just got lost," he says. "That's all. It's easy to do. Hell, it still happens to me and I been traipsing through them swamps more'n sixty years. I know they's a lotsa unanswered questions and maybe even a little of what looks like evidence that it was somethin' else, but trust me—they were over they heads before they ever stepped one foot in there, and the deeper they went the more over they heads they gots. Weren't prepared. Weren't supplied. Weren't dressed right. Weren't ready. People come up with theories, try to sensationalize it and what not. Why, I don't know. Boredom I suppose. Nobody does hard work no more. But it's a tragic accident. Nothin' more."

As he's talking, I see Meagan Gaines and a group of her friends walk into the lakeside park across the way, find a bench down by the water, and proceed to begin to smoke. I decide to wrap things up with Maurice so I can try to talk to her while her parents aren't around, but I have one more idea I want to get his take on.

"Their bones and backpack were scattered all over the place," I say. "Some eight to twelve miles from where they entered Cottonmouth Creek."

"Yeah," he says. "Scavengers got at 'em after they's dead."

"But that's a very, very long way from where they started," I say. "And we know based on their phone data and camera photos that they were alive and moving for several days before they died."

"Fact that they's movin' what made it impossible to find 'em," he says. "They'd'a stayed put . . . search and rescue woulda probably located 'em."

"I was looking at a map," I say. "And when I marked where they entered the swamp, where most of their remains were discovered, where the backpack was discovered, and where Chipola Campgrounds is located . . ."

He tilts his huge head back and his eyes widen beneath the wide brim of his sun hat. "Son of a bitch," he says. "Son of a bitch."

"One of you son of a bitches care to let me in on it?" Merrill says.

"They coulda been on their way to the campgrounds," Maurice says. "Probably were. Must've wanted to check it out themselves or . . ."

"Or maybe they were meeting somebody there," I say. "Think it's something we should keep in mind."

10

"**I**s it true they're making a movie about the case?" Meagan asks.

"It is," I say. "Merrill and I were on the set last night talking to the star and the director."

After leaving Maurice, Merrill and I walked down to the bench by the lake where Meagan and her friends are smoking, introduced ourselves, and asked if she minded talking to us about Naomi and Sasha.

"I *adore* true crime," she says. "I've tried and tried to figure out exactly what happened to Naomi and Sasha. Tell you what . . . If you can get me and these losers on the set and you swear not to let Jay and Robbie know that anything I said came from me and you're willing to do it in front of my friends while we smoke . . . Sure I'll talk to you about them."

She is sitting on a large wooden bench with five other young twenty-somethings, two guys and three girls, smoking like it's about to be outlawed forever.

The heavy, soft, curly haired blond boy is vaping, as is the goth girl in the black hoody. Meagan and the skinny stringy black-haired boy have joints they only begrudgingly share, and the other two girls, who look like former cheerleaders and future Daughters of the American Revolution, are chain-smoking cheap cigarettes.

"Aren't you a cop?" Skinny Stringy Black-Hair says. "You got no problem with us enjoyin' a little herb?"

I shake my head.

"We're gonna need an audible response for the recording," Soft Curly Blond says. "Could you speak into his left tit?"

Both the quantity and quality of smoke and smokers creates a pungent fog that for some reason hovers around them instead of floating away.

So far the only thing the disparate group seems to have in common is a passion for smoking. Of course, friendships have been based on less.

"What can you tell me about Naomi and Sasha?" I ask.

"They were cool," she says. "Lot more than I expected them to be. Naomi was sweet and sort of quiet and Sasha was wild and funny as fuck. We had a good time together."

"What'd y'all do?"

"Hung out a lot and talked. They stayed with me in my room. It was like a sleepover with two older cool kids. Nothing like hanging with these losers."

The losers laugh.

We've only been here a few moments and I can already tell that Meagan is the alpha of this crew. She appears to run it with a playful, light touch, but she runs it.

"I'm serious," she says. "You guys suck."

"We're better than smokin' alone," Soft Curly Blond says.

"I used to think so," she says, "but now I'm not so sure."

From the moment we walked up, Meagan has been stealing surreptitious glances at Merrill and she checks his reaction to everything she says.

"What else?" I ask.

"Went to the beach," she says. "Shopping. A football game.

A bonfire. Horseback riding on the cape. Think the only thing I didn't do with them was go to the bar—I was underage—and go into the swamp with them."

"Which, *thank Goddess*," one of the cheerleader-looking twins says. Her voice sounds like that of an overly dramatic young gay guy. "You'd be dead now too."

Meagan shakes her head. "Nah, I'd've kept their stupid asses alive."

The city park is mostly empty—a walker or two on the cement walking path that encircles it and a mom or two with a small child or two over on the playground equipment. Behind us, the lake is calm and still, its glass-like surface refracting the bright morning sun and the clear, cloudless sky it appears to be affixed to.

"Did y'all have any problems with anybody during any of those activities?" I ask.

She shrugs. "Not really. Sasha got some attention she didn't want—she was a knockout and the life of every party—but you could tell she was used to it and knew how to shut it down pretty fast. The worst of it came from my creepy foster brother."

"Dylan?" I ask.

"Yeah," she says, nodding. "He had a yin for her the moment she walked in the door. You could tell she sort of put up with more of it from him than she normally would. Guess 'cause she was stayin' with us. He drank too much at the bonfire and acted basic as fuck. Rest of the time he just sort of followed her around like a little puppy."

"A sick puppy," Goth Girl adds.

"The only place he couldn't follow her into was the Oasis," she says. "He was underage at the time too. So his lame ass just waited outside for her—*for hours*."

"If that's the case," I say, "it surprises me he'd let them go into the swamp by themselves."

"I'm not so sure he did."

"Oh yeah?"

"Look, he's a little creep and I don't like him," she says, "but I'm not tryin' to get anybody in trouble—'specially if he's innocent, and he may be. I've read all about this case and questioned him and I don't know for sure. But . . . and this could mean nothin' . . . but when I woke up . . . he wasn't there."

"What time was that?"

"Not sure exactly," she says. "But I was the only one in the house. Not sayin' he was with them, but his room is across from mine and his door was open and he wasn't in it."

"You have no idea what time it was?" I ask.

"My phone had died during the night so I don't know for sure, but it had to be after ten and before twelve-fifteen, 'cause that's when the 'rents and the little hellions are at church."

Merrill says, "I'm sure you plugged your phone in to charge as soon as you saw it was dead. What time was it when it came back on?"

"I checked messages, not the time," she says, blushing a little from speaking with him directly.

"Okay," he says. "How 'bout this? Was it a long time or a short time between the time you woke up and the time your parents got back from church?"

"Wasn't long at all."

I nod toward Merrill, then ask Meagan, "How long was it before you saw Dylan again, and where was he?"

"I left," she says. "I wasn't around for any of the . . . I went to Petra's and hung out. Didn't get back home until that night."

"Petra?" I ask.

"Me," Goth Girl says, raising her hand. "I picked her up after those basic bitches left her behind."

"You were upset Naomi and Sasha didn't wake you up and take you with them?" I ask.

Meagan shrugs. "I don't know. We hadn't made any plans. Said we'd talk about it once we all woke up. We were wiped out from all we did on Saturday. But, yeah, I was surprised they left without me. We had been inseparable before then—except for the bar, and they tried to sneak me in there."

"When you got back home that night was Dylan there?" I ask.

"He had been, but he was gone again," she says. "He took Biscuit back out there looking for them. He and Dad had been in the yard when Biscuit came up without them. Dad tried to stop him, but he went tearing off out there to find them."

"I bet he thought bein' a hero might get him in Sasha's pants," Petra says.

"Or he coulda just been concerned about them," Soft Curly Blond says. "You know, like, cared like a decent human being."

The others laugh at that.

"Not everybody's got an angle," he says.

They laugh even harder at that.

"How long did he stay out there in the swamp?" I ask.

"A while," she says. "Eventually Dad had to go out and get him. But there were so many people around by then—cops and search and rescue and game wardens—I don't know when it was they finally made it back."

"Do you have any idea why Naomi and Sasha went out into the swamp in the first place instead of waiting to go with Horton Joshua the next day?"

"I don't know why they went when they did and I don't know what they were thinking going dressed the way they were and with the few supplies they had, but I do know they had no intention of going out with Horton the following day or any other time."

"Why's that?"

"He creeped them out," she says. "Gives me the creeps too. I'd never go into the swamp or anywhere else with him and I told Mom that. He has a reputation for only taking young women out on his little ecotours and there've been a lot of complaints about him over the years—sexual harassment stuff. Inappropriate behavior."

"Didn't he head up one of the search parties?" Merrill says.

I nod. "*And* discovered Sasha's remains."

"Sounds like ol' Horton needs to hear a who from you and me," Merrill says, his voice low enough so only I can hear him.

"You said you've studied the case," I say to Meagan, "and you had a front row seat for most of it. What do you think happened?"

She shakes her head and shrugs. "I go back and forth. I want to think someone killed them. It's the romantic in me. But there's a lot of evidence that argues that it was just a stupid, unnecessary accident. They should've never been out there alone to begin with. So I'm like seventy-five or eighty percent sure their dumb asses just got lost and killed by the swamp, but . . . there's definitely evidence that you can't explain away that says they could've been killed."

"Such as?"

"Cellphone data, photographs, the backpack, and the bones."

I nod, knowing I don't know enough about them yet to ask her about them. Perhaps I can when we take her to the set of *Lost Innocents*.

"Is there anything else you can tell me?" I ask. "Anything I should've asked you but haven't? Anything you know that no one else does? Any impressions or ideas you have even if there's no evidence for them?"

Her eyebrows arch as her mouth drops open slightly. "There is this . . ." she says. "Sasha was up to something. Have no idea what, but she kept slipping off and whispering on her phone—and though it was obvious she didn't want any of us to know what she was up to, she really, *really* didn't want Naomi to know."

"And you have no idea what it was?"

"None."

"What did you think at the time?"

She shrugs. "Not just one thing. I thought she's trying to leave. Another time I thought she's trying to score some drugs. It always felt yucky to me and I had the feeling she was out of control and in some trouble."

"That's huge," Ben is saying. "All big pieces of the puzzle we didn't have before. And each piece answers some extremely important questions."

Dad, Ben, Merrill, and I are sitting in a booth at Rudy's Diner having lunch and talking about the case. Taylor's in preschool and Johanna is in Tallahassee shopping with Verna.

Dad and I are above-average-sized men, Merrill is taller and bigger than me, and yet Ben looks as if he's at a small table having a tea party with kids—if we were the sort of kids who played tea party, which we are not.

It's the prison's admin shift's lunch break and Rudy's is filled with several officers and staff members Merrill and I used to work with at Potter Correctional Institution.

"We always wondered why they went into the swamp alone," Ben continues. "Why they didn't just wait to take the tour the next day with Horton. Where they could've been going. Why no one saw them leave. Why the Gianeses didn't want us talkin' to their kids. And that thing about Sasha bein' up to something . . . that's . . . that could be a game changer. "

"All we have are some possible answers and a potential theory on where they might have been headed," I say. "It could all be bogus, but even if it's not, it raises more questions than it answers."

Rudy's smells like it always does—like old grease with the sweet tinge of pancake batter. I look around and think about how many sleepless nights I spent here in a booth in the back, reading and thinking and keeping an eye on Carla, Rudy's young, motherless daughter who he made work nights. And though it's not the same without her here, I'm so very grateful she got out.

"Gotta wonder why Meagan was so forthcoming," Merrill says.

"She's never been allowed to talk, "Ben says. "Probably been wanting to—*needing* to—all this time."

"Sure gave up her foster brother awful quick," Merrill says. "Gonna need to hear his side of things."

"I think what she's sayin' is legit," Ben says. "He was seen with or near them by several witnesses the entire time they were here. I know he was at the bonfire and the thing about him waiting outside the Oasis for them is true. I put in my book how Meagan and Dylan and Naomi and Sasha were inseparable during those three days, which I found a little odd. Meagan I could see, even though she was younger, but Dylan . . . Makes a lot more sense if he was just following them around. Makes sense him having a crush on or even being obsessed with Sasha. Seems like just about everybody commented on not only how pretty she was but also how vivacious. She really was one of those rare beauties whose personality was as good as her looks."

Dad says, "Whether they're the actual answers or not and no matter how many more questions they bring up, I'm just glad to be getting some movement on the case. That's always

He walks over to our table as the others make their way

the best chance of clearing it—stirring things up, getting people talking and thinking and remembering it."

I nod.

"No question," Ben says.

Merrill looks from Dad to Ben and back. "We keep hearing how attractive Sasha was," he says. "Anyone ever say anything about Naomi being jealous or feeling overlooked?"

"Just the opposite," Ben says. "As different as they were, they seemed to have a really great relationship. Naomi really seemed to appreciate and even adore Sasha. And it seemed like it went both ways. And Naomi was a pretty girl in her own right. She got plenty of attention from boys too. It was just quieter and in the background."

The cowbell above the front door sounds as the cast and crew of *Lost Innocents* walks in. Nearly everyone in the diner stops talking and eating and turns to look at them.

There's a brief, awkward beat when no one seems to know what to do before Simien Eggers takes a step forward and slips into character.

"Greetings people of Pottersville," he says. "We the cast and crew of the riveting film *Lost Innocents* are here to enjoy your local cuisine and to put even more of our money into your local economy. We have a very tight shooting schedule today, so we would ask that you save all your questions and requests for pictures and autographs until the premiere of our film, which we will do here and to which you are all invited."

Merrill can't hide his amusement, which draws Simien's attention.

He walks over to our table as the others make their way to two booths in the back corner, Haliee Benson waving to Merrill as they do.

Simien's eyes widen when he nears the table and sees that Dad is with us.

"*Sheriff Jordan*," he says. "My good man. Oh, how I have longed for the day that I'd run into you and here it is. Fate has destined it to be today. The film I'm making, which has every promise of being a masterpiece, isn't just the sad, tragic story of Naomi Newman and Sasha Grande, but of the seasoned veteran sheriff who searches so diligently to find them and failing that, at finding the vicious killer who stole their innocence from them. Benjamin, tell him. We need him. Without you this film will still be a masterpiece but with you it will be . . . transcendent."

I had asked Dad not to give Eggers a hard *no* so we could stay in touch with the production and monitor what's going on with it. That doesn't mean that's what he'll do, though.

"I'll certainly consider it," Dad says. "I'll have John give you a call and we can get together and talk about it."

"You have but to name the time and place and I will be there, though it means halting production to do so. Thank you very much, kind sir." He starts to move away, then stops and turns back around. "Mr. Monroe, may I have a quick word?"

"Sure," Merrill says, but doesn't move.

"In private, if you don't mind. It's a somewhat delicate matter."

Merrill nods and rises and the two men step through the front door.

"He always talk like that?" Dad asks Ben.

"He tries real hard to constantly remind everyone he's an artist."

"Seems more like an actor than a director to me," Dad says.

"He's definitely a showman," Ben says.

We are quiet a moment.

"Sheriff," Ben says, "I want to say again how sorry I am about all this. I had no idea it would be like this. I wish I would've never sold the film rights to my book. I wish someone else was making the movie. And I wish they couldn't just do whatever they wanted to with it."

Dad nods. "I know," he says. "No need to apologize."

"I swear I do you right in my book," he says.

"I know," he says. "I read it."

"You *did*?"

"You did a fine job all the way around. Made me proud."

"It did?"

"Very much," he says. "I know it's not easy, but you gotta let go of the things you have no control over." Pausing a moment, he adds, "Not doing it can give you cancer."

Ben looks a little confused, and I'm not sure whether or not he knows that Dad has cancer or if he does, if he realizes Dad's playfully confessing to not having been very good at letting things go himself.

Before anything else is said, Merrill returns to the table.

"He going back into porn and want to cast you?" I ask.

He smiles. "Yeah, but I told him I charge by the inch and he realized he couldn't afford me."

Ben says, "Length or girth?"

"He can't afford either."

Merrill takes a big swallow of his tea and then another.

"What did he really want?" Dad asks.

"Says he's bein' stalked," Merrill says. "Wants me to protect him and find out who's doin' it."

"You've always wanted to work in show business," I say.

"Yeah," he says. "It's right up there with politics and Klan rallies."

"You gonna do it?" Ben asks.

"Says he's a true artist who suffers for his art so neither he or the production have any money for the services he's asking me to provide. Asked if I'd consider doing them as a contribution to the cause. Says I'd join the long line of honorable and distinguished patrons of the arts. Started to tell him from what I could gather it was his so-called art that caused the suffering, but then I thought if I'm around I could see what he's up to and maybe even exert a little influence on how he handles the sheriff's portrayal, so instead I told him it'd be my honor to suffer from his art too. And he looked at me like I was the dumb negro he thinks I am and said, 'No, my good man. Not *from*. For. *For* my art.'"

12

It seems as though every community, organization, and institution has a Horton Joshua—a sleazy, manipulative mover and shaker who no one trusts and everyone seems repulsed by, yet who remains in a position of power and pseudo popularity.

Horton, a sixty-something-year-old lifelong bachelor, has never run for public office, but has served in a variety of city and county government positions as a political appointee. Among his many and varied roles, he has served as city manager for Pottersville and as head of the Potter County Tourist Development Council, which is the position he held back in 2014 when Naomi and Sasha went missing.

Always involved in several ventures at once, in addition to heading the TDC, Horton had a fledgling ecotourism business at the time. He had been scheduled by Robbie Gaines to take Naomi and Sasha on a river swamp tour on Monday, September 29, 2014—a tour that never took place because the young women went missing on the day before, a tour that Meagan Gaines says wouldn't have happened even if they hadn't gone missing.

Big Ben and I find Horton driving his golf cart through the pecan grove at the front of his property. From the side of the golf cart he gathers pecans by pulling a rolling nut harvester behind him, the plentiful pecans popping up into the oblong wire-spoke basket at the end of the four-foot handle he's holding.

It's just me and Ben because of the bad blood between Dad and Horton over decades of county politics skirmishes and because Merrill is following Simien Eggers to see who might be following him.

Horton is a fat man with no discernibly human shape. He has no neck, so the thick jowls of his huge, balding head seem to sit directly on his rounded and sloped shoulders, and since his back is nearly as beefy as his front, he resembles a blob of melting ice cream more than a man.

It's rare to find Horton alone. He's nearly always in the company of either aging good ol' boys or single young women —the latter at the Oasis where he buys their drinks until they can't drink anymore.

Ben told me on the drive out here that it was at the Oasis on the Saturday night before they went missing that Naomi and Sasha had encountered Horton, which given what Meagan said, must have been when they also decided they would most definitely *not* be going out into the wilderness with him.

We park on the tree-lined drive and get out. Horton drives over to us but stays in the golf cart.

"Pecan?" he asks, holding up the nearly full basket. "Best in the county."

"No, thanks," I say as Ben shakes his head.

"Seein' you two together like this can only mean one thing," he says. "Those poor wilderness camp girls who got swallowed up by the swamp."

We nod.

"Well, y'all wasted a trip out here," he says. "Not gonna talk about that."

"Why not?" I ask.

"Ben knows," he says. "Surprised he not only let you throw effort after foolishness like this but joined you in the endeavor. I won't talk about the case for two reasons. First, though it's as cold as those girls' bones are wherever all they may be buried, the case is allegedly still open, and that bein' the case, you never know when somebody's gonna get desperate enough to pin it on someone—and I'm not gonna aid and abet the misguided into that bein' me."

"And the second reason?" I ask.

"There have been some awfully nasty comments made about me on those true crime online forums and podcasts and the like. Never knew people could be that vicious, that confident in their own cockamamie theories. So, no, thank you, but I won't be tossing fuel on my own funeral pyre."

"Not even off-the-record to us if we give you our word it won't go any further?"

He shakes his head. "Not even then. And please don't take offense. I know you are both trustworthy men of your words and on the whole I'd say Ben's book was reasonably fair to me, but . . . I'm just not going to make any exceptions to my no-talk rule. It's nothing personal. And has nothing to do with any past politics between your dad and me."

"Did you hear they're making a movie out of my book?" Ben asks.

"Oh, yes, not much goes on in this county without me knowing about it, and they asked to interview me for it, which I declined."

"Whatta you think about it?" Ben asks.

"If it brings money and the right kind of attention to our county, I'm all for it, but . . . my guess is it'll be too obscure to do either."

"What made you start an ecotourism business?" I ask.

Not only does he not seem the type to enjoy the outdoors, but I can't imagine he'd be physically capable of a hike through the swamp.

"When I started it, Potter County was at a crossroads," he says. "If you remember, it hadn't been long since the paper mill had shut down. Paper company was selling all its land. Timber industry was going away. We had an opportunity to transition into a tourist economy. I was tryin' to show what we might become, what was possible. The recession hit and everything stalled and it appears as if our little county isn't going to willingly move in the tourism direction, but . . . I've hung onto my little ecotourism business 'cause I just can't give up on what we could become."

"Do you have much business?" I ask.

"Hardly any at all."

"Do you have any help or do it all yourself?"

"I have access to help when I need it," he says, then nodding toward Ben adds, "Tried to hire this guy back in the day, before he started with Fish and Game. Man, aren't you glad you took that path instead?"

Ben sort of nods and shrugs and I can tell he's trying not to give offense.

Ben had briefly worked for a different ecotourism outfit that most people in the area considered to be the only legitimate one.

Horton looks back at me. "Bet you've heard I only take out pretty young girls."

"Huh?"

"On the tours," he says. "If it's a family, men, or unattractive women I use one of my subcontractors to do it, but if it's attractive young women like Naomi and especially Sasha, I do it."

I nod.

"Even if it's true," he says, "so what? What's wrong with it?

What if I set up this entire business to be close to attractive young women walking through the woods in short shorts? Wouldn't be anything wrong with that, would there? I mean, not in and of itself. Would there? And it wouldn't make me a murderer, would it? You're the expert, but I would think a murderer would find victims he has no connection to, not ones that leave a record of hiring him."

I nod again, hoping he'll keep talking.

"Let me tell you fellas what my sixty-three years on God's green earth have taught me," he says. "Everything, and I mean *everything,* is transactional. There is nothing else. We are selfish creatures pursuing our own pleasure."

"You don't think true altruism exists?" I ask.

He shakes his head. "I don't. You do?"

"I know it does," I say.

"It's an illusion. Everybody wants something. Everybody's after something—even if it's to feel good about themselves for being such a good, unselfish person.

Years ago I had heard Scott Peck, the author of *The Road Less Traveled* and perhaps the father of the self-help revolution, speak at a conference, and he had said something similar, though not as cynical. He said there is good selfishness and bad selfishness and our goal should be to only practice good selfishness. Though I understood what he was saying and saw the subtle truth in it, I didn't completely agree with him then and I certainly don't agree with Horton's argument now, which strikes me as a shallow form of self-justifying rationalization and moral equivalency.

As far as I know, Horton Joshua had never had a long-term intimate relationship and had never had children—two of life's greatest gifts of opportunity for the practice of ego dethroning and unselfishness. Of course, many of the most self-centered among us are impervious even to these.

"You're both attractive young men," Horton says. "Well, Big

Ben's still a baby and you probably seem younger than you are, but the point is you're both attractive in your own way. I'm not. Never have been. Nothing to be done for it. Genetics is a lottery. I'll never be a model, but I'm smart and a hell of a hard worker and I'm ruthless, which is in itself a gift. I have money. I have position and a certain amount of power. If a beautiful, tight-bodied little blonde is willing to trade some of her time, attention, affection, even her body for some of my money or power or what those things can do for her, then I think it's an honorable transaction and one I'm willing to make. It's no different than two beautiful people exchanging beauty for beauty, body for body, or two powerful people exchanging power for power. I just exchange power with other powerful men and money with beautiful young women."

"Were you trying to make a transaction with Naomi and Sasha at the Oasis the night before they went missing?" Ben asks.

He shakes his head. "Not Naomi. Just Sasha."

"What did you say to her?" he asks.

"Just made her an offer she could refuse," he says. "Happens all the time. No harm. No foul."

"Had to be more than that," Ben says. "Her reaction was too extreme for it to have just been that. She actually bitched-slapped you across the face. She cut her night short and left the bar then. And canceled their tour with you."

I had heard talk of this incident, and though Ben had told me he had seen it happen, it surprises me he confronts Horton about it so directly.

"No," he says. "No one canceled the tour. But as I said, I'm not going to talk about the case. Already said more than I should have."

"Had to embarrass you to get slapped like that in public," he says.

Horton shrugs and shakes his head. "Happens more than

you might think, and I don't get embarrassed. It's another one of the genetic gifts I *did* receive."

"So you didn't pay her back and it's not suspicious that you're the one who found her remains?" he says.

"See what happens?" Horton says. "I welcome you onto my property and try to have a pleasant chat with you and then you're leapfrogging to accusations. I'm going to get back to enjoying my afternoon. I wish you gentleman a good day."

Without another word, Horton presses the pedal, his golf cart comes to life, and he drives away, this time holding the nut gatherer out like a baseball bat in the outstretched hand of a juvenile delinquent searching for mailboxes to smash.

"We're just trying to get to the truth," Ben yells after him. "What kind of transaction does it take to get to that?"

13

The girls and I are in the middle of an epic game of hide-and-seek, or as Taylor used to call it *hidin'-and-seekin'*, when the doorbell rings.

The girls shriek and squeal and run to hug her when they see it is Sam Michaels, an FDLE agent from Tallahassee who I had worked with on homicide cases over the years and who had lived with us while recuperating from a near-fatal gunshot wound she sustained as we attempted to apprehend a suspect down near Tampa a few years back.

"Sam, Sam, Sam," they shout as they accost her.

"Now, that's my kind of greeting," she says. "Wow. I can't believe how big y'all've gotten."

Not exactly sure how strong and stable she is, I gently guide the girls off her. "Okay, let's let her in the house. Come on."

Johanna and Taylor rush back into the kitchen, leaving Sam and me alone in the mudroom for a moment.

We embrace and I close and lock the door.

"Hope you don't mind me dropping in like this," she says.

"Are you kidding? I'm happier to see you than the girls are —and that's saying something."

"Daniel drove over to record with Merrick, so I hitched a ride so we could catch up and talk about the case some more."

She had been the FDLE agent assigned to assist with the investigation of what happened to Naomi and Sasha and I had called her earlier in the day to get her take on the case.

Sam's partner, Daniel Davis, is an amateur sleuth and has a true crime podcast with journalist Merrick McKnight, who also happens to be the boyfriend of the sheriff of Gulf County and my boss, Reggie Summers.

"I'm so glad you did," I say. "Truly."

We make our way into the kitchen where the girls are eagerly awaiting our arrival.

"Did you come to play hide-and-seek with us?" Taylor asks.

"*You know it,*" Sam says.

As much fun as we were having before, we have even more with Sam in the mix. She is so slight she's not much bigger than Johanna and can hide anywhere. The girls adore her, and with their mom away and the chaos of the post-hurricane world just outside our door, her presence is even more calming and comforting.

Though Johanna and Taylor would play hide-and-seek all night, we eventually get them settled down with snacks and a movie so we can talk.

We sit at the kitchen table with cups of coffee, the girls snacking and watching a short distance away in the living room, their movie turned up a little louder than usual to cover our conversation.

"So how are you?" I ask. "You seem like you're doing amazing. Not many people can keep up with the two of them."

"I'm a miracle," she says. "According to my doctor."

"You're unbelievably strong and determined and you've obviously been working your ass off."

She nods. "I'm grateful just to be here," she says. "Everything else is icing. But I like icing. How are you? How is Anna?"

"We've been better," I say. "But things are improving."

She asks for details and I tell her what we've been dealing with lately.

"Oh my God, John, I'm so sorry. That's . . . Life can be so . . . It's never easy, is it? And it's always changing, so even when things are good you know they won't last. It's like Florida weather. Don't like it? Give it a minute. It will change."

I smile. "Exactly," I say, "but thankfully it's true of difficult things too. Everything is always changing—good and bad. Nothing lasts long."

"Making a relationship work well is hard enough," she says. "Not sure why life finds it necessary to pile on."

"Ain't that the truth."

"Can't tell you how many times Daniel and I almost pronounced TOD, and Merrick and Reggie actually did, though I understand they've had a resurrection of sorts."

I find it interesting that a cop would use a term like Time of Death about her relationship.

"They have indeed," I say. "It was a Christmas miracle that happened right here in this very house."

"Maybe it means your house is magic," she says. "Next time Daniel and I are having issues, don't be surprised if we show up at your door asking if we can stay here until we get our shit together."

"Y'all are welcome anytime," I say.

"It's not the house so much as the love in it," she says. "Certainly saved my life. I can never thank y'all enough for taking me in while Daniel was missing. All y'all did for me . . . You and Anna are going to be okay. You have to be."

I hope she's right, but right now I'm not so sure.

We talk about life and family and work a little while longer, but eventually I get up, check on the girls and get us more coffee, and we transition into Naomi and Sasha's case.

"You ever had a case where you can't be certain whether or

not it's even a homicide or not, and it drives you crazy because half the time you're convinced it's a tragic accident and the other half you're convinced it's murder?" Sam says.

I nod.

"I sympathize with your dad," she says. "We took it as far as we possibly could at the time and never could say definitively which it was. Some cases are just like that. The world's full of open and unsolved cases—and most of them never will be solved. That's the sad fact of it. And you hear people talking about what a shame it is that the family won't get closure—and it is, and there's no comparison—but the cops that worked it don't get closure either, and that's a unique kind of hell."

"Yes, it is," I say. "Sorry."

"Part of the job," she says. "But it's a bigger part than most civilians know."

I nod. "It certainly is."

"So I'm not sure how long we have," she says. "Can't text Daniel 'cause they're recording. So tell me what you most want to know about the case right now."

"Let's start with the phones."

"Sure," she says, nodding and narrowing her eyes in concentration. "This is from memory so double-check me on it, but it's so seared into my brain I think I'll get it right. Sasha had an iPhone and Naomi had a Samsung Galaxy. Both phones were found in Naomi's backpack, and we know what we do because of the data retrieved from them. The backpack's a whole other mystery, but I'm guessing we'll get to that later. There's a lot that is fascinating and mysterious about the phones. Both of them remained in service for almost ten days."

"How?" I ask. "There was no mention of a portable charger in their things and the Gaineses have never mentioned them having one in the things they brought with them."

"We don't think they did," she says. "The data recovered shows they powered them down when they weren't using them to conserve the batteries and only powered them on occasionally to check for signal. Many days they only turned them on once."

I shake my head. "Says a lot about their discipline and desire to survive."

"Doesn't it? They were really remarkable young ladies."

Like so many other victims from cases I've worked on in the past, I wonder what they would have done with the rest of their lives, who they would've become, how they would've developed the largely untapped potential they died with.

"We don't know what happened to Naomi and Sasha," she says, "but we know whatever it was—or whatever the first thing to happen to them was—happened early on. Within a matter of hours of them venturing out into the swamp on their own, they were attempting to call for help. We think they left the Gaineses' sometime between eleven and twelve. By a little after four they were placing their first 911 calls."

"That *was* quick," I say. "But it happening so fast doesn't really narrow down what it was that happened. It could still be encountering someone—witnessing something illegal or—

"Remember the Remington James case?" she says. "Makes me think of it."

Remington James was an amateur wildlife photographer whose camera traps had captured the murder of a young woman in the same swamps Naomi and Sasha died in.

I nod. "Absolutely," I say. "Could've been something like that or one or both of them could've gotten injured, had an accident of some kind, or been stung, bitten, or attacked, or just gotten thoroughly and completely lost."

"Yeah, the timing doesn't help us with what happened, but is interesting that it was so soon after they went in—especially in relation to them being alive for so many days after that."

"I'm assuming there's still no cell service in the swamp," I say.

"That's right," she says. "There's not any today, let alone six years ago. And because there was no service there was no GPS so the data can't tell us what paths they took, where they were when, or anything else like that."

I frown and think about how helpful it would be to know their movements.

"During the days the phones still had power, several 911 calls were attempted. I can pull up the exact number but it's a lot. And yet the most disturbing and confounding thing that happens with the phones happens only with the iPhone and only at the very end of its life."

I try to imagine the mental and emotional state they must have been in and the panic and desperation to continue to call emergency services over and over again without success.

"The iPhone lasted a little longer than the Samsung, but we have no idea how much charge they had when they started. Sasha's iPhone required a four-digit security code to unlock it, but Naomi's Samsung didn't require one. Let me bring up the data logs from the phones so I can get the details right."

As she begins swiping and tapping her phone, I step over and look in on Johanna and Taylor.

They are snuggled up together beneath a pink blanket watching their movie with heavy heads and blinking eyes. For a moment I imagine them lost in the river swamp together and am seized by the iron grip of a palpable fear.

When I return to the table, Sam looks at me with widening eyes. "What's wrong?"

I shake my head. "Just an overactive imagination."

She glances toward the living room and nods. "Not overactive," she says. "Just powerful. It's what makes you such a good investigator, so empathetic."

"Don't know about all that, but thanks," I say. "You find the logs?"

She nods, glances down at her phone and begins reading.

"On September 28th, two phone calls were made. Naomi's Samsung was first used at 4:13 p.m. About ten minutes later, Sasha's iPhone was used. Both attempted 911. Both calls failed due to no reception. They then switched their phones off and tried calling again nearly fourteen hours later.

"On September 29th, the following day, a Monday, the phones were powered back up and calls were made at 6:58 a.m., 10:53 a.m., and 8:14 p.m. The 6:58 a.m. call was made from Naomi's Samsung phone and it actually managed to connect to 911 somehow but only for a second or two before it disconnects. We always assumed this was from lack of signal, but it's possible it was manually disconnected. After it was disconnected, the Samsung phone was switched off again about thirty-six seconds later. The 8:14 p.m. call was attempted with Sasha's iPhone and after it failed, a screenshot was taken of the phone's screen. Of course, we can't know whether it was intentional or accidental, but if it was on purpose, we can't figure out why it was done. After that, the phone is powered off and no more attempts are made—well, actually the phones aren't even powered up again until the following day.

"On the third day of their disappearance, September 30th, an attempt is made to call 911 at 9:33 a.m. Sasha's iPhone is switched on for one minute before that call attempt and switched off right after it. At 1:50 p.m. Naomi's Samsung is switched on for fifty seconds to check for signal. She does this two more times around four in the afternoon. Sasha's iPhone is switched on once around 4:00 p.m., presumably to check for signal because no call is attempted.

"On the fourth day, October 1st, Sasha's iPhone is again switched on at 10:16 a.m., then turned off a few seconds later. She does this at 1:42 p.m. also. Naomi's Samsung phone is not used at all that day.

"Then on the fifth day, October 2nd, Naomi's phone is switched on at 4:50 p.m. and is turned off almost immediately.

It is turned back on for the last time at 5:00 p.m. The screen lights up, then the battery dies. The Samsung phone is never used again. Remember how I said that Sasha's iPhone had to be unlocked every time it was used with a four-digit security code?"

I nod.

"Well, from September 28th until October 1st her phone was consistently activated by entering the code correctly. It's not turned on again until Friday, October 3rd, the day Tropical Storm Fritz hits, but when it is the wrong security code is entered so the phone is not opened, can't be gotten into. And, in fact, the correct security code is never entered again."

I think about what that might mean.

"Between the 3rd and the 5th, when the storm is actually on top of them, Sasha's phone isn't even turned on. Then on Monday night, October 6th, one week and a day since they first entered the swamp and went missing, on the same night that nearly ninety nighttime photos were taken, no less than seventy-seven attempts were made to get into the phone. Seventy-seven times. All unsuccessfully."

I think about the desperation involved in attempting to get into a phone seventy-seven times in one night and the frustration and hopelessness that had to follow doing so unsuccessfully.

"Then nothing until Wednesday, October 8th, when the iPhone is suddenly switched on again at 10:51 a.m. It remained on until 11:56 a.m. when its battery finally died."

"Eleven days," I say, shaking my head. "The iPhone lasted eleven days."

"Would've lasted longer," she says. "If they had continued to manage it the way they had been."

"Of course, we don't know if they were still managing it at that point," I say.

"True."

"So much we don't and can't know," I say. "We can make some deductions based on the phone evidence but it would mostly be guesses, leaps, and suppositions. And there's no way to prove them right or wrong."

"Make them anyway," she says. "I want to hear your initial reactions and conclusions."

"My overwhelming reaction is sadness for those poor girls and what they went through—no matter what it was. It was a harrowing and horrific end to young lives just getting started. And it's highly likely they were alive for a long time while search parties were out there looking for them."

She nods and frowns.

"I'll start with it being a tragic accident," I say. "No foul play and both girls staying alive and together. If that's the case, and to me the evidence says it's not, but if it is, we have to explain why Sasha stopped being able to get into her phone."

"Exactly," she says.

"She could be alive but incapacitated," I say. "Didn't give Naomi her security code before she lost consciousness. Or, she could be the one trying to access her phone. She could've been so sick or out of it from eating or drinking the wrong things out there—bad water, mushrooms, poisonous plants—that she was unable to remember her code or properly enter it. But I think it's far more likely that she wasn't conscious, wasn't with Naomi, or wasn't alive at that point."

"I agree."

"Second scenario based on the phone evidence not involving foul play—" I say. "Sasha got injured or killed. We know that very early on in their hike they felt the need to call for help. If it wasn't because they encountered someone wanting to do them harm, then it was either because they were already hopelessly lost by then or, more likely, one of them got hurt or injured. Let's say it was Sasha. She gets bitten or stung or breaks a bone or something. Naomi stays with her and they both try calling for help with their phones. And then either Naomi eventually leaves her to try to go get help or Sasha dies and Naomi takes her phone with her when she tries to find her way out of the swamp. If Sasha dies without giving Naomi her security code, she could've taken it with her and tried to use it when her Samsung died. That would explain all the wrong codes entered. Knowing her friend the way she did, she could've thought she could figure it out. Or she could've thought she knew it and maybe Sasha had changed it recently and forgot to tell Naomi. But, since we have days where neither phone is turned on, I think it's also possible that Sasha was alive but injured and unable to move and Naomi went to get help. Sasha kept her phone and continued trying to call 911 occasionally. The two girls are separated. Naomi is lost in the swamp. Her phone dies. And either because she knew her way back or more likely she was walking around in circles, she arrives back to where Sasha is and finds her dead and takes her phone and continually attempts to get in it while trying to find her way out of the swamp."

"Oh wow, I hadn't thought of that last one. And I'm not sure anyone else has either. I haven't come across anyone online who's put it out there. That's good. And it fits."

"I'm sure it's out there somewhere," I say. "I'm definitely not the first to think of that theory. If foul play was involved it would explain why there were so many wrong security code attempts but it wouldn't explain why the killer would keep trying to get into the phone. Or why he or they would leave the phones and camera in the backpack to be found. If you say he was trying to access the phone to see if there was any incriminating information in it—photos, texts, notes—it would make sense, but it would make far more sense if the killer destroyed it, if he just destroyed everything."

"Exactly," she says. "Why would their killer or killers stay in the swamp that long? Why would they keep calling 911? They wouldn't. Why wouldn't they just destroy everything?"

"So although we can't know for sure," I say, "I can see why Dad came down on the side of it being death by misadventure."

"And if you only had this phone data evidence, I'd agree, but the clothes and the backpack and bones and especially the photographs tell a very different story. It's very hard to explain them away without foul play being involved."

14

I 'm lying on a pallet of blankets and sheets on the living room floor, the girls fast asleep on either side of me. They had nodded off watching a Disney princess save her people, and I hope they're dreaming of the princesses, heroines, and saviors they can become.

I had planned to study the case file some more when Johanna and Taylor went to sleep, but by the time they actually drifted off, I was in no condition to do it.

I'm tired, both mentally and physically depleted, but it's my emotional state that provides the biggest impediment.

My sense of isolation and misery is overwhelming. I miss Anna—and I did even before she left for her retreat. She hasn't been herself for a while, and I've felt the singular and acute pain that comes from being lonely within a relationship.

And now with the girls and the world asleep and Anna halfway across the country, I feel a heightened sense of seclusion and sadness.

Was this inevitable? Was what I had with Anna until recently just the honeymoon phase of the relationship? Had I fooled myself about what we had? Had it been an illusion? Is it over now for good? In spite of everything, I didn't believe so. I still believed in us, in what we had—that it was who we are, that the recent difficulties were the anomaly, the exception that proves the rule, the result of Anna's illness and not the end of a false honeymoon period signaling the arrival of a ruthless reality.

I hear a key being entered into the lock and the easing open of the side door.

Climbing up gingerly, careful not to wake my little princesses, I cross the living room and make my way into the kitchen in time to see Merrill letting himself in.

"Just came from tucking Simien in and knew you'd be up," he says. "Za's workin' a late shift at the hospital," he adds of his new wife who's a doctor at Sacred Heart Hospital in Port St. Joe. "No reason to hurry home."

"I'm glad you stopped by," I say. "You hungry?"

"Always."

I pull a beer out of the fridge and hand it to him, and he leans on the counter drinking it while I take out a couple of steaks and drop them into a frying pan on the stove. Turning the burner to low, I cover the pan with a lid, grab a bag of seasoned french fries and empty about half of the bag into the air fryer and turn it on.

"Simien's an odd dude," Merrill says. "Can't tell which is stranger . . . him or his production."

I lift the lid, flip the steaks, and replace it.

"I know I've only seen a little of what they're shooting," he says, "and I realize they're shootin' out of sequence, but . . . none of it makes any sense and a lot of it seems to contradict itself."

"That's not surprising, considering how bad the writing was on the scene we saw."

"One of the crew members—Simien's assistant, though they all do several jobs—says Simien is a genius and is shooting the story several different ways and won't decide until he edits it all together which scenario he's going to go with. Says he might even show the different theories and let the audience decide what they think happened. He's definitely shootin' some shit with a killer chasing them through the swamp and other shit that makes it look like they got lost and had an accident. The boom mic operator or audio guy or whatever he is said that Simien is rewriting the script every night and giving them new pages each morning."

I nod. "He seems like the type that would."

"Seems like the type that don't know what the hell he doin'."

"That too," I say.

"But his ass can direct the hell out of some porn," he says. "You looked at any of his work?"

I shake my head. "You?"

"Yeah, but purely for professional reasons," he says with a smile. "Whatchin' his ass try to direct that shit today I kept wanting to tell him to make it easier on himself and tell the actors to take off their clothes."

I flip the steaks again and step over and shake the french fries in the air fryer basket.

"And the atmosphere of the shoot . . ." he says. "You'd except the actors to be frustrated, resentful, or resistant or something, but this goes way beyond irritation or tension. The hostility on that set is palpable. And it ain't just directed toward Simien. Everyone seems to hate everyone else, though the majority of it is definitely between the main actress Hailee Benson and both Simien and the main actor Logan Taylor-Johnson. Hell, she hates the crew too. Simien and Logan act awkward around her, handle her with kid gloves, let her do whatever the hell she wants. Like they scared of her."

"She seemed so nice and laid back when we talked to her," I say.

"That's what makes it so strange. She not like that with anybody else."

"Anybody following him tonight?" I ask.

He shakes his head. "But he definitely bein' harassed by somebody. Showed me the threatening notes and other shit he's done. Keyed his car and slashed his tires. Broke into his trailer and cut up all his clothes, wrote shit on the walls. Left messages on his phone sayin' he'd be dead before he could finish the film. I'm not sure how much danger he's really in. Most people serious about popping somebody just pop 'em, they don't tell 'em they gonna do it. 'Course . . . if somebody take his ass out, it'll show how much I know."

15

On Friday, November 21st, Naomi's blue backpack was discovered by an elderly lady fishing with a cane pole from the banks of the Apalachicola River near Potter Landing—a spot nearly twelve miles away from where Naomi and Sasha entered the swamp near Cottonmouth Creek. Inside were Naomi's Canon SX270 HS camera and her Samsung Galaxy, Sasha's iPhone, two bathing suit tops, a partially empty bottle of water, a compass, and seventeen dollars—all dry, packed neatly, and in good condition.

"How could an inexpensive, non-waterproof backpack stay in the swamp for nearly two months, go through a tropical storm no less, and float down a river, and it and everything in it be in pristine condition?" Ben asks.

"Always bothered me too," Dad says.

Dad, Ben, and I are heading to White City to talk to Thelma Washington, the elderly lady who found Naomi's backpack near Potter Landing. We're in Dad's truck but I'm driving. Our route takes us out of Pottersville down through Wewahitchka, Honeyville, and Dalkeith, and the destruction of Hurricane Michael that is still so evident. Downed trees. Ditches still filled with debris. Mangled mobile homes. Battered houses with blue tarps where once were shingles.

"To me it's clear evidence of foul play," Ben says. "No way that backpack was in the swamp that entire time. No way it floated down the river."

"It seems unlikely," Dad says, "but without more evidence you can't say for certain there's no way it could have."

"How?" Ben asks. "How could it stay in the swamp that long after Naomi and Sasha died? How it could it be so far from where their remains were found? How could it be in the condition it was in?"

"I've already said I don't know," Dad says. "That's the point. Not having an answer doesn't mean I'm supposed to make one up."

"I'm not making one up."

"I'm not saying you are," Dad says. "I'm just telling you what I'm doing. And that's saying I don't like this piece of evidence or lack thereof. It bothers me. But ask John—every case has details that bother you. Questions you can't answer."

"It's a pretty big dang detail," Ben says.

"Okay," Dad says, "we don't know and that's the point, but what about this— What if before they died, the girls hid the backpack in the hollow base of a cypress tree. The swamp is full of them. It would protect it. Keep it dry."

Ben nods. "Sure, but how does it get out of that safe, dry spot and down to Potter Landing?"

"It's not out of the realm of possibility that the girls left it a lot closer to the landing than we think," Dad says. "Just because their remains were found far away from it doesn't mean they didn't get that far with it. They could've hidden it intending to come back to it and kept hiking, or they could've been killed closer to where it was found than we think and animals could've dragged their remains to where they were eventually found. If the backpack was closer to the landing than we have previously believed, then a bear or some other animal could have found it and pulled it out and dragged it to the landing. So it never went into the river. Never was exposed to the tropical storm or much of anything else. Do you think that's more farfetched than someone killing the girls and later leaving their backpack near the landing?"

"No, sir," he says, "I don't."

"And if someone did kill them," Dad says, "why couldn't he just destroy their things instead of leaving them to be found? If he's the kind of killer who would stalk and kill women in the wilderness, he'd be the kind to keep trophies from it."

Ben nods. "Also true."

"But here's another scenario for you," Dad says. "Let's say the girls hide the backpack somewhere out in the swamp—closer to where their remains were found. And eventually someone finds it. Could be a hunter, a grower, one of the volunteers helping us search. And for whatever reasons—and there are plenty—they take it, actually leave the swamp with it. Then because they realize what they have or if they had known all along, they change their mind about it and place it at Potter Landing to be found. I'd say that's at least as likely as them encountering a vicious killer who does what he does to them and then two months later leaves their backpack near the landing to be found."

"It certainly is," Ben says. "You're right. I've been making assumptions and drawing conclusions—"

"That might be right," Dad says.

"But might not be," Ben says. "And that's the part I've been leaving out. Of course, it may all be moot anyway. It's possible the backpack wasn't even found at Potter Landing."

"What makes you suspicious of Thelma Washington's story of finding it where and when she did?" I ask.

"At the time she supposedly discovered it, she was Horton Joshua's housekeeper."

"Really?"

"Are you sure?" Dad says. "We never knew that."

"It was very secretive and she was paid under the table," Ben says. "Nobody much knew. The talk is that she was more than a maid. She's never been willing to talk to me. I found all this out after my book came out. But I'm hoping she'll talk to us now because she doesn't work for Horton anymore. Evidently they had some sort of falling out and she moved to White City. I think he found the remains *and* the backpack but faked Thelma finding it to hide the fact—and why would he do that unless he's hiding something else too? I think he did far more than just find the girls' remains."

"Miss Thelma, we just wanted to ask you some questions about that backpack you found near Potter Landing back when those girls from Jacksonville went missing," Dad is saying.

We had decided that Dad should do the interview because of his rapport with her.

We are standing on her porch, she behind a latched screen door.

She is an emaciated-looking, elderly black woman with skin that appears as thin and fragile as parchment. Her shortish hair is pulled back from her gaunt face and her makeup is thick and somewhat misapplied. She's in a navy blue sheath dress but has no shoes on.

"You mind if we come in for a few minutes?"

"Sheriff, you always been good to me and my boys and I owe you, that's a fact, but . . . I . . . I can't talk about that. No sir. I'm sorry, but . . . I just can't."

Thelma raised two boys on her own, and Dad had helped her in a variety of ways over the years—everything from bringing them home to her instead of the county jail when they were arrested, to helping with groceries and clothes and rent from time to time when the two jobs she worked weren't enough to cover the barest of necessities.

"Miss Thelma, you mind tellin' me why?" Dad asks.

"I'm real sorry for what happened to them girls, I am, but I didn't have nothin' to do with it and don't know anything about it."

"We don't think you did," Dad says. "We just want to talk to you about the backpack. Is there a reason you won't talk to us about it?"

"Sheriff, you probably know well as most . . . they's bad people in this world."

"I surely do," he says. "And I've always done my best to protect you and your boys and the rest of the good people I served from them."

"You certainly did that the best you could," she says. "But you ain't the sheriff no more and . . . and well they's some people don't answer to nobody. Not in this life they don't. And some of those people genuinely love hurting others. And they good at it—the pain of others. Gets good at it the way people who enjoy a thing does. Sorry, Sheriff. I truly am. But I ain't gots many good years left. Don't want to spend them in pain."

16

As we walk back toward the truck, Dad takes the keys from my hand and climbs into the driver's seat.

He's weak and unsteady and drives like it—but at an aggressively high rate of speed.

"I knew it," Ben is saying. "I knew that old, sick, fat bastard had something to do with it. She's scared to death of him."

I nod but speak to Dad. "You sure you don't want me to drive?"

"If I wanted you to," he snaps, "I wouldn't've taken the keys from you, would I?"

I don't respond. He's visibly upset and in his condition doesn't need to be. I don't want to do anything to upset him even more.

"Might want to slow down on this curve," Ben says. "It's easy to get away from you on this bad boy. Happened to me more than once."

Ignoring him, Dad drives even faster.

We race through Dalkeith, Honeyville, and Wewa as if we have emergency flashers and a siren going. We have neither.

When on the outskirts of Pottersville, Dad turns down a

side road. I know what he's doing and it concerns me far more than his reckless driving.

Horton Joshua's place is just off this road.

"We've already questioned Joshua," I say. "He won't talk."

"Ain't interested in talkin'," he says. "I'm sick to goddamn death of evil bastards like him preying on the weak and vulnerable of this world. I was wrong not to lock his ass up when I was sheriff."

"Dad, if he did it, we will get him for it," I say. "This is not the way. This will actually work against us getting him."

"Won't have to get him if he's in the ground."

He slings the truck into Horton's driveway, tires squealing, gravel flying, spots Horton on his golf cart and races toward him.

Horton is on the driveway heading toward us and seems to speed up when Dad does, as if the two men are playing chicken —one in a golf cart, the other in a full-sized pickup truck.

"Slow down," I say. "If you hit him, you'll kill him."

"And the world'll be a better place," he says.

He doesn't slow down. If anything, he speeds up.

The distance between the two mismatched vehicles steadily decreases, and I can tell that Dad is about to drive right through Horton and his golf cart and keep going.

At the last second, Horton snatches the wheel and veers off to his right, bouncing through a ditch and coming to a stop between two thick-bodied pecan trees.

Dad slams on the brakes, jumps out, and rushes toward Horton.

Ben and I jump out of the truck and follow him.

As he reaches the golf cart, Horton is stumbling out of it.

"What the fuck is wrong with you?" Horton says. "You coulda killed—"

"You're not going to hurt another person," Dad says as he steps directly in front of the rounded blob of a man.

Their faces are within inches of each other now.

"I'm making it my life's work to making sure you don't," Dad says.

"From what I hear you don't have much life left," Horton says. "So you better get busy, old man."

Horton then brings up both of his short, fat arms and shoves Dad in the chest.

As Dad is falling backward, Horton hits him in the face with the bottom of his fist, bringing it down hard like a hammer punch.

I reach out and grab Dad and keep him from hitting the ground.

As I do, Big Ben steps in between them, and though I can't see what he does because of the way he totally eclipses everything on the other side of him, he makes a sudden movement and a moment later Horton goes down and doesn't get up.

Dad's breathing is labored and his clammy skin has a distinctly gray pallor.

Ben turns and gets on the other side of Dad and we help him to stand.

As we make our way back over to the truck, Dad coughs and spits and stumbles.

"Stupid, weak old man," he says. "Sorry fellas. Lost my head for a minute there. There's no fool like an old fool."

Ben says, "Sheriff, I've never been more proud of you or had more respect for you in my entire life—and that's sayin' something."

———

17

By the time we reach Dad and Verna's farm, a deputy is waiting for us.

He's a youngish, tall, slender black man with huge hands and long, bony fingers. Dad had hired him back when it was his department and it's obvious he feels awkward and unconformable about being here.

"Sheriff," he says when we get out of the truck. "John. Ben."

"Hey, Chaquille," Dad says. "How's everything with you?"

"Been better," he says. "Hate bein' here about this."

"About what exactly?" Dad asks.

"Sheriff—the new sheriff, Sheriff Glenn, asked me to bring you in," he says. "Horton Joshua's accusing you of assault."

Hugh Glenn, an employee of Dad's, had defeated him in the last election, and is now in the position Dad had held for consecutive decades.

I start to say something but Ben beats me to it. "Horton Joshua is the only one to commit any kind of assault on anyone and he did so in front of two sworn law enforcement officers. Get your boss on the phone for me."

Chaquille taps a few buttons on his phone, tells the sheriff that Ben Brooks wants to speak with him, and hands Ben the phone.

"Hey, Sheriff," Ben says. "Ben Brooks here. How are you? Listen, Chaquille's here, says you told him to bring Sheriff Jordan in, but you need to know that an officer with Florida Wildlife and an investigator with the Gulf County Sheriff's Department witnessed the entire incident. Sheriff Jordan didn't lay a hand on anyone. In fact, Horton Joshua shoved and then struck Sheriff Jordan. The only other thing that happened after that was that I subdued the attacker, Mr. Joshua. I'm not sure if Sheriff Jordan is going to pursue charges, but he's the only one who can. He never touched anyone and yet Joshua shoved and struck him. And both the sheriff's investigator and the wildlife officer will swear to such in court. I'm just tryin' to avoid any unnecessary complications and embarrassment for your department." He waits a moment, then says, "Okay. Very good. Thank you, Sheriff."

He hands Chaquille his phone.

"Yes, sir," Chaquille says, then listens. "Okay. Yes, sir." He then disconnects the call and says to us, "Sheriff says not to bring you in but to warn all of y'all to stay away from Horton Joshua. Says even if Horton was the only one to throw a punch, y'all were on his land and he felt threatened. Says if it had only been John's word we'd still be bringing you in, but since Ben was there he'll smooth things over with Joshua."

"Smooth things over," Dad says, shaking his head. "Needs to be arresting his evil ass. But . . . guess I shouldn't expect him to take care of my unfinished business. Thank you, Chaquille. Can you stay for lunch?"

"I'd like to," he says, "but I've got to respond to a call over where they're shooting that movie about those girls that got killed in the swamp. Somebody killed an animal and left it in the director's trailer."

18

"Correct me if I'm wrong," Merrill says. "You the expert. But this does qualify as escalation."

I smile. "Certainly does."

"I mean, this shit's way beyond keyin' a car and cuttin' up some clothes."

"Certainly is."

"Motherfucker who'll do that to a—what is that?"

A mass of blood and fur dangles from a noose on the door of Simien Eggers's Airstream.

Merrill and I are standing about ten feet away from where Chaquille is carefully examining the poor creature hanging in front of the door, but even if we were closer we wouldn't be able to identify what kind of creature it is.

"Not sure," I say.

The large, old Airstream is in the back corner of Oak Grove Campground, a small, rustic campground surrounded on all sides by thick woods. A handful of other older campers that house the rest of the cast and crew are spread throughout the secluded campground. Though there are empty sites, only the crew in town making *Lost Innocents* are staying here.

"Anyone who'll do that to a little fur ball," he says, "capable of cuttin' up a hack director."

"I'd say so."

Behind us in small groups of two or three, the cast and crew look on in both fear and fascination.

"The hell I get myself into?" he asks.

"Not easy being a patron of the arts, is it?"

"Oh, shit, that's right," he says. "I'm doin' this shit for free."

Though Chaquille had called for an investigator and a crime scene unit, he is examining the door and the bloody fur at the end of the short nylon rope as if it's his job to do so, poking and prodding the small critter with a fountain pen.

"I can't tell what it . . ." Chaquille is saying. "Looks sort of like a—"

He jumps back, losing his footing and dropping his pen, which hits the ground a moment before he does, as the bloody mass begins to move.

"*What the fuck*?" Merrill says, his voice airy and high.

The nylon rope begins to bounce up and down as angry hisses, squeals, and shrieks emanate from the writhing beast.

As I start toward it, the noose loosens and a flap of animal hide drops down, releasing the angry cat that had been inside.

The cat, a small blue-gray whirring blur, lands on its paws and darts away, growling as it goes, quickly disappearing into the woods beyond the clearing.

"It's a . . . deer skin," Chaquille says.

Part of a deer hide had been gathered and tied at the top to form a pouch that held the cat. It's unclear if the red substance the deer skin had been smeared with is animal blood or something else, but it doesn't appear to be the cat's, who besides angry and annoyed did not seem injured in any way.

19

"Should've stayed in porn," Dale Kohler says as he walks up to me and Merrill.

He's a skinny twenty-something in white drawstring capri pants and a pink T-shirt so tight he had to have purchased them in the boy's section of the department store. He's wearing black-and-white faux alligator-skin loafers with no socks and what looks to be about ten black bead-and-leather-band bracelets on each of his tiny wrists. His hair is bushy and long and in need of washing and he has a large auburn-tinted handlebar mustache.

Kohler is Simien's director of photography and camera operator and assistant director and a few other things going back to his days in porn.

"Who does something like this?" he says.

"A sick fuck," Merrill says.

"There's some strange shit in porn," he says. "But never anything like this."

"Any ideas who may've done it?" I ask.

"Like I told him," he says, nodding toward Merrill, "this shoot is cursed. Everything that can go wrong *has*. I mean everything. It's as if someone is secretly sabotaging the production."

"Who would want to?" I ask. "And why?"

He shrugs. "Anyone who doesn't want the film to get made. Who knows? A family member or friend of the victims, whoever killed them—if someone killed them. Simien has been very vocal about his promise."

"His promise?" I ask.

"That the film will reveal the identity of the killer."

As if on cue, Simien walks up and joins us.

"That poor little creature," he says. "What kind of depraved, demented mind could come up with such a thing?"

"You have any ideas?" I ask.

He shakes his head. "All I know is that great intellects and artists are always misunderstood and mistreated by the inferior individuals whose fear and insecurity make them feel threatened."

I resist the urge to ask him how that applies here.

"Any inferior individual in particular?" Merrill asks.

Simien shrugs. "They're all part of the nameless, faceless uncreative crowd to me."

"We tryin' to stop one of those nameless, faceless ones from stepping out of the masses and punchin' your ticket," Merrill says. "Be helpful, we had some idea who it might be."

"Can't tell you something I don't know. But it's obviously someone who doesn't want the truth out there."

"The truth as in what really happened to Naomi and Sasha?" I ask.

"Sure, that," he says, "but also the deeper truth of what it says about us as humans, about crime culture, and the systemic misogyny that pervades our particular patriarchy."

It's difficult not to laugh at everything he says—even when there is some truth in it. His relentless self-aggrandizement makes him seem to be playing a role parodying an overly earnest young filmmaker and undercuts even his accurate observations about society. Of course, it's also the way he says what he says.

"Is it true you're telling everyone that you're going to reveal the identity of the killer in the movie?" I ask.

"I'm not making anything nearly so crass or commercial as a movie," he says. "I'm making a work of art. *Film* is a far more appropriate term for what I'm creating. But yes, I will reveal what happened to these tragic young ingénues and who is responsible."

Merrill says, "And it ain't occurred to your genius ass that said killer might want to stop you from doin' that?"

"Well . . . of course," he says hesitantly, and it's obvious this hasn't even crossed his mind.

"So you don't think it was an accident?" I ask.

"There are no accidents."

"You believe they were murdered and that you know who did it?"

"You'll have to watch my film to find out," he says.

Merrill says, "Careful being too coy. Could get you killed."

"You don't think I'd gladly die for my art?"

As we are talking, Renadale Hanan walks up and stands several feet away. Serving as the PA, script supervisor, and responsible for craft services, she is the youngest member of the entire production.

She is nineteen but looks more like she's fifteen—or younger, her juvenile figure having nothing particularly female about it. She's kind of quiet and shy, but hardworking and seems to worship Simien.

She waits while the great director talks, obviously not wanting to interrupt the genius's flow, and only comes over when he motions her to.

"Everyone's asking if we're still going to shoot today," she says.

"And of course they sent you over," he says.

"Yes, sir."

"None of that now," he says. "We're all co-collaborators on my set. It's my vision we're bringing to life but we're doing it together. I'm not above anyone else and age is irrelevant, so no need to call me sir."

"Yes, si—" she begins, then stops. "Okay."

"Okay what?" he asks, as if she's a child, and I guess in many ways she is.

"Your highness?" Merrill says.

"Okay, Simien," she says.

"Of course we're going to shoot," he says. "The philistines will never win—not so long as I'm at the helm. Tell everyone to make ready for battle. We beat the bully today. You know what, never mind. I'll tell them myself. Come on."

He takes her by the hand and they head off together, almost skipping as they do.

"That may not be the creepiest thing I've never seen," Merrill says, "but then again it just might be."

s the cast and crew are dispersing to prepare for their first shoot of the day, Merrill and I walk over to Hailee Benson.

"Is this the most bizarre shit you've ever seen?" she says.

"No, but we've seen more than our share of bizarre shit," Merrill says.

"This is without a doubt the worst experience of my life," she says. "I've actually been in some decent movies. Have y'all seen *Campground Killer 3*?"

Merrill smiles. "Must've missed that one."

"It's a terrible title, I know," she says, "but it's actually a good little movie. And I'll tell you why—because the writer-director on it wasn't a no-talent hack posing as an auteur. He knew he wasn't making art, so he concentrated on making a good movie. I may not know much, but I know pretension kills creativity."

"Your mom called me again last night," Merrill says. "Said she still hasn't heard from you."

"I just . . . You told her I'm okay, right? You can see that I am. I'm just going through some stuff right now."

"Really?" Merrill says with mock surprise. "'Cause you hide it so well."

"You're kidding, but I am actually holding my shit together pretty well, all things considered."

"Your rage at Simien, Dale, and Logan seems about a lot more than dissatisfaction with how the production is going."

"It is," she says. "They're pigs. Vile reptiles. I detest them more than I can say."

I say, "Why not quit?"

"I would if I could," she says. "But I just can't."

"Well, can you at least call your moms?" Merrill asks.

She shakes her head. "Not yet. I'm just not ready yet. She's my agent and manager. She's the reason I'm in this shit show. I promise you she doesn't want me to call her. She thinks she does, but she doesn't."

A huge black SUV pulls into the campground and Hailee turns to watch it, visibly excited by its arrival.

"Who's that?" Merrill asks.

"Naomi's parents' attorney," she says. "He's tryin' his best to shut this shit down—and I'm pulling for him."

21

Merrill and I make our way over to Simien and are standing with him when the small attorney climbs down out of the back seat of the big black SUV.

His driver remains in the vehicle.

Thomas McCloud is a short, slight, middle-aged man with a pointed, balding head and small round glasses. He's in an expensive black suit, crisp, bright white shirt, and a narrow black silk tie.

"Mr. Eggers," he says as he walks up.

"You know the answer," Simien says.

"But you don't know the question," McCloud says.

"If it's *will I stop production on this film*, the answer is *no*."

"I've come with a new proposal," McCloud says. "One I can almost guarantee you're going to like. Is there somewhere we can talk?"

Simien nods. "Right here."

McCloud glances at Merrill and then me.

"These gentlemen are part of my security and investigative staff. Feel free to speak freely in front of them."

Merrill shoots a look over at me and mouths *security and investigative staff*.

The other members of the cast and crew have stopped what they're doing and are looking on, but none of them venture over any closer so that they could actually hear what's being said.

Unlike over in Gulf County, the trees here in Potter County are still standing, still straight and unbent, and the early afternoon sun shines down through their branches, limbs, leaves, and needles to dapple the uneven ground.

"I understand you're financing this film yourself," McCloud says.

"Can't expect anyone else to invest in your art if you won't," Simien says.

"I also understand that your hope, like so many independent filmmakers, is to sell it to a distributor, which I understand is a very, very long shot."

"You seem to understand a lot—or think you do," Simien says.

"I'm just saying that the prospects of you winding up with a mountain of credit card debt and a film you can't sell are enormous."

"Everything in life is a gamble."

"Sure, but some things far more than others," McCloud says. "Some with far, far less odds than others."

"I realize you're paid by the hour," Simien says, "but I'm gonna need you to get to the point. I'm losing daylight while you circle around to what you came to say."

"I'm merely pointing out the reality of the situation," he says. "As you no doubt know, my clients still aren't satisfied with the lack of answers they've gotten and are raising the reward for information leading to the arrest and conviction of their daughter's murderer. We're hosting a huge fundraiser rally this weekend and they are going to match every cent that is raised.

We're already at near fifty-thousand and we believe we will be well over one hundred by next week. And the thing is, since my clients believe that your film would have an adverse effect on them finding out the truth of what happened to their daughter and her best friend, they feel as though a good use of some of the reward money would be to purchase the film and TV rights to the book from you."

I'm not sure exactly how much of the reward money McCloud is offering, but Simien's production budgets must be even more micro than I realized if even the entire amount could not only pay off this production but fund his next one.

"You're saying for me to stop my production and I've already told you my answer to that."

"What I'm saying is . . . I'm offering to purchase from you the rights to *Lost Innocents* for enough to pay off all you owe on this production and to fund your next film. Surely you have many other stories to tell. You could simply move on to the next one with the entire budget to actually make it without going into any more personal debt. It's the offer of a clean slate and a fresh start and the resources to achieve your vision on your next story—something that now has to be obvious even to you isn't happening on this one."

Simien doesn't respond, just appears to be considering the bribe being offered.

"No need to answer me now," McCloud says. "Mull it over for a day or two and let me know. We and our resources aren't going anywhere."

22

"He actually seemed like he might take the money and run?" Ben asks.

"Certainly seemed to be considering it," I say.

"That would be . . . incredible."

"You wouldn't be disappointed?" Dad asks.

"I'd be relieved," he says. "There's no way to know what the finished film will be like, but based on what we know of Simien and the shoot, I'd say chances are good that it will be horrendous. And even if by some cinematic miracle he pulled off making a good movie from a production-quality standpoint, I still believe his point of view will be so skewed that it would do more harm than good to everyone involved—you, Sheriff, those poor girls, and even my book."

Dad, Ben, and I are sitting at Dad's dining room table. Verna and Johanna have gone to pick up Taylor from school. Merrill is watching over Simien on the set of *Lost Innocents*. And Anna is still thousands of miles away at her meditation retreat. Dad, Ben, and I are waiting for Chaquille, who had called and asked if he could meet with the three of us together.

"I'm not convinced he's going to do it," I say, "but it wasn't an automatic no like before."

"I wish he would," Ben says.

"He'd pay a high price," I say.

"To his ego?" Dad says.

"It'd show what a hypocrite he is," Ben says.

I say, "It'd expose him. Reveal how nearly everything he's ever said about his art is BS. Of course, if he does it, he'll find a way to justify and rationalize it."

"True," Dad says.

"I don't even care," Ben says. "He can tell himself and others whatever he wants as long as he pulls the plug on the production."

"Do you think the Newmans are just purchasing the rights to kill it?" Dad asks.

"What do you—"

"That they're not going to do anything with them," he says. "Not make a movie of their own or . . . anything else."

"That's interesting," Ben says. "I hadn't even considered that. I can't see them doing anything with them. But they'll be free to do whatever they want. All they're concerned with is finding out exactly what happened to Naomi and Sasha. If they thought a movie or docuseries or whatever would help with that, then they'd make it in a heartbeat. I just don't see how it would do that."

"How well do you know them?" I ask.

"Just a little," he says. "They refused to let me interview them for the book, but we've gotten to know each other some since it came out."

"I'd like to talk to them if possible," I say.

He nods. "I'll see what I can do."

"Thanks."

"There's Chaquille," Dad says, nodding toward the driveway through the window. "Let's see what this is all about."

By the time Chaquille is out of his patrol car and walking over to the house, we are standing on the porch waiting for him.

"Sheriff, Ben, John," he says. "Afternoon."

"Afternoon, Chaquille," Dad says.

"I'm sorry to have to be the one to do this, but the sheriff thought it'd be best coming from me."

"What would?" Dad asks.

"Horton is petitioning the court for a restraining order against the three of you," he says. "There's a hearing in five days. In the meantime, Judge Simpson issued a temporary restraining order against y'all. I'm sorry, but I'm here to serve y'all with the petition and the temporary order."

"No need to be sorry about it," Dad says. "Got nothing to do with you. And it's not like we have any desire to be around that fat bastard. Just wanted to stop him from hurting some vulnerable people and find out if he had anything to do with what happened to Naomi and Sasha."

"I know that, Sheriff. I do. And I know Horton's filing this to prevent you from doing that. He's not fooling anybody. So . . . just between us . . . if you need me to do anything just let me know."

23

That evening I drive down to Gaines Landing to meet with Denise Denaro of the Wabi Sabis.

Wabi sabi is an ancient Japanese art form that embraces imperfection. The Wabi Sabis are an all-female band out of Panama City known for lively and fun performances of their own unique brand of acoustic folk-pop and Americana, and their profoundly positive energy.

They are headlining the reward money fundraiser being organized by Naomi's parents.

I had worked with the group recently at a Hurricane Michael fundraiser, but already had a connection to Denise through our mutual friend Dave Lloyd.

Denise is in town to check out the stage and finalize the details for their upcoming performance and had called to see if I had a moment to answer a few questions she had. Instead of having a conversation on the phone or having her come by Dad and Verna's farm, I had offered to meet her at the landing.

Gaines Landing is part of Jay and Robbie's property, but on the opposite side and a few miles from where they live with their wild child foster boys.

Like most of the many landings along the Apalachicola River, Gaines consists of a simple cement boat launch at the end of a county-maintained dirt road. Though private property, the public uses the landing as if it is a public boat launch, and as I pull in there are a handful of trucks with empty boat trailers attached to them scattered about.

Instead of a large, empty clearing cut out of the woods lining Florida's longest river, the landing now holds a huge stage, a few temporary pavilions, and a smattering of wooden and aluminum picnic tables. A long row of porta potties runs along the tree line on the far side.

The stage, constructed on top of a rusted, old flatbed semi-trailer, is parallel to the river. The cypress trees lining the banks, both in and out of the water, provide a picturesque back-drop and sound barrier.

When I park and step out of my truck—a new magma red metallic Ford F-150 Anna had surprised me with following a big settlement she had obtained for a client she was repre-senting in a medical malpractice lawsuit—Denise leaves the small group she is speaking with over near the stage and bounds over to me.

"*John Jordan*," she sings out.

Energetic and bubbly, she is the kind of person who makes you feel like she's genuinely happy to see you.

We embrace.

"I can wait if you need to finish with them," I say, nodding toward the small group.

"We've *been* finished," she says. "This is their first event like this and they're nervous, so they're just going over everything a few hundred times."

"How're the other Sabis?"

"All good," she says. "Just living the dream. Nobody told us it was this much fun being rock stars."

Born out of the Ukulele Orchestra of St Andrews and

gigging together since August of 2017, the Wabi Sabis is comprised of Julie Bullock on upright bass, Valerie Woods on vocals, uke, and mandolin, Jennifer Rollins on guitar and vocals, and Denise on washboard, percussion, and vocals.

Denise glances back at the group then looks at me and lowers her voice. "I just wanted to ask you about this whole thing," she says. "Someone mentioned you were working the case and I knew you'd have a much better feel for what's going on over here."

"What do you mean?"

"We're just getting some strange vibes and some red flags about this event and wanted to make sure we need to be doing it. We're always down to support a good cause."

"Y'all are extremely generous and I can't tell you how much you're appreciated."

"We just wanna make sure it is a good cause, you know?"

I nod. "Of course."

"Obviously, helping the family find out what really happened to their daughters is worthwhile, but is that what we're doing? One of the organizers mentioned the film that's being shot here and said something about some of the money raised may go to buying it so it doesn't come out."

"I heard something about that for the first time this morning," I say.

"Really? So it's true? What's the deal?"

I tell her what I know.

"What do you think?" she asks. "Should we still be involved?"

"There's no way to know if the film would help or hurt the investigation," I say. "It's entirely possible it'll be too obscure to do either. I know that the author of the book it's based on hopes that the family is able to buy the rights and stop the production so it doesn't come out. To me, what y'all are doing is a very good and generous thing. It will increase awareness of the case and give comfort to the community. And if stopping the production provides the suffering family with any solace at all, I can't see how that's a bad thing."

"That's all we needed to hear," she says. "We'll be here doing our perfectly imperfect best."

24

After leaving the landing, I drive around the Gaineses' property hoping to see Meagan or Dylan without their parents around.

It takes a little while, but eventually an old Camaro pulls off the highway and onto the dirt road leading back to the Gaineses' house.

For a long moment the car just sits there idling, but eventually the passenger door creaks open and Dylan climbs out in a cloud of smoke.

As the loud car speeds away, Dylan, dressed in black biker boots, black jeans, and a black T-shirt, begins walking toward the house.

The dirt road leading back to the Gaineses' home is long and straight and empty, thick woods on either side of it.

I pull up beside him.

"Want a ride?"

He shakes his head.

Though technically an adult, he has yet to fill out and still has the body of a boy, and he actually looks taller than his slightly below-average height because of how thin he is. His wavy black hair is too long and stands high on his head in a kind of big, soft pompadour that undulates as he walks.

He continues moving and I follow along beside him, leaning out of the window slightly.

He seems unkempt and maybe a little uncared for, a lone, vulnerable young man in a merciless world, and something about the figure he casts hurts my heart. Life is difficult enough without being abandoned by your parents, and I feel sorry for him, even as I'm grateful for what the Gaineses are doing for him.

I'm also—and not for the first time—filled with gratitude for my parents. In spite of their issues, even Mom's alcoholism, they gave me so much—and never gave me up.

"Hop in," I say. "I'm headed that way anyway and I need to talk to you."

"You the guy lookin' into what happened to Naomi and Sasha?"

"One of them," I say. "John Jordan. I think I've spoken to about everyone around here except you."

"Can't imagine what they've told you about me," he says. "Ain't walkin' 'cause I got no ride. Need to air out and I like to get my head together before I go back in that place. But I don't mind talkin' to you if you want to ride alongside me."

"Cool," I say. "Thanks."

"It's all good, man."

He's obviously high, but not so excessively that I think it'd be a waste of time to talk to him.

"Why do you have to get your head together before going home?" I ask.

He shrugs. "It's just . . . kinda chaotic. All those little kids. And Robbie can be a little much. Jay's cool, but everybody else is a little . . . intense."

I nod and give him an understanding expression. "I get that."

"It's funny, man, but . . . you called it home. Doesn't feel like home to me. Not really. They adopted me and everything but . . . don't think it will ever feel like home. Guess no place does."

"You'll have your own place one day," I say. "And when you do, you'll know what home feels like."

"Hope so. I just need some space and some quiet, you know?"

"I absolutely do," I say. "I'd go crazy if I didn't have that."

"That's what it feels like a lot of the time. Like I'm losing my mind 'cause I never get any time with just it. Can't ever just hear myself think. It's too much, man."

"Sounds to me like you're an introvert," I say. "Extraverts like having people around all the time—they draw their energy from them. Introverts need time alone—that's where we draw our energy from."

His expression seems to indicate he's considering what I've said.

"One's not better than the other," I say. "Both have strengths and challenges. The earlier in life you can figure out which you are and live your life accordingly, the better your life will be. You ever come out here by yourself? Walk out in the woods and sit and think?"

"Try to," he says, "but usually one of the little brats follows me. Before long they're all out here."

"It gets better," I say.

"That's what they tell the gay kids," he says.

"It's generally true for everyone," I say. "Get older and gain more autonomy and—"

"More what?"

"Get to be your own person, make your own decisions, decide what you want your life to be like."

"They think I'm weird," he says. "Don't know why they adopted me. Must've felt like they had to."

"I really don't think that's the case," I say. "Robbie doesn't seem like she does anything she doesn't want to."

"That's for damn sure."

"They speak about you with genuine love and real affection," I say, "and they've worked hard to protect you from questions about what happened to Naomi and Sasha."

"That may be for their protection as much as mine," he says.

"Why's that?"

He shrugs. "Don't know exactly. Just . . . Doesn't matter. I know a lot of people think I had something to do with it."

"Did you?"

He doesn't seem surprised or offended by the question.

Turning and looking at me directly, he says, "No, sir. I didn't. Some of what's bein' said is true. I did crush on Sasha pretty hard, but how that could make anyone think that'd make me more likely to hurt her . . . I just don't know."

"Do you have any idea what happened to them or who may have hurt them?"

He shrugs.

I wait.

He doesn't say anything.

"Do you?"

"I don't guess so," he says.

I decide to come back to that.

"Did you go with them into the swamp that Sunday morning?"

"Started to," he says. "Should have. Wish I would have. But I could tell they didn't want me to. Treated me like I was a little puppy dog following them, so I sent Biscuit with them."

I start to say something, but he continues.

"And I'll tell you this," he says. "No way he just left them alone out there. Something happened."

"Any idea what?"

He frowns and shakes his head. "No, not . . . specifically, but I . . . I really believe he came to get help. I don't know if someone took them or they got hurt or something, but they weren't just lost. He would've led them back home. He wouldn't've left them unless they couldn't come or were separated from him and he came to get help. That's why I went back out there with him, searching."

"Where'd he lead you?" I ask. "What'd you find?"

"He took me to a couple of spots, but there was nothing there. He looked so confused. It was like they had been there but were gone, and he'd try to follow the scent but kept getting turned around. Eventually I ran into Jay, and he made me come back with him. I tried to tell everyone that we needed to go back out there, that Biscuit coming back on his own meant they were in trouble and needed us now. Some people believed me. I know Jay did and a few others like the guy who wrote the book and some of the search-and-rescue guys did, but the sheriff— that's your dad, right?—it was his call and he said we wouldn't start the search until the next morning. Always wondered what woulda happened if we'd'a gone out that night. They both might be alive today."

"It was heroic of you to go out looking for them and to try to convince the others to go back out too," I say.

He shakes his head. "Wasn't heroic. Wasn't . . . anything. Just . . . needed doing. I didn't even think about it. I just did it."

We are nearing the house and I know I don't have much time left with him.

"Earlier you seemed like you might have an idea of what happened to Naomi and Sasha," I say.

"I just know there was a reason why they didn't mind me and Meagan tagging along the rest of the time but didn't want us going that day."

"What was that?"

"They were meeting someone," he says. "Well, Sasha was. I don't think Naomi knew anything about it."

"Who?"

He shrugs. "I don't know. A guy. She used to talk to Naomi and text in her phone in this . . . like code. I listened to it and snuck enough glances at her texts to figure out part of it. She had been talkin' to this guy online. He was from over this way somewhere—farther west, like PCB or Fort Walton. I think a big part of the reason she came was to meet him. I think he had something to do with it—because if not, why not come forward and tell what you know. You know?"

25

"People say there's nothing worse than losing a child," Reese Newman is saying, "but they're wrong. Losing a child and not knowing what happened to them and who's responsible is worse."

Dad, Ben, and I all nod and acknowledge the truth of what she is saying.

Naomi's mom must have had her when she was very young. Reese Newman is still a young woman, somewhere in her early forties, with long black hair, sad, dark eyes, smooth olive skin, and a youthful appearance.

From a distance and at a glance, especially sitting in her plush hotel suite high above Panama City Beach, Reese Newman looks to be an attractive, pampered woman living the good life—and perhaps partly she is—but a second, closer look reveals a childless mother broken open by loss and grief.

She is seated in an oversized leather club chair. Framed by the sliding glass door of the balcony, the Gulf of Mexico, some sixteen stories below, expands out toward the vanishing horizon and the setting sun sinking toward it.

Dad, Ben, and I are seated around her on the matching

leather couches that form the seating area atop the muted colors of an authentic Persian rug. The three of us have come to Reese's hotel room to talk to her about our new investigation into what happened to her daughter and her daughter's best friend. The only other person in the room is her attorney, Thomas McCloud, who set up the meeting—something I don't think even he would've been able to do if Ben weren't with us. He is standing over near the wet bar along the far wall.

Hurricane Michael had wiped out many of the hotels and motels closer to Pottersville and filled the rest, but I suspect Reese would've stayed out here regardless. Nothing over in our area comes close to providing this level of luxury.

"I can only imagine," Dad says.

"But that's the thing," she says. "It's unimaginable. So you can't."

"I guess it is," Dad says, nodding slowly. "I guess I can't. I wanted to apologize to you again in person for not being able to give you more answers during our first investigation. I honestly did my very best and have never stopped working on it."

"I received your email, of course, but I do appreciate you coming here and saying it in person. I truly do."

Of the many critics of Dad's handling of the case, no one had been more outspoken than Reese Newman.

"We're very hopeful we'll get you more answers this time," he says.

"I don't just want answers," she says. "I want justice."

"The one will lead to the other," he says.

"I certainly hope so," she says. "But I've nearly lost all hope."

"Please don't do that," he says. "Not yet."

"I'm encouraged that you're working with Mr. Brooks," she says, nodding toward Ben. "I take that as a very encouraging sign. Does it mean you've finally come around to seeing that it couldn't just be a tragic accident?"

Dad starts to speak, but she cuts him off.

"'Cause I'll tell you this . . ." she says. "There's no way—no way—my tough, scrappy little girl wouldn't survive that swamp if that's all it was. Someone killed her and Sasha and I want his head."

"I am leaning toward that," Dad says.

"Leaning?"

"I have to remain open and follow the evidence where it leads—no matter where that may be—but I do believe someone is responsible for what happened to them."

"Well, I guess that's something."

Ben clears his throat. "I wanted to apologize to you too," he says.

"You have nothing to apologize for," she says. "Nothing whatsoever."

"I do," he says.

She looks at me and then Dad. "Do you know he sent me an advance copy of his book and expressed a willingness to change anything I had an issue with?"

We nod at Ben.

"The thing is," he says, "I wouldn't have sold the film rights if I didn't think it would help us find out what happened."

"I know that."

"I'm afraid I made a huge mistake by selling them to Simien Eggers. He talked a good game, but . . ."

"We'll sort it out," she says.

"I feel horrible that any of the reward money would have to be used to buy back the rights," he says.

She starts to say something, but stops as Ben reaches into his shirt pocket, pulls out a check, and hands it to her.

"What's this?" she asks, looking down at it.

"The option and film rights money I was paid by Simien," he says. "It's not much, but I want you to use it toward buying back the rights and stopping his production."

"That's awfully generous of you," she says, "but there's no need. Truly. We have more than—"

"The only thing I care about is finding answers and getting justice for Naomi and Sasha. I could never profit over what happened to them."

"But you already have," Thomas McCloud says from over by the wet bar.

Ben shakes his head. "No, I haven't. Not that it's any of your business, but the little money that has come in from the book sales, I've already donated to the reward money fund."

"Oh," Thomas says.

"*Ben*," Reese says, "that's so . . . Thomas, you owe Ben an apology."

"I certainly do," Thomas says. "Please forgive me, Mr. Brooks. I spoke out of turn, and, as it happens, out of ignorance."

I nod at Ben and give him an expression of respect and appreciation.

"Don't any of you go making this anything more than it is," he says. "None of it amounts to much money. And I don't need money. I have a good job and plenty put up."

"But the gesture," she says, "means more than you'll ever know."

"Certainly does," Thomas says.

We all fall silent for a moment, and it's obvious that Ben is embarrassed and uncomfortable.

"The world is full of good and kind and generous people," I say.

"In spite of everything, I have to agree," Reese says.

"We won't keep you much longer," Ben says, "but could we ask you a few questions first?"

"Of course," Reese says.

Ben's timing is genius. He could've easily waited until we

were leaving to give her the check, but by doing it when he did, he assured her cooperation.

He glances at Dad.

"First," Dad says, "can we start with . . . Is there anything the investigation or the media reports have gotten wrong about Naomi or Sasha that you feel needs correcting?"

"So much," she says. "So very much."

"I mean that would have a direct bearing on the investigation and finding out what happened to them."

"There was nothing frivolous about my Naomi," she says. "She was a sober and serious-minded young woman. And she was tough as they come. She wasn't a party girl and she wasn't there partying it up those three days before she disappeared. She wouldn't have risked her or Sasha's life by going into that swamp. She wouldn't have gone farther than she was supposed to. She wouldn't. She was careful and cautious and vigilant. She wasn't a boring person—I don't mean to make her sound like that—but she was an extremely responsible one. And she was a fighter, a survivor. No way she didn't make it out of that swamp unless someone killed her in it. And that's not just a mother's misguided belief in her daughter. When Naomi was just seven years old, my father-in-law took her fishing. Made a big deal of taking her to his secret spot, this prime fishing hole that no one else knew about. To make a very, very long and harrowing story short, he suffered a heart attack and died at this secluded lake in the middle of nowhere outside of Jacksonville and no one knew where they were. Naomi survived for almost four days in the wilderness on her own—*at seven*. Don't tell me she couldn't do it at twenty-one. It breaks my heart that she survived all she did in life, including that, just for some evil fuck to kill her in the swamp and for everyone to believe she just got lost and gave up."

"Was Naomi seeing anyone?" I ask.

Reese shakes her head. "She had a boyfriend her freshman

year, but it was never serious. She had been concentrating on her studies since then. She went out on occasion, mostly in groups."

"What about Sasha?" I ask.

"I honestly don't know much about her," she says. "They were college friends . . . so I didn't get to know her well. I understand she was very . . . active . . . socially. As far as I know she wasn't seeing any one person, but, like I say, I don't know for sure. Why? Do you think someone followed them or . . ."

"Just gathering information," I say. "Trying to accumulate as much as we can. You never know the one point that causes all the tumblers to click into place."

"Well, I haven't found Sasha's family to be particularly helpful, but you could ask them."

"Why do you think?" I ask.

"They're satisfied it was an accident and want to move on from all of it. I can't."

Ben looks from Reese to Thomas and says, "Could you all put out the new reward total amount? The more it is, the better chance we have of getting some useful info. It will increase the crank calls and the bogus tips, but I think it's worth it."

"Absolutely," she says, then to Thomas, "Make that happen by the morning, would you? And double what we've put into it."

26

D riving back to my place from Panama City Beach we are quiet, each seeming lost in our own thoughts, presumably about the case and what Reese Newman has just told us.

As soon as we cross the Hathaway Bridge, leaving Panama City Beach and coming into Panama City, we are surrounded by the damage and devastation wrought by Hurricane Michael. Piles of debris. The flashing lights of work crews. Abandoned buildings, widows blown out, roofs ripped off. Traffic filled with trucks and trailers hauling heavy equipment. Chaos. Confusion. Claustrophobia.

"So often over the years I've worked cases alone," I say.

My voice sounds small and disembodied in the darkness of the truck cab.

"It's very different getting to work it with you guys," I say. "And I want you to know how much I appreciate it."

They both sort of nod and mumble an acknowledgement, as if they've not fully come out of their thoughts or what I'm saying makes them uncomfortable.

"I also want you both to know how inspiring I find you," I

say. "Your desire and commitment to close the case. Dad, your openness to having been wrong and wanting to get it right no matter what that is. And Ben, your generosity is heartening and affecting."

"It's just not that much money," he says. "And it's only money. I have everything I need. I can't fathom making money off of what happened to those two poor girls. I've never understood benefitting from the tragedy of others. I mean, I guess people who do it professionally—authors, journalists, filmmakers, podcasters—have to make a living, but an amateur like me . . . I just needed to write about it. Couldn't let it go. I did this for me. I'm not generous. I'm selfish."

"That's not how I see it," I say.

"Me neither," Dad adds.

"Why did you ask about Naomi and Sasha being in relationships?" Ben asks.

I can tell he wants to change the subject, so I let him.

I tell them about talking to Dylan and what he said about Sasha trying to meet someone.

"That's . . ." Ben says. "Victims are much more likely to be killed by someone they know than a stranger. If one or both of them had a jealous or possessive boyfriend they were going to meet out there . . ."

"But why meet him in the swamp?" I say. "Seems like they'd've had him or them come into town—to the ballgame or the Oasis or the bonfire, not the swamp."

"That's true," he says.

"Unless," Dad says, "she wanted to keep him a secret. Could've been something about him that she didn't want anyone else knowing—or just the fact of his existence."

I nod, though they can't see me do so in the dark cab. "Doesn't necessarily have to be a *him*."

"True," Dad says. "That in itself could be the reason for secrecy."

"That would explain why Sasha shot down all the guys who gave her attention," Ben says.

"But she didn't seem to have the personality type to care what other people thought," I say.

"Maybe it wasn't her but him who wanted to keep it a secret," Dad says.

"To me that fits better with what we know."

"There's just so much we *don't* know," Ben says.

"Too true," Dad says.

We fall silent a moment as we pass through Callaway, which was hit even harder by Michael than most areas around here, the devastation and decimation more pronounced, more complete.

"I feel really bad that we didn't start the search that night," Dad says. "That may be the single biggest mistake I made in the entire case."

"There was no way to know," Ben says. "It was just a judgement call. All you knew was that there were two girls lost in the swamp. Not wanting to risk getting more people lost or injured or even killed because they were out there searching at night wasn't wrong. It was wise."

"But you wanted to search that night," Dad says. "You agreed with Dylan and—"

"Yeah, but I was young and stupid," he says. "Like Dylan. And like Dylan I thought Sasha was something else. Wouldn't've minded looking heroic in front of her or Naomi. Sitting here tonight, at least a little older and wiser, I believe you made the right call given everything you knew at the time. Sending your deputies, search and rescue, and volunteers out into the swamp that night doesn't guarantee we would have found them. It's more likely one of us would've gotten hurt or killed."

"I wish I had known the stuff about the dog," Dad says. "If I had known there was a possibility he was trying to lead us to them . . ."

"But Dylan said they weren't at the spots where he led him to," I say.

"I still feel horrible about it," Dad says.

"You feel horrible?" Ben says. "Think about how I feel. I've always thought Dylan did it."

"We don't know for sure he didn't," Dad says. "We can't just go by what he said or the fact that John feels bad for him and sees the best in him. He does that for everyone."

27

"Naomi's camera didn't have the same battery problems as the girls' phones," Sam is saying. "It was a Canon SX270 HS and was found in good condition in the backpack and actually still had battery life left on it. There were 133 photos from their time in the swamp. Each had a time and date stamp—though we think the time was off, but none of them had any GPS location info because this model of camera doesn't come with that option."

"So the only way we can establish or guess at any of their locations," Ben says, "is by studying their surroundings—the backgrounds of the photos themselves. But because many of the shots are at night and so much of the swamp environs look exactly the same, we haven't been able to tell much."

"Exactly," Sam says.

When Dad, Ben, and I had returned from Panama City Beach, we found Sam at my place. She had hitched a ride over with Daniel, who had come to record another podcast with Merrick. The four of us were supposed to have dinner and go over the camera evidence in the case while Verna kept the girls, but Dad was tired and not feeling well and decided to go home, so it's just Sam, Ben, and me. Merrill is supposed to stop by when he finishes with Simien for the day.

After a bite of pizza and a sip of her Blue Moon, Sam continues, "The first photos from the afternoon they left—Sunday, September 28th—show both girls smiling and happy. The weather was good—plenty of sunshine, no rain. Though it's difficult to tell based on the background of the photos—as Ben said, so much of the swamp looks the same—it appears as if they are on their way to Cottonmouth Creek."

Sam had brought the pizza and beer and even oranges to slice up and put into the Blue Moons.

"There's not an actual trail to the creek," Ben says, "but the Gaineses' boys go to it enough that there is a certain worn path that is somewhat visible if you look closely enough."

"But even on a clear day with the sun shining," Sam says, "the river swamp's thick canopy of trees doesn't allow much sun through."

She wipes her fingers and withdraws some photographs from a file folder.

Ben slides the pizza box over and she spreads the prints out on the kitchen table.

The enlarged photos show the two young women walking, smiling, and pointing at various trees, plants, animals, and other objects of interest along their hike.

It is obvious from how they are dressed that they hadn't planned for anything more than a short walk in the woods.

My heart hurts at how young and carefree, innocent and happy they appear, and I'm reminded that in a few short turns of calendar pages Johanna and Taylor will be their age.

Sasha is as beautiful as everyone has said—and photogenic, her personality and attitude shining through the images, but Naomi is just as attractive, only in a very different and far more subtle way. You have to take a second, closer look, but for many beholders her beauty and allure would be far greater than the more obvious and out-front nature of Sasha's.

I think of Dylan's loner, introverted personality type. From everything I've heard and read and what I'm seeing here, Naomi would've been a far better match for him.

"They only took a few photos as they walked through the swamp toward Cottonmouth Creek," she says. "We can't tell exactly where they were, but because we know where they entered the swamp we have a pretty good idea."

Sam takes another sip of her beer.

Ben says, "We know they made it to the creek. The next set of photos shows them there. Within a span of about three minutes, they took eight photos—all in the vicinity of the creek."

Sam gathers the first group of photos and stacks them to the side, then removes the prints of the eight shots Ben has just described from the file folder and spreads them out on the table in front of me.

I study each one carefully.

"But they're kind of odd," Sam says. "Some of the pictures were just a few seconds apart and all of them were taken very closely together and yet in some of the pictures their hair is pulled back in ponytails and others it's loose and sort of windswept. In some of the photos the creek is directly behind them. And others to the side and others it can't be seen. To take the shots they did, they would have had to have been running around changing their hair and shooting from different angles —all very quickly."

"We estimate it would have taken them about two hours to hike to the creek," Ben says. "Maybe a little longer depending on how much they stopped and how long it took to take the pictures on the way. That would put them there around 2:00 p.m. If they had turned around then and headed back the way they came, they would've made it back to the Gaineses' well before dark."

"But that's not what they did," Sam says.

"We don't really know what they did, where they went, or why," Ben says. "They didn't take a lot of photos at first, and the ones they did don't show enough to tell us much about where they were or what they were doing."

Sam picks up the eight photos on the table and replaces them with four others.

"These were taken about two and a half hours later," she says.

The four photos show four different but similar images of the swamp—what appears to be random trees and bushes. Taken in low light, the dim pictures seem arbitrary and unremarkable.

"Am I missing something?" I ask.

Ben says, "If you are, we all are. Everyone from forensic photo experts to thousands and thousands of armchair detectives have studied these without finding anything but some trees and bushes in the late-afternoon dimness of the swamp."

"But this one," Sam says, placing another photo in front of me.

"Is that blood?" I ask.

The image is of several cypress knees growing near each other, each between one and three feet high, the closest one to the camera seeming to show a smear of blood on the top and side.

"We believe it is," Sam says. "And we believe this is the source."

She places another photo beside the cypress knee one—a closeup shot of what appears to be Sasha's forehead with a scrape and cut on it, blood flowing from the cut. But it's difficult to tell for sure. Not only is the picture dark but the angle is bad and Sasha's hair is hanging down to cover most of it.

"So," I say, "Sasha fell and hit her head on a cypress knee?"

"Possibly," Sam says.

"That's what it looks like to me," Ben says.

"How close is this to the first 911 call?" I ask.

Sam says, "Either right before or an hour before—depending on if the time stamp on the camera was set to the correct time."

"They were from Jacksonville," I say. "On Eastern time. The camera, which wouldn't automatically reset like their phones, would've been an hour ahead unless they manually reset it."

"Exactly," Ben says.

"Why did you say 'possibly'?" I ask Sam.

"Because," she says, removing another photo from the folder and placing it in front of me, "this next one seems to contradict it."

She's right. This photo appears to show Sasha's forehead with no blood or abrasion on it.

"You're showing me these in the order they were taken?"

She nods.

I look at them again, studying, thinking. "Could it be mud? Could she have tripped and fallen in the mud, gotten it on her forehead and on the cypress knee as she pulled herself up?"

"It's possible," she says. "It's just impossible to tell for sure because of the quality of the photos."

"I still think it's blood," Ben says.

"If it is," I say, "then mystery solved. Sasha gets injured. Naomi stays with her or tries to help her hike out and they get even more lost and die from dehydration or the attack of a predator. Death by misadventure. Dad was right. It was a tragic accident."

"Certainly possible," Sam says, "but there's additional evidence on the camera and in subsequent photos that seems to contradict that."

I smile. "Figured there might be."

Ben says, "I'd love to be wrong and for it just to have been an accident," he says. "But if one or both of them were injured, how did they survive so long? How did their remains get so far from where they started? And why didn't the search teams see any sign of them anywhere? Not to mention the other photo, phones, and bones evidence."

"Okay," Sam says, gathering up the photos on the table, "so . . . all the photos we've seen so far were taken on Sunday, September 28th, their first day in the swamp. No photos were taken the next two days. Then on Wednesday, October 1st, these."

She places three new photos in front of me on the table.

These images are even darker than the previous ones. Every element within them is faint and difficult to discern. One appears to be a watering hole surrounded by deer, bear, and boar tracks. A cypress tree stands behind it, broken off at about ten feet up, its top a jagged point like a primitive, inexpertly whittled spear. The next seems to show a tree line in the distance. The third looks like the dried-up bed of a narrow tributary or slough.

"These could be attempts at photographing landmarks," Sam says. "For reference to make sure they weren't walking in circles. Or because something significant happened here or they left something here they had to come back for. We just don't know."

"Have these locations been found?" I ask.

Ben shrugs. "Maybe. Some people think they have, but these could be a thousand different places in the swamp, and if the right places were actually found, nothing notable was discovered there."

"Look at the bottom of the second shot," Sam says.

I look back at the image that seems to show the top of a tree line in the distance.

"See anything?"

"Just shapes," I say.

"What about this?" she asks, pointing at one of the shapes at the bottom center of the photo.

I shrug. "A fallen tree maybe."

"A lot of people are convinced it's a body," she says. "And not just online citizen detectives. Even some experts."

I study it again, moving it to different distances and angles from my eyes.

"I don't see it myself," she says.

Ben says, "I think it could be, but it's far too dark to be able to tell for sure."

I shake my head. "I don't know. I guess it could be, but . . . It could be a lot of other things also."

"Ready to move on?" she asks.

"Yeah, but I want to come back to all of them and really study them with good light and a magnifying glass at some point."

She nods. "You should. Won't do any good, but you should. These were taken the next night."

The first photo shows some twigs with what looks to be strips of plastic and candy wrappers on top of a fallen tree. The second shows what looks like toilet paper and a mirror on a stump.

"Not sure what to make of these," she says. "There are plenty of theories of course, but . . ."

Ben says, "Some people say those are strips of flesh, but I find that ridiculous. It looks like bits of plastic to me. And people say, well, they didn't take any plastic into the swamp with them—but that doesn't mean they didn't find any while they were in there. Other humans have been in there before."

"Say it is strips of plastic . . ." Sam says. "And candy wrappers or whatever. Why take a picture of it?"

"That, I don't know," he says.

"You know what it could be," I say, "is strips of flagging."

Ben's eye widen and he nods vigorously.

"Flagging?" Sam asks.

"Plastic ribbon used to mark trees," I say.

"Loggers use them to mark the trees not to be removed," Ben says. "Biologists use them to mark dangerous or invasive species."

"But why photograph them?" she asks.

"What if they used random items they could find to mark something?" I say. "Taking a picture of them could be an attempt to document it—or communicate it in the event that something happened to them."

She nods. "That could be it. Makes more sense than anything else I've ever heard."

"Were any of these items ever found?" I ask.

They both shake their heads.

"Nothing," she says.

"I'm not sure about the toilet paper—if that's what it is," Ben says, "but I'd guess the mirror was used as a signal, maybe trying to get the attention of the search team."

I nod.

"That's what I've always thought," Sam says, "but I've never understood the toilet paper or why they'd take a picture of it."

"Since the photo of what looks like Sasha's head," I say, "there haven't been any others of either woman. Are there any more of them?"

Sam shakes her head.

"That's very interesting," I say. "And no videos or—"

"No videos of any kind on the camera or the phones," she says. "The next picture is perhaps the scariest."

She pulls out another photo and places it in front of me.

It's another dark, fuzzy night photo, but in the center is a faint, oblong image of what could be the distorted face of a man. It has a slight resemblance to a copy of a copy of a copy of a copy of a bad charcoal rendering of Edvard Munch's *The Scream*.

"This one is the most bizarre by far," Ben says. "It's been said to be everything from an alien to an attacker lunging at them. Of the possible people it could be, the online consensus is that it looks most like Jay Gaines."

"It's frightening," Sam says, "but I don't think it's a person at all—just some trick of light, the flash reflecting off the forest."

"It could be almost anything," Ben says. "Or nothing. It's impossible to tell. But it's been fodder for the most fringe online investigators."

"I can tell you this," Sam says, "you can enlarge or shrink it, look at it for a brief moment or for hours at a time and study it for years as I have, and you still won't know what it is for sure—and you'll think it's a thousand different things."

I nod. "I'd like to study all the photos some more," I say, "but I can't imagine determining anything for certain."

"It's the nature of this case," Ben says. "Each item of evidence—the cell phone data, the photos, the backpack, the bones, on and on and on—is a microcosm of the entire case, confusing, contradictory, crazy-making."

"That's straight out of your book," Sam says.

He smiles.

"And it's true," she adds.

I frown and shake my head. "I can see us getting to the end of this investigation and not having any better an idea of what happened than the initial investigation did."

"The difference is," Ben says, "the first investigation didn't have Simien Eggers. Don't forget his film is going to reveal the culprit."

Sam shakes her head. "We're fucked."

"I'm actually cautiously optimistic we're going to reach some more definitive conclusions this time," Ben says. "We already know more than we did."

Sam's phone vibrates on the table and she leans down and reads it.

"Daniel's on his way," she says. "Let's try to finish the camera evidence before he gets here. The next photos to be taken are the most spooky and disturbing of all and were taken in the middle of the night on Monday, October 6th," Sam says. "The same night that seventy-seven attempts to get into Sasha's iPhone were made. That night some ninety flash photos were taken between 1:00 a.m. and 4:00 a.m., apparently deep in the swamp and in near total darkness. Think about that. Ninety photos in three hours in the middle of the night and every single one of them nothing but blackness."

Ben says, "You know how on the other photos, no matter how dark they are, there's still some faint images? There's nothing like that on these. Just darkness. It's almost as if the lens cap is on, but the Canon XS 270 HS is a point and shoot. There is no lens cap."

"There are a lot of theories, but you can read about them," Sam says. "Let's go ahead and get to the missing photos before I have to go. All of the images on the camera are numbered sequentially. And even though there are some bad shots early on in their vacation, Naomi didn't erase any of them. However, images 509, 510, and 511 are missing, and they fall between the image that looks like an alien or a man screaming and the series of ninety blackness shots."

"The thing is," Ben says, "when you delete a picture from a camera, it isn't really deleted, it's just space made available for an image to be written over it. So even if Naomi had decided to delete three images in the middle of the swamp, they'd still be on the camera's memory card. For them to have been completely deleted, the card would've had to have been taken out of the camera, placed in a computer, and the images permanently deleted that way."

"It's one of the most compelling pieces of evidence of third-party foul play," Sam says.

"But," Ben says, "it raises other questions. If someone else was involved or responsible, why just delete three images? Why put everything in the backpack and leave it to be discovered? Why not destroy everything or bury it and the girls?"

"And yet," Sam says, "it still remains that those three images couldn't have been deleted from the camera itself."

28

"Think I know how Simien's financing his film," Merrill says.

He has just arrived and is eating a cold slice of pizza and drinking Blue Moon from the bottle, a small slice of orange floating around in it.

Daniel had picked up Sam a few minutes before, so it's just Merrill, me, and Ben. I only have a few minutes before I have to go pick up the girls from Dad and Verna's, but want to catch up with Merrill first.

"And if I'm right," he says, "he ain't gonna sell back the rights and halt the production. He has no need to."

"Well, hell," Ben says.

"How?" I ask.

"Porn," he says. "The thing, like drugs, that sells itself. He never stopped making it."

"That could certainly do it," I say.

Merrill makes the cold pizza look so good, I have another slice myself. A moment later, Ben grabs one too.

"Thing is . . ." Merrill says, "I don't think it's just that he never stopped making porn. I think he's doing it with this production."

"*What?*" Ben says. "Are you serious?"

"I could be wrong," Merrill says. "I don't have a lot of proof yet. This is mostly deductions and suppositions, but . . ."

"God, I hope you're wrong," Ben says. "I can't even fathom how surreal my book about the tragic death of two special young women would be as a porn film."

Merrill shakes his head. "Don't mean he's turnin' your book into a porn film. I think he's shooting two films at the same time —Naomi and Sasha's story and a porn film."

"Using the same actors?" I ask.

"Some of them. Some of the same crew. Some of the same sets."

"It would explain why what we've seen him shoot so far doesn't make any sense," I say.

"That slimy son of a bitch," Ben says. "Wonder if he is, if we can use that to shut him down?"

"Let me find out if it's real first," Merrill says.

"He still getting harassed?" I ask.

Merrill nods. "Nothing happening while I'm around, but when I'm not . . . he's getting threatening notes, shit left on his steps—little, nuisance stuff."

"I hate to even say this out loud," Ben says, "but . . . you think it's possible Thomas McCloud and or Reese Newman are behind the harassment? As part of their strategy to shut him down?"

I nod. "It's possible. Certainly something we've got to consider."

"Y'all already thought of that?" Ben says.

"Merrill did," I say.

"I the brains of this here operation," Merrill says in his best Stepin Fetchit voice.

29

Both Johnna and Taylor fell asleep on the drive back from Dad and Verna's and are snoring on either side of me on our blanket pallet in the living room.

I lie wide awake, wishing Anna was here with us, reading Ben's book by the light of my cell phone about how and where Naomi's and Sasha's remains were found.

After Thelma Washington allegedly discovered the backpack, the search for Naomi and Sasha or their remains ramped up again, and eventually the swamp began begrudgingly giving up a few of its secrets.

Though many search teams were involved, nearly every occurrence of evidence being uncovered involved Horton Joshua.

He and his team, mostly young men and woman who worked for his ecotour company, discovered bones and shoes belonging to both Naomi and Sasha near the Apalachicola River.

In what is yet another strange, mysterious, even eerie element of this case, the jeans shorts were found nearly fourteen walking-distance hours from where the backpack had been discovered. They were on the opposite side of the river, neatly folded on a fallen cypress tree.

And though this is the official version in the record, rumors and subsequent witness statements claim that the jeans shorts weren't found neatly folded at all, but rather floating in the river itself.

The first bone remains were found on December 10th near a boar bog deep in the swamp. Not only were they found a few miles from the river where the backpack, clothes, and shoes were found, but they were discovered upstream. A pelvis bone and a left sneaker with an intact foot still inside were the first remains to be found. The foot showed multiple fractures of the metatarsals. DNA tests revealed that both the pelvis and foot belonged to Sasha Grande.

The laces of the shoe were still laced and a sock remained inside. Both the pelvis and the foot still had flesh on them.

Forensic examination of the remains discovered that the cuts of talus, tibia, and fibula bones were surprisingly clean and no blood was present. The bones themselves showed no signs of nicks, scrapes, hacks, gunshots, teeth or claw marks.

In the same vicinity, though not at the exact same location, some thirty-three bones, mostly left leg bones, were also discovered.

Very few of Sasha's other bones or remains were found—and the ones that were, were found scattered over a mile away, all downstream.

On the other side of the river, and several miles away, Naomi's pelvic bone was also found, though unlike Sasha's hers was broken and no flesh remained on it.

Later, and not far from the partial pelvic bone, Naomi's right rib bones were also discovered, as were her femur, tibia, and fibula.

In stark contrast to Sasha's tissue-covered remains, Naomi's bones were bare and bleached bright white.

Even later, a rolled-up ball of skin from Naomi's shin was also found. The section of skin was still in early stages of decomposition according to the forensic pathologist who worked the case.

While Naomi's bones were fully bleached and clean, Sasha's were dry and un-decomposed, the bone marrow inside them intact and unaltered.

Many questions remain about the bones, especially how different the decomposition was between the two women.

Dr. Harriet Price, world-renown forensic anthropologist and best-selling author who studied the case, said in her opinion foul play was unlikely.

"In my opinion," she said, "accidental death is most likely when all factors and findings are considered. A river swamp habitat isn't one environment, but many microenvironments. Decomposition can occur quite rapidly in some microenvironments, while in others, due to other factors, like variance in river current, flora growing on the banks, and transport by scavengers, it can be much slower. In such a plethora of microenvironments, preservation or decomposition of various body parts can occur at different rates. With bodies decomposing in water, dismemberment follows typical patterns with the head and limbs detaching first. Further damage from animal scavenging can be very diverse due to multiple transport modes."

And yet despite Dr. Price's confidence in her conclusions, she notes that many forensic mysteries remain in this case, including the lack of abrasions or trauma during a microscopic examination of the remains. "I'd expect to see damage due to animal scavenging," she said. "I'd also point out that it's almost unheard of for drowning victims to break up into tiny fragments. And while it's possible that Naomi's bones could be bare and bleached after only two months, it is unlikely. It's at least possible it points to some sort of human intervention. I also have to wonder what caused Naomi's pelvic bone to break in two."

30

"See how contradictory this case is?" Ben says. "One piece of evidence seems to prove it was foul play and then the very next one makes you think there's no way it could be anything but a tragic accident."

Ben, Dad, and I, dressed in jeans, long-sleeve shirts, and snake-proof hiking boots, have just entered the swamp near the Gaineses' place and are heading toward Cottonmouth Creek, attempting to follow the same path that Naomi and Sasha did.

Not only are we dressed far more appropriately than they were, but we each have a backpack full of supplies.

Ben, who knows the terrain the best, is leading the way and turns his head back toward us when he speaks.

Dad is in the middle and I am bringing up the rear.

"No question," I say. "I keep going back and forth."

Glancing back over his shoulder, Ben says, "Of all the evidence that it really was just a tragic case of death by misadventure, probably the most convincing is the timeframe. Well, that along with the calls and pics. If someone abducted them . . . why keep them alive so long? And why let them keep their phones and camera?"

"He wouldn't," Dad says. "That's why I think it was just an accident. But even if it was, I'd still like to know more about exactly what happened to them and why the evidence is so contradictory."

Ben slows and leads us around a fallen tree.

The route we're taking isn't a trail or path at all, just the only passable way into the dense cypress swamp.

Not only is Florida almost completely surrounded by water, but most of it is lined by rivers and streams, dotted by lakes and ponds, and submerged beneath wetlands and swamps. Our ecologically unique and diverse state has both the largest freshwater lake, Lake Okeechobee, also known as Florida's inland sea, and the largest freshwater spring, Wakulla Springs, in the contiguous United States.

Swamps are low-lying wooded areas of uncultivated ground where fresh water collects and actually stands for much of the year. They are similar to bogs and marshes, though usually involve far more forestation. They are a huge and vital part of Florida's freshwater wetlands and interior aquatic ecosystem.

Cypress swamps, like the one we're in, are the most common freshwater swamps in Florida. They take shape along rivers and around ponds that have cypress trees growing in and around them—like the Dead Lakes in Wewahitchaka. Swamps usually occur in huge depressions within the terrain. Pond swamps have a dome-like appearance when seen from a distance—the tallest trees near the center of the pond—while strand swamps form in areas where the depression is longer than it is wide. Since strands are longer and narrower, they resemble a tree-filled riverbed with the tallest trees in the deepest parts of the depression.

The enormous North Florida swamp we're in right now has rivers, ponds, strands, bogs, and marshes, between and around which are pine flatlands and hardwood hammocks. It is a wide, wet wilderness, both wondrous and dangerous, singularly treacherous and stunningly beautiful.

"It's a wonder those young girls were able to even get back here," Dad says. "Must've been awfully determined."

"No doubt about that," Ben says, "but I'm also guessing that Biscuit led them through the best way."

"Would explain why they were completely and utterly lost when he left them," Dad adds. "If they were."

"Certainly would," Ben says.

We walk a while longer in silence.

Ben looks over his shoulder and says, "Sheriff, you let me know when you want to stop and take a little rest."

"I will. I'm good right now."

We trod along damp, soggy ground, around bogs and thickets, over fallen trees, under vines and spiderwebs.

Every few minutes I remove my phone and check for signal. We had lost service shortly after stepping into the swamp, and haven't had any our entire time in here.

Eventually we stop to catch our breath and drink some water.

"Those poor girls never stood a chance back here, did they?" Dad says.

"If they had just gone to the creek and back and kept Biscuit with them," Ben says, "they might have made it. But even then a lot could've happened."

"If we had just started the search that night," Dad says.

"In a way we did," Ben says. "John, I don't know if many people know this, and I've never heard your dad use it as a defense when he's attacked, but . . . once he made the difficult decision to start the search early the next morning and the other law enforcement officers and search-and-rescue volunteers went home to get some sleep, he could tell that Dylan, Jay, and I were considering going back in here looking for them anyway. He had me get in the car with him and we stayed up all night riding the roads around the swamp, going from landing to landing—looking for them, calling, yelling, sending up signal flares. We even launched a boat at Gaines Landing and slowly drove upstream near the banks with a search light."

"It was too dangerous to come into the swamp," Dad says, gesturing to the thick, wet woods around us, "but that didn't mean we couldn't circle around the outside—on the roads and in the river—looking for them."

"We stayed up all night doing that," Ben says. "Only to join the others in the search in the swamp at first light the next morning." He turns to Dad. "So don't tell me you didn't do enough or that your decision cost them their lives. It didn't. As usual, you made the right decision and did the right things— the above and beyond things—and didn't try to take any credit for any of it and took all the blame instead."

I look at Dad and nod appreciatively.

"You've always been my hero," Ben says. "You've never let me down."

"Mine too," I say. "Same here."

Dad shakes his head and waves off our sentiments. "I ain't dead yet. Save that shit for my funeral."

It's obvious he's embarrassed and attempting to dissipate the awkwardness he feels, but it's equally as obvious that he's touched and genuinely moved by the expression.

I'm extremely grateful to Ben, and whether he's doing it because of how Dad might look in his book or the movie or because Dad is dying, it's an act of kindness I won't ever forget.

"You sissies ready to keep going?" Dad asks. "We don't get a move on, I may actually die before we get there."

We continue, Ben leading the way through the moist jungle-like environment.

Passing beneath ancient oak, pine, and cypress trees well over two centuries old, we swipe aside thick vines dangling down from them with our hands and forearms as if passing through rows of beaded curtains in the entryway of a retro novelty shop.

As if on an ecological obstacle course, we wind around hardwood hammocks, weave our way through cypress knees fields, and climb over or crawl under giant felled trees.

Eventually we arrive at Cottonmouth Creek and stand approximately where Naomi and Sasha had when they took the series of snapshots.

Dad is out of breath and sits on a pond pine tree stump, unaware of or more likely unconcerned about the sticky sap seeping into his pants.

"It's hard to imagine that after fighting their way through all that," Dad says, "that they would consider anything other than heading right back the way they came."

"I agree," Ben says. "That leads many to believe that someone forced them to continue."

"Look over there," I say pointing to a dried-up slough bed. "Something like that, that appears to be a path, could've made them think they could find an easier way out of here."

Ben nods. "At least one of the photos looks like it was taken in a dried-up tributary."

"One of the first and most important mysteries to solve," Dad says, "is why they didn't turn back from here."

"We have to consider the possibility that they thought they did," I say. "It's easy to get turned around. And look at in how many directions everything looks exactly the same. And remember how quickly and from how many different angles they took the pictures here. They could've easily gotten turned around and headed in the opposite direction from what they thought they were."

"That makes a lot of sense," Ben says.

"But so does someone forcing them to," Dad says. "Or that they were meeting someone, so they kept going because of that. All of it just keeps us going in circles like we're the ones lost out here. It's so fuckin' frustrating. I don't think we're ever going to really know."

His rare use of profanity shows just how frustrated he really is and how desperate he is to solve the case before time runs out for him.

"Anyway," he adds, "I'm sorry, but I don't think I can go much farther. I'm gonna head back. Y'all can keep going and let me know what you find when you get out."

I shake my head. "No, we'll head back too. I want us to stay together, and this is a good start for today. We'll come back another time and explore some of the other possible paths they could've taken."

31

When we pull up to Dad's farmhouse, Thelma Washington is waiting for us.

She's sitting on the front porch in one of the old wooden rocking chairs, and though the chair is smaller than average, it seems to swallow up her tiny frame.

She's in the same navy-blue sheath dress she was wearing when we went to her house in White City a few days ago but has added an old, worn pair of black dress shoes, which she wears without sox or stockings.

She stands and walks toward us as we park and is at the truck by the time we're climbing out of it.

"Sheriff," she says, nodding toward Dad. "Boys."

"Miss Thelma," Dad says, "this is a nice surprise. Won't you come in? We're about to have some lemonade."

"No, sir," she says. "It's a kind offer. That's a fact, but I got some errands to run directly. I surely do. And I best be goin.'"

"Well, that's truly a shame," he says, "'cause Miss Verna makes the best lemonade I've ever had the privilege of putting in my mouth—and I'm a connoisseur."

"Sheriff, I tol' you I's real sorry for what happened to them girls and I didn't have nothin' to do with it or know anythin' about it. No, sir. And that's the gospel on the matter, but . . ."

"Yes, ma'am?"

"Well, they is somethin' I wanna come clean about to you on findin' that there backpack."

"Yes, ma'am," he says. "And what might that be?"

He has adopted a type of speech that mirrors her own.

"I wish I'd'a never found it. No, sir, I don't. And I found it just like I said I did and right where I said I did. That's the God's truth."

"But . . ." Dad says.

"But Mr. Horton," she says, "he tol' me to look around there for it when he gave me the day off to go fishin'. Never gave me no day off to go fishin' or anythin' else before. Tol' me to look for it and what to do when I found it. Now you know much about the matter as I do—and maybe I can look at myself in the mirror again and go to bed without a guilty conscience tonight."

She turns and begins to walk away, standing taller, moving less hesitantly, not appearing nearly as frail or skeletal, as if the unburdening has unbound her somehow.

"Did he ever say—"

She pauses and looks back. "Sheriff, I done tol' you that's everything I know on the subject, and that's the truth. Now, I'm goin' shopping so I can get back home. Only other thing I want to hear from you is your word that if that evil fat bastard hurts or kills me, you'll square it for me."

"I give you my word," Dad says, "that I won't let him harm you in any way."

"And?" she says, lifting a long, bony hand and cupping it to her ear.

"And if he does anything at all to you I'll square it," he says.

"And if I'm not around any longer to do it, these fine young men will."

"And you have our word on *that*," Ben says.

32

"Someone's following me," Hailee Benson is saying. I'm on my way to Tallahassee to talk to one of Naomi and Sasha's friends, and have stopped by the set to see Merrill.

As he and I are talking, Hailee walks over as soon as Simien yells *cut* and without preamble makes her pronouncement.

"What makes you think that?" Merrill asks.

"I don't *think it*," she says. "I *know it*."

They are shooting in a small clearing in a tract of state-owned wetlands on the outskirts of town, the small, young cast and crew resembling a student production more than anything else, and it occurs to me that Simien has saved a ton of money on sets. Which is probably why he thought he could pull off this production on such a shoestring budget.

"What makes you *know it*?" Merrill says.

"I can *feel* him," she says. "Plus I've seen and heard him a time or two too."

"What's he look like?"

"Only got a glimpse," she says. "He was running away. Sort

of short, trim. It was night and he was wearing all black. It was hard to see."

"Has he done anything? Said anything? Left you any threatening messages? Vandalized any of your property?"

She shakes her head. "Nothing like that. Just follows me. Watches me."

"How long it been goin' on?" Merrill asks.

She shrugs. "Not sure. Thought I was imagining it at first. A week maybe. I don't know. I've only been sure the past few days. What should I do? Do you think it's just a shy fan, or some kind of obsessed crazy man? Can you protect me?"

"Can you afford me?" Merrill asks.

"Well, no," she says in genuine surprise. "I don't have any money."

"They's lots of that goin' around."

"I just thought . . . Well, I don't know. You protect people, right?"

"Sometimes," Merrill says with a smile. "Sometimes just the opposite."

"The *opposite*?" she asks, seeming genuinely alarmed.

"Sure," he says, "as in the case of stalkers and the like."

"Oh," she says. "Oh, yeah. Right. Of course, that's . . . good. That's real good. Well, do you think . . . I mean since you're here anyway protecting Simien . . . Do you think you might be able to watch over me too?"

"I'll see what I can do," Merrill says. "Has he ever come to the set?"

"My stalker? No."

"When does he usually do his stalkin'?"

"At night," she says. "He only comes out at night."

"Not sure how much I can do for you," Merrill says, "so do what you need to do to protect and take care of yourself. Definitely report it to the sheriff's department. But I'll look into it, do what I can."

"Oh, thank you so much," she says. "You don't know how much this means to me. I haven't been sleeping or eating. This is such a relief."

"Don't be relieved," Merrill says. "There's not much I can do, as I'm only one man and I'm already committed to protecting Simien. Notify the authorities. Have someone stay with you or stay with someone if you can. Act as if you are solely responsible for protecting yourself. And I'll see what I can figure out."

As she lumbers away downcast and dejected, Merrill turns to me. "What the odds they's two stalkers on the same tiny little micro movie shoot?"

"Not very good, I'd say. But we've seen stranger things."

"This some fucked-up shit right here now," he says.

"The stalkings or the—"

"The entire production and everythin' around it," he says. "Never seen nothin' like it."

"Ah, show business," I say. "I'll try to get back to help you tonight."

He shakes his head. "You got the girls by yourself and the real case this fake shit is based on. Ain't got time for this."

I nod. "I've got help with the girls and the other case," I say. "And I can't resist the magnetic pull of the motion picture industry."

33

M adison Urich works at Guitar Center in the Tallahassee mall off Monroe Street.

But long before she did that, she was a roommate and friend of Sasha Grande and Naomi Newman's at the University of North Florida in Jacksonville.

Guitar Center is a big-box chain music store with something for everyone—singers, drummers, keyboardists, bassists, DJs, recording engineers, and, of course, guitarists. Though the store carries a ton of gear, it has more guitars than anything else—giant walls of them hanging four and five rows high.

The first thing I notice when I step inside is the noise.

Several guitarists on electric guitars plugged into loud amps play different riffs in different keys in different times, all seeming determined to outdo the other, while from a room to the left, unseen drummers bang out beats and pound out rolls and fills out of sync with each other and the guitarists.

The chaos of the overstocked store and the cacophony of wannabe juke box heroes is irritating and frustrating, and not conducive to conducting an interview.

Fortunately the guitar gods are feeling benevolent, and I find Madison in the acoustic room.

As the wood-framed glass-paneled door closes behind me, I'm in a much smaller, more soothing soundproof room with rows and rows of acoustic guitars. Fewer than a handful of customers on stools playing their potential purchase are scattered throughout the room.

"Let me know if I can help you with anything," Madison says from the back corner where she is returning a Gibson six-string to its wall hanger for a customer.

She doesn't look like she belongs in the acoustic room.

In her mid-twenties like Naomi and Sasha would now be, she is extremely petite with short, jet-black, spikey hair, a face full of piercings, and arms covered in tattoos. Her red Guitar Center polo-style shirt and name tag say minimum-wage retail-hell shop girl, but everything else about her screams rock and roll—maybe even punk.

I cross the small room and introduce myself.

"Oh, yeah," she says, "you called about Naomi and Sasha. Such a shame, man. I mean *fuck*. Right? I won't ever get over that shit. I'm not sure how much I can help you, but I'll do what I can. I've always wondered what the hell really happened to them."

Her hair, ink, and piercings may say rock and roll, but her smile and helpful manner are more merch-table mensch.

"It's a while before I go on break," she says. "Mind if we talk in here?"

Her blue eyes are big and bright and shine with interest and intelligence.

"Not at all."

"You should let me sell you a new six-string while you're here."

I smile. "I don't play."

"*Really*? I'd've sworn you were a musician."

"I actually thought about getting a guitar after the hurricane to try to learn to play, but some things came up."

Thinking back to Johanna and Taylor being kidnapped, Father Andrew's murder, and the serial killer swept in with the storm, I realize what a laughable understatement *some things came up* is.

"Well, it's never too late," she says. "Making music helps your mind and your soul, man. Few things in life are more fun or fulfilling. I'll make you a killer deal on a little Fender acoustic to get you started."

"Thanks," I say. "I'll think about it."

"Sure, I get it," she says. "But just so you know, I don't work on commission, so I'm not hustling you. I just know how life changing learning an instrument can be."

"Sold," I say. "You've convinced me. Let me ask you a few questions about Naomi and Sasha, then we'll talk guitars."

"Sure," she says. "Shoot."

"Mind just telling me a little about them?" I say. "I'm trying to get as complete a picture of them as possible."

"I wasn't their roommate long," she says. "Actually, Naomi and I were roommates before she and Sasha were. Sasha moved in and took my place, but there was some overlap— Sasha crashed on the couch for about a month before I left and she took my room."

"Did you and Naomi have a falling out?"

"Oh, no," she says. "Nothing like that. I thought the world of her. We got along great. I transferred here to attend FSU. So I knew Naomi a lot better than Sasha, but I knew them both pretty well. We stayed in touch and they actually stopped here and hung with me on their way to . . . on the way to do that camp thing, so I saw them like three days before they died. Or before they went missing or whatever."

"Oh, really?" I say. "I didn't know that. I don't think that's in the case file. Who interviewed you?"

She looks confused, shaking her head and shrugging. "No one. Don't guess anyone knew they stopped in here to see me. Either that or didn't think it was relevant. Anyway . . . They were opposites in nearly every way. Naomi was the sweetest person I think I ever knew. That sounds bad—I don't mean Sasha was the opposite of that. She wasn't. I mean their personalities were opposite. They were both good people. Sasha was just so outgoing and kind of like a magnet or something. Naomi was more quiet and reserved. But she was so very kind and thoughtful. I still can't believe they're gone. Doesn't seem real."

I nod. "I'm sorry again for your loss."

"Thank you," she says. "I appreciate that. You're . . . If you don't mind me sayin' . . . you're very different from any cop I've ever seen. Like . . . I mean, I already said I thought you were a musician and . . . I don't know . . . It's like you really care about Naomi and Sasha."

"Well, I do," I say. "It breaks my heart they didn't get to grow up."

She nods. "That's it," she says. "That's the real truth—twenty-one is legal but it's not grown up, is it? They didn't get to grow up. I guess in a lot of ways Naomi was already a grown-up, but Sasha . . . she wasn't at all. Here's how—this'll give a good idea of their personalities and how different they were. They were both going to get community service hours for doing the camp, right? Sasha's were to meet her probation obligation and Naomi's were for her school scholarship, but . . . the thing is . . . Naomi already had more than she needed. She was volunteering to work with those kids—kids that were a lot more like Sasha than her—because she was . . . because that's just who she was."

I nod and smile.

"You know how these things go . . . on the face of it, Sasha was more fun, but only at first. Then one of two things will happen. Either she'll wear you out and you'll just be like I can't keep up. I need a break. Or she'll just sort of disappear on you —even when you're out together partying—and you have to call Naomi to come get you. And she will, of course. She always will be your DD, the person you can count on. Both are great. Just different. So very different."

"Why do you think they were such good friends, being so opposite and all?" I ask.

She twists her lips and gives a quick shrug. "No idea. I guess it's like some couples—on paper you're like, this could never work, they're too different, but then . . . it does. Just a mystery, I guess. And I'm not saying they're a—were a couple. They weren't. Just really close friends."

"Why do you feel the need to say that?" I ask. "Were they gay?"

"No. Well, Sasha was—I guess that's why I said it—Sasha was bi. And since I said the thing about some couples . . . but anyway. No. They weren't. But Sasha . . . she just hooked up a lot. Some people do. Sort of have sex like other people have conversations. Had all these apps and groups and connection thingies . . . 'cause she was always hookin' up. Hell, she hooked up with someone from one of her apps the night they were here."

"She did?"

She nods. "It was a rare day when she didn't."

"Do you know who she was with here?" I ask.

She shakes her head. "No idea. We were—the three of us were at this bar on Tennessee and her phone buzzed and she was like *my date's here* and she got up and went out the back door. Few hours later, she reappeared. Truth is, it wasn't that long—probably not even an hour. Don't know why I said that. Yes I do. A few hours sounds more like a date. A few minutes definitely says hookup. I'm so programmed and conditioned. Dammit, man. I have no problem with her hookin' up if she wants to. And I shouldn't care if you do. I guess . . . I just . . . I mean, they were really great girls. And I wouldn't want you thinking less of them because Sasha was . . . prolific."

"I don't," I say. "The only reason it's relevant is if they were killed, then every person they intersected with is of interest."

"Oh, I see, well, then, you should know she made a joke about already havin' some cornpone country pussy lined up over in Pottersville."

34

On the drive back from Tallahassee I call Sam Michaels.

"You should've let us know you were coming to town," she says. "We could've had dinner."

"Sorry," I say. "I'm rushing back to see the girls before they go to bed, then I'm helping Merrill with a stakeout."

"I could've interviewed Madison for you," she says.

"I should've let you," I say. "I was so happy to have found her, so focused on getting to her and getting any info she had, I didn't even think about it."

"Well, next time you come to town let's get together," she says.

"It is ironic that I was just there and I'm calling you on my way back home."

"And if you need anything done over here again, let me do it."

"I will. Thanks. Sorry I didn't think of it."

"I'm just glad you found her. And it sounds like she had some helpful information."

"Was there any evidence of Sasha seeing anyone while she was staying with the Gaineses?" I ask.

"No. None. Just the opposite."

"Yeah, I thought the same thing," I say. "Everyone I've spoken to says she was continually being hit on but that she shut everyone down."

"Maybe it was because she had some rendezvous set up."

"Could be," I say. "Do you think we could power up Sasha's cellphone?"

"Maybe," she says. "What for?"

"I'd like to look at the apps she had on it and her texts."

"I've got printouts of all of that," she says. "I can get them to you, but I bet they're in the file you have—and if not, I bet your dad has them."

"I'll check," I say. "Thanks. Is there a way we could see who in the area was on the same hookup apps she was? And if she communicated with any of them?"

"Leave it with me and let me see what I can do."

35

Ordinarily, Merrill provides security for Simien Eggers during the day while he's shooting and stays with him until he is safely secured away in his Airstream for the night, returning the next morning to rinse and repeat.

Tonight, after tucking Simien in, Merrill gets in his car and drives away like usual—but instead of leaving the area, he drives around to the back of the campground on an access road and joins me in a tree stand.

The tree stand belongs to a friend of ours whose hunting lease backs up to Oak Grove Campground, and from it we have a good view of both Simien's Airstream and Hailee Benson's small travel trailer.

A cross between a tree stand and a high hide, the six-by-six enclosure is made of dark green painted plywood on a metal platform some twenty feet in the air, with a metal round-rung ladder leading up to a small door in the floor. More an elevated blind than anything else, it stands next to but is not attached to a large oak tree. Narrow horizontal openings on each side allow for both spotting and shooting wildlife, mostly deer.

"Man, I's hopin' you'd have a pizza or somethin' waitin' on me up here," Merrill says as he climbs up through the hinged plywood door in the floor.

"I've got a peppermint in my pocket."

"Good to know," he says. "Wouldn't want to have bad breath while assaulting a stalker."

I'm sitting in a padded folding chair looking through an opening at the campground below.

As he closes the door, I offer him the seat, but he declines and takes a seat on the floor, leaning against the back wall.

"Why don't you go eat and get some sleep?" I say.

"And miss out on all the fun?"

"You could at least eat," I say. "Probably be a while before any stalking commences."

"You think somebody really stalking her?" he says.

"Hopefully we'll get an answer to that tonight."

"I half figured she be the one harassing Simien," he says.

"She may be," I say.

"She the most hostile toward him," he says.

"Could be her way of deflecting suspicion—*Hey, I'm being followed too.*"

"Don't know many actresses like deflectin' attention from they selves."

"Good point. Did you figure out if Simien's definitely making a porn film as well as *Lost Innocents*?"

He nods. "Yeah, and the dumb ass plans to call it *Lost Innocence.*"

"Wow."

"Uh huh. And he ain't gonna take the Newmans' offer to buy him out and finance his next film neither."

"Why would he?" I say. "He's already got his financing."

"Says it's the new model he gonna use goin' forward. Says porn gonna be the patron of his art."

"That's—"

I stop as I see a figure in black step out of the shadow of a thick-bodied pine tree not far from Hailee's camper.

Merrill slides over to the opening and follows my gaze down to the figure.

"Guess she wasn't just deflectin'," he says.

"Guess not. What do you want to do?"

He shrugs. "Not sure. Was thinking either watch him for a while and see what he does or try to sneak up on him and ask the young man his intentions."

"Your case. Your call."

He smiles. "Roles usually reversed, aren't they? Let's see . . . usually in these situations I ask myself WWJJD?"

"I had really hoped you'd come up with a better method than that by now."

"Haven't found one that works as well," he says. "So what would you do?"

Now it's my turn to shrug. "You might be more patient than me."

"You right, let's go have a little chat with him," he says, standing and opening the door.

As we climb down the ladder, he says, "I'll drive back around and come at him from the front. You walk through here and approach him from the back. Just give me a minute to get around there."

I do.

Walking through the wooded area between the tree stand and the campground, I find a place to hide along the tree line and watch the figure.

When Merrill has parked around front and is walking toward the guy near Hailee's camper, he texts me.

From the tree line where I'm watching the watcher, I'm about thirty yards away.

As I start toward the figure, a car pulls into the campground, its headlights sweeping over Merrill and then the stalker and then me.

Whipping his head around toward Merrill, the figure darts in the direction of Hailee's camper, running around it and between two campers behind hers, disappearing into the darkness.

Merrill and I take off running after him.

The car, which must have just been turning around, pulls back out of the parking lot and returns the way it came.

Within a minute we're coming up behind the campers—me on this end, Merrill on the opposite end.

Behind the row of three campers, spaced about twenty feet apart, is a grassy area of about twenty feet and then the woods begin again.

Merrill and I both scan the area. There is no sign of the man we're chasing.

We continue toward each other, looking back and forth from the campers to the woods.

Near where the figure came between two of the campers, a branch is broken at the edge of the woods and a bush is waving as if someone ran past it.

"I ain't chasin' his ass through the dark woods at night," Merrill says. "But what we can do is wake everybody up . . . make sure it's not one of the cast or crew."

We do.

While keeping an eye on the woods, we go from trailer to trailer banging on the doors and yelling for everyone to get up and come outside.

In a matter of moments, the small cast and crew are assembled outside in front of their campers.

Everyone is present and accounted for.

When we explain what is happening, Simien says, "Well, it's good for you all to know that it's not one of us. We already knew that, but I'm glad it's confirmed for you, so you don't waste time looking for the wrong person. But the question still remains, who is it? What does he want? Why is he doing this? And is he the same stalker stalking me?"

"That's way more than one remaining question," Merrill says. "But we gonna try to answer all of them in due course. For now, I think it's a good idea for y'all to bunk in with each other so nobody's alone."

"I'll stay with Hailee and protect her," Logan Taylor-Johnson says.

"The hell you will," Hailee says.

The others laugh.

"I'm going to remain alone," Simien says. "I must have my space to create. Besides, I work late into the night. Never know when my muse is going to sing to me."

In a few minutes, all the arrangements have been made, and Alison Miller, Hailee's co-actress who's playing Sasha, and Rena Hanan, the shy PA, have agreed to stay with Hailee in her camper.

"That's it," Simien says. "Safety in numbers. Now, let's all get back into our trailers and get some rest. We have a big day of shooting tomorrow. And some very pivotal scenes. Night night, thespians and artisans."

As Merrill and I walk back toward the tree stand he says, "Little dude's pretty fast. Should've been our first clue that he wasn't a thespian or an artisan."

He does his best Simien impression on *thespian* and *artisan*.

I laugh.

"Speaking of his size," Merrill says, "he remind you of anybody?"

I think about it. "Who?"

"Don't know if he spry enough for it to be him," he says, "but he built like Reese Newman's attorney. Thomas McCloud."

"Certainly is," I say. "You're absolutely right."

"You imagine what she got to be payin' him . . . have him out here doin' shit like that?" he says.

"Not enough, whatever it is," I say. "We need to take a closer look at him. See if he's a runner."

BECAUSE I KNEW I would be helping Merrill, I had arranged for Dad and Verna to keep Johanna and Taylor tonight, so instead of going home after leaving the campground, I drive to the farm and creep into the dark, quiet farmhouse and into the spare bedroom the girls think of as theirs.

My plan had been to crawl into the bed between them, but seeing the odd angles they are lying at and the massive amounts of pillows and toys surrounding them, I decide instead to lie on the floor beside their bed so I can be close to them throughout the rest of the night.

I search around for a pillow and blanket but the best I can find is a large plush Minnie Mouse doll and a Moana bathrobe that covers less than half of my body.

I'm exhausted, and not even the hard, uncomfortable floor can slow the fast, relentless approach of the sandman.

I can feel that I'm only instants away from falling off the precipice of consciousness into the deep, mysterious underworld of dreamscapes, and spend my final moments in this realm mouthing prayers of gratitude and protection for Anna, Johanna, Taylor, Dad, Verna, Merrill, Jake, Nancy, Sus . . .

36

"Have you given much thought to what the camera evidence means?" Ben is asking.

It's two days later, and we are back in the swamp, searching for possible paths Naomi and Sasha could've taken, and any evidence that might still be out here. Both are very, very long shots, but just being out here gives me a better sense of what the two young women encountered and experienced.

This morning it's just the two of us, so we hope to cover far more ground than we did during our first trip. Our plan is to bring Dad with us again when we enter the swamp from the river side and most of the journey will be by boat.

"Giving it and everything else about this case lots of thought," I say. "Too much probably. Sometimes it seems as though it's all I'm thinking about these days."

"Any theories?"

"No theories," I say. "Nothing that fully formed. Just random thoughts and questions."

"Such as?"

"Everything about the photos is a mystery to me," I say. "I really wonder why they didn't shoot any video with the camera or the phones. Why they didn't leave messages for their families or friends or even authorities."

He nods. "Yeah. Makes me think of Remington James."

"Yeah," I say. "I've thought about him a lot lately—especially when being out here and looking at the photos."

Remington James was the amateur wildlife photographer whose camera traps had captured the murder of a young woman in these very swamps some fifteen or twenty miles from where we are right now.

"And of course I wonder about the image that looks like the distorted face of a screaming man."

"That one gives me nightmares," he says. "Do you think it could be Jay Gaines?"

"Certainly could be. Looks like him. Of course, it could just be a lens flare or a shadow or reflection."

"Yeah, but it'd make sense if it was him. He could've been helping Dylan or have some motive we don't yet know about for doing it himself. It's so distorted it could be anybody— including Horton Joshua."

I nod.

"Oh, and about Jay and or Dylan . . ." he says. "I was thinking last night—and I don't know why this didn't occur to me sooner . . . and I'm not saying it's them, just that there was opportunity—what if when your Dad and I left their place on that first night, they went back out into the swamp anyway? They say they didn't. They told your dad they would do what he said and go inside and get some rest so they'd be ready the next morning, but . . . what if while he and I were riding around the roads and up the river . . . they had gone right back in with Biscuit? They were home the next morning when we gathered there to begin the search, but we have no idea what they did during the hours between then and when the sheriff and I left them. Again, I'm not accusing them. Just surprised I haven't thought about it before."

"You're right," I say. "We need to keep that in mind as we compile more evidence. Dylan could've killed them when he was out here the first time and then took Jay back in with him to help cover it up."

"Like you say . . . need to keep it in mind. What else?"

"Well the two biggest mysteries of all relate to the camera evidence," I say. "The deleted photos and the series of ninety black images taken between 1:00 a.m. and 4:00 a.m. on Monday, the sixth."

"You come up with anything on either of those?"

"Mostly more questions," I say. "And maybe dismissed a few of the theories out there."

"Like what?"

"I've read that some people say the ninety images were the girls just using the camera's flash to light the path they were walking or running, but . . . I think doing that would've only made them night blind, causing them to see less not more."

"Yeah, that's definitely one of those theories espoused by people who've never tried it," he says. "One of the theories that I think might be a possibility is that they were trying to scare off or blind an animal or a person trying to attack them—sort of like at the end of *Rear Window*."

"Guess it's possible," I say, "but it's hard to imagine it going on that long."

"True."

We finally arrive at Cottonmouth Creek and pause for a moment to stretch and drink some water from our thermoses.

"One of the more interesting theories," he says, "is that whoever was taking the photos—whether it was Naomi or Sasha—was hallucinating and taking pictures of what they thought they were seeing."

"That *is* interesting," I say.

Images of a dehydrated and deranged Naomi imagining all manner of scary creatures coming at her and trying to take pictures of them as she stumbles through the treacherous swamp fill my mind.

"I think the most likely explanation is that they were trying to use the flash as a signal," I say. "Were probably just pointing the camera up into the dark night sky and clicking."

He nods. "I agree."

"Did y'all use signal flares that night?" I ask.

"Not then, but earlier, sure."

"Could've given them the idea," I say.

"But why'd they wait so late to do it?" he says. "That's what I can't understand."

"Yeah," I say, "that's the part that makes me question it. Why do it when no one is looking?"

"May not have known what time it was," he says. "Or didn't feel like they had a choice. Knew they were about to die. But . . . that little flash wouldn't've been seen for more than a few feet away. It's sad thinking of them spending so much valuable time doing something so futile."

That thought lingers around us as we finish our water and return our thermoses to our backpacks.

Once we are both watered and rested, he says, "Which direction do you want to take first?"

I pull out my phone, on which I have loaded all the photos Naomi and Sasha took. "I was thinking . . . What if we look at the last picture they took here and see which direction they were facing and take it?"

"That's not a bad idea," he says, "but the person taking the picture will be facing the opposite direction from the one in it."

"Let's look at both and see if one looks more promising than the other."

"Sounds good."

I scroll to the final photo taken here and study it, zooming in and out, as I look around us. Eventually, we find as best we can the approximate location, step over to it, and gaze in both directions—the ones each woman was facing.

"Well, that's easy," he says.

We can't go the direction that Naomi was facing because it's the creek itself. The direction that Sasha was facing as she took the photo is of the dried-up slough bed, which we had believed was a good possibility for the path they took when they left here anyway.

"I'm sure y'all searched down that direction on those first days after they went missing," I say.

He nods. "Seems like we searched in every possible direction. How we didn't find them I'll never know."

"Did y'all find anything? Is it worth us going down again?"

"It definitely is," he says. "Remember, all we were doing was tromping through here yelling their names and quickly scanning everything. We weren't deliberate. We didn't pause and ponder anything, we just rushed through frantically yelling."

"Then let's head down that way."

W e step down into the trough of the dried-up slough and begin to make our way down it.

Though there's no standing water in the slough, the ground is soft and soggy, slick and slippery.

Extending out from both sides of the banks are bushes and tree limbs and the thick undergrowth that seems to be stretching across the narrow divide to its counterpart on the other side.

We move slowly, pushing aside the natural barriers that buffet our progress.

"It's hard to imagine them walking very far through this," Ben says. "'Course, we said the same thing about the trek to the creek, didn't we?"

"Different time of year," I say. "From the photos it doesn't look like it was nearly as thick then."

We are making our way down the dried-up slough bed in late February of 2019. Naomi and Sasha were here in September of 2014. And though I'd expect the foliage to be thicker in fall than the spring, the photos show that for some reason it was actually less overgrown then. Perhaps because the slough had dried up more recently then.

He shakes his head. "That's right. It wasn't. I need to try to keep remembering what it was like back then."

"Will definitely be helpful for all of us. Need to remind Dad to do that too. You've been looking at this a while . . . Anything else that makes you suspicious of Jay and or Dylan?"

"Obviously, the way Robbie serves as a buffer for them and keeps us away from Dylan completely. I'm so glad you got to talk to him. Different ways Jay and Robbie acted and contradictory things they've said over the years, none of them very big in and of themselves. Just sort of all add up. The other thing is . . . Have you seen Dylan and Meagan's posts about Naomi and Sasha?"

I shake my head, but he's too busy fighting through the underbrush to see it. "I haven't."

"It's alarming. Meagan has done a series of posts about how close she was to them, how it was like losing sisters. It may just be typical teenage melodrama, but seems way over the top and . . . And Dylan . . . he actually wrote a song for them and posted a video of himself playing guitar and singing it. Again, maybe it's just wanting attention or something, but I think it could speak to something deeper—like guilt. Some of it seems almost confessional."

"I'll definitely check it out," I say.

"This case has never had traditional prime suspects," he says. "Hell, we don't even know for sure anyone was involved, but if I had a list, the Gaineses and Horton Joshua would top it."

"They all warrant more focus as we continue to gather information and evidence."

"Speaking of . . ." he says. "You never said what your thoughts were about the missing photos—images 509, 510, and 511."

"Don't have anything new to add to the subject," I say. "But either we're wrong about the tech and somehow Naomi or Sasha were able to delete them or it's definitive proof that a third party was involved. I'd really like to hear from an expert on that model of camera and the whole issue of deleting images."

"Yeah, that would help," he says. "I just find the sequence that's missing—what they fall between, the image that looks like Jay screaming and the ninety photos of darkness—too suspicious to be a coincidence. And I've never found anyone who says there is any way to delete photos like that from the camera itself."

The slough bed peters out and we find ourselves in a dank tree-canopied bog.

As if in the tropics, this area is warmer and wetter than any we've encountered so far. Suddenly, as if in a sauna, our skin is damp and our boots are sinking farther into the ground.

"So much ecological diversity back here," Ben says. "It's like we just stepped into a different part of the world. It makes sense that decomposition would occur at different rates."

"There really is," I say. "There's nothing quite like a North Florida swamp, is there? But decomposition rate is one thing. Bleached is another. And how there's no scavenger marks ..."

"No scavenger marks, but no knife, club, or saw marks either."

We continue walking for a while in silence, our labored breaths joining the desultory sounds of the swamp.

In the absence of conversation, I get lost in my thoughts, chasing ideas and images down rabbit hole after rabbit hole, and I have no idea how much time has passed or how far we've walked when I emerge from the echo chamber in my head.

Eventually, the damp ground beneath our feet begins to slope.

"We're heading toward the river now, aren't we?" I say.

Ben nods. "Yeah, you can feel the slope, see the plant species begin to change."

"But I didn't realize we had changed directions," I say.

"We didn't," he says. "At least not intentionally. That's the thing about the swamp. We had no idea we had turned. Probably did so very gradually. And if you didn't know that the slight slope of the ground or the changing of the species means you're angling toward the river, you'd think you were walking in the same direction. It's what happens to so many people out here."

"As far as we know, Naomi and Sasha had no prior experience with hiking in swamps," I say. "They could've walked for miles in a direction opposite or other than they believed they were."

"Most likely did," he says. "We just did, and we're supposed to know a thing or two about this place. Me, especially."

A while back, we were surrounded by long leaf and loblolly pines. Before that laurel oaks were scattered about, and now I'm noticing more magnolias, maples, and sweet bays.

In and around and between all of these trees are bushes and grasses and flowers and other trees that I've seen my entire life and still have no idea what they are.

Even though we're now headed toward the river—or I believe that we are—if Ben suddenly vanished I'd find it very difficult if not impossible to find my way out of the swamp or even to the river. And I've lived here my entire life and spent a fair amount of time in this or similar terrain. How could Naomi and Sasha have ever hoped to negotiate their way through this claustrophobic quagmire, let alone navigate their way out of it?

I stop suddenly.

Ben spins around, alarmed. "*What is it*?" he asks, his voice rising, coming out ragged.

"Look," I say, pointing to a small piece of metallized film partially submerged in the muck.

"What is it?" he asks again, calmer now.

"Is it a candy wrapper like the ones in Naomi and Sasha's photos?" I ask.

"*Is* it?"

I step toward it, removing a latex glove from my pocket and snapping it on my right hand. Squatting down in front of it, I carefully lift it out of the damp dirt and standing water.

Ben shakes his head. "Long after humans are gone, all the plastic shit we made will still be here not biodegrading."

I stand and hold up the small wrapper.

It's completely faded to the point of being nearly see-through.

"It's the right size and shape," he says, "but there's no way to know since it's completely faded. It *is* how you'd expect a candy wrapper that had been out here that long to look, though. Of course, in miles and miles of swamp, what are the odds that we'd find one of their wrappers?"

"Not good," I say, "*unless* . . . we're on a path similar to the one they traveled."

He nods. "That's true. That'd certainly make the odds go up."

I bag the wrapper and place it in my backpack, and we search the area for others.

Finding none, we continue.

"Wonder if it is possible that we're on the same or a similar path to the one they took?" Ben says. "What if walking down that slough and continuing inevitably guides you toward the river?"

"Certainly possible."

He shudders and lets out an involuntary squeal. "It's just . . . After all this time to possibly be on a similar path as they were. There's no way to know, but . . . even at a very, very long shot . . . it give me chills."

I nod. "It's just hard to imagine them getting this close to the river and not making it to it, and if they made it to it, why they didn't just wait and flag down a passing boat for help."

"Like Remington James did?" he says. "How well'd that work out for him and Mother Earth?"

"That's true," I say. "They could've encountered the wrong person or people on the river."

"But again, what are the chances? It's not like there are serial killers roaming the river looking for prey."

Now it's Ben who stops suddenly.

Up ahead, in a thick stand of sweetgum, needle palm, and tupelo, a large, homemade houseboat, seemingly completely intact, leans on its side at a slight angle.

It's odd to see a houseboat out of water, appearing trapped in the tree branches of the thicket. The swamp is littered with abandoned boats, carried inland during periods of flooding, trapped in trees and beached as the risen river returns to coil within the boundaries of its banks.

I've seen several over the years, but none this big and none this far back.

"Look at that," Ben says.

"Are we closer to the river than I thought?" I ask.

"No," he says. "Have no idea how this big boy could've gotten so far back here. Let's check it out."

We make our way over to it.

"You'd think if they saw something like this, they'd take a picture of it," he says.

"Maybe they did. Could be one of the images that got deleted."

"That's true."

"How high was the water when they were out here?" I ask.

"Seems like it was pretty high at the time, but not at flooding levels," he says. "We can look it up to be sure. But it was nothing like what it would take to put this big boat back

here—and I'd say there hasn't been since the time of Noah, but
... don't know how else it could've gotten back here."

He steps over and pulls himself onto the lowest corner of
the front porch of the houseboat.

"I'm gonna put my weight on the opposite side and see if I
can get it to drop down some so it's more level, then we'll see if
we can get the door open and see what's inside."

"Hold on," I say, "those floorboards look wet and slick with
mold and mildew."

He climbs the slanting floorboards like ladder rungs,
making his way toward the opposite end of the porch, but after
he's a little more than halfway across, his boots slip and he hits
the floor and begins to slide down the sloping porch.

As the weight of his enormous frame falls on the porch and
slides down, the boat shifts in the branches, convulses, and the
front door swings open—revealing the skeletal remains of
several people inside.

38

"The one time I don't come," Dad is saying, "and you find a boat full of bodies."

It's late evening, and he, Ben, and I are standing some thirty feet back from the houseboat, which is now swarmed by FDLE crime scene techs and investigators from the ME's office, FDLE, and the Potter County Sheriff's Department. Hugh Glenn, Dad's replacement, is standing across the way watching it all.

"You're here now," Ben says, "and this is when we actually find out something."

After discovering the remains in the boat, Ben and I had hiked to the river, flagged down a fisherman, and gotten a ride back to Gaines Landing. From there we hitched another ride far enough inland to get a signal and called the Potter County Sheriff's office. While waiting for them, we called Dad so he could join us.

"This has to be connected to what happened to Naomi and Sasha, right?" Dad says.

"Doesn't have to be," I say, "but I'll be surprised if it's not."

"Why couldn't we have found this during the initial investigation?" he says.

Ben says, "I bet you anything some of our searchers walked right past it."

"Is this area a hunting ground or a dumping ground for a serial killer?" Dad says. "Is that old boat his mausoleum?"

"If it is," Ben says, "and he killed Sasha and Naomi, why aren't their remains in there?"

"Some of them might be," Dad says. "But I get what you mean. Why were even some of their remains out in the swamp instead of in here?"

Ben looks over at me. "You're awfully quiet."

"That's what he does," Dad says. "He thinks instead of talking. The rest of us stand around blabbing away, tossing around theories and speculation, and he takes it all in and keeps thinking and eventually solves it."

"Can you tell us at least a little of what you're thinking?" Ben asks.

"Not much," I say.

"Oh, I know better than that," Dad says.

"It's true," I say. "I don't disagree with the possibilities y'all are talkin' through, but until we know exactly what's inside that boat we don't know enough to—"

Sam Michaels steps over to us.

She is still in her white hooded bunny suit, which given how short and small she is makes her look like a kid dressed as CSI for Halloween.

"I'll tell y'all more later," she says. "The politics of this is tricky since this is Sheriff Glenn's investigation. They think I stepped over to tell you y'all could go and I'll come get statements from you later. But real quickly . . . we've got the skeletal remains of six young females."

"And only them?" I ask.

"Huh?"

"No partial remains."

"Right," she says. "So no Sasha or Naomi. They appear to have been handcuffed and shackled, and from a cursory examination of their clothes and jewelry I'd say they weren't US citizens."

"Any IDs or anything else present in there with them?" I ask.

"Just some empty food and candy wrappers and bottles of water."

"Are the—"

"And yes," she says, "the candy wrappers match those in the pictures Naomi and Sasha took. Okay, I need to get back. I'll stop by later and—"

"Just one more thing," I say. "Any idea how long they've been in there?"

She shakes her head. "Not really. A few years, but I can't be more specific than that at this point."

39

"No tellin' how many bodies are buried in those swamps," Merrill says.

We are sitting in his car at the Oak Grove Campground keeping an eye on Simien's and Hailee's camper trailers.

"Generations of bones," he adds. "This earth just one big graveyard."

I nod. "Won't be long, it'll be swallowing up our bones too."

"Be here lot sooner than I'd like. Promise you that."

"One hundred percent," I say. "So what's been happening here?"

"Well, we ain't found no boats full of bones," he says. "Simien gave McCloud his official answer of *no*, which clearly displeased both McCloud and his boss. Oh, and guess how ol' Thomas McClound keeps his little high school figure?"

"Intermittent fasting?"

"Not sure he on that particular bandwagon, but he is a runner."

"Did he say whether he enjoys a little stalking before his runs in the woods?" I ask.

"*Shit*, I knew there was something I forgot to ask his ass.

Don't know if it's related or not, though my black ass long since quit believing in coincidences, but since Simien rejected Reese's offer . . . they been lot less incidents of stalkin' 'round these parts."

A few moments later, Sam pulls up, parks behind us, and climbs into the back seat.

"Evenin', gents," she says.

"Bet your skinny white ass didn't wake up this mornin' thinkin' you's gonna be trampin' through the swamp tonight," Merrill says.

"That's a bet you'd win," she says. "If you could find someone dumb enough to take that action."

"Always somebody dumb enough," he says. "Hell, the cast and crew of this here film ain't got a high IQ between them."

"Ah, show business," Sam and I say simultaneously.

We laugh and then fall quiet a moment.

"So," Sam says, "my skinny white ass is muddy, mosquito-bitten, and exhausted, and I'm heading back to Tallahassee to my Daniel who has a late dinner ready for us."

"You give him my best," Merrill says, "and tell him how sorry I am again."

"I'll give him your best," she says, "but you gotta quit apologizing. It wasn't your fault."

A few years back, Daniel Davis, Sam's partner, was abducted while being protected by Merrill, and though he has been back safe and sound for years now and everyone agrees Merrill wasn't to blame, he still apologizes to Daniel every time he sees him.

"Don't know how you figure it that way," he says, "but we ain't got to get into it now."

"No, we don't," she says. "Anyway, before I head home I wanted to stop by to tell you that there's not much else I can tell you. I may know more after the autopsies, but maybe not even then. Hopefully in a day or two we can track down who owns that boat and how it got way back there, but for now I only have one rather interesting bit of information other than what I already told you."

"Let's hear it," I say. "Interesting bits of information are our favorite kind."

"It appears as though all six young women died of natural causes."

"*Natural causes*?" Merrill says. "The *hell*?"

"Not much natural about being cuffed and shackled and left in a beached houseboat," I say.

"You're right," she says. "Poor choice of words. What I mean is . . . there are no signs of violence or trauma to the remains."

"So they were cuffed and shackled and locked in there and left to die?" I say.

"What it looks like," she says. "Which makes it hard for me to see how it has anything to do with what happened to Naomi and Sasha."

40

"Are you sure?" Hailee Benson is saying.

Merrill has just told her that no one has been following her since a few nights ago when we chased her stalker away.

He and I are with Hailee, Alison, and Rena in Hailee's trailer.

"I've felt so much safer having these great girls staying with me each night and you two out there watching over me," she says, "but . . . I don't know . . . I've still felt like he was out there . . . still watching, biding his time until you all leave me and I'm alone again."

The three young women are sitting on a small couch, framed posters of Hailee's films, including *Killer Campground 3*, hanging on the wall behind them.

Hailee notices me looking at the posters and glances back at them.

"Never thought I'd be livin' that shit," she says.

"Nobody been killed," Merrill says. "And now even the followin' and watchin' has stopped."

"It hasn't stopped," she says. "He just knows they're inside here with me and y'all are outside watching over us. If you leave me now he'll be back, and if he comes back he'll get me. I can feel it. Please don't leave me."

"Ain't leavin'," Merrill says. "Just thought you'd be relieved to know you not bein' stalked. Miscalculation on my part."

"No, it's not that. I just . . . I am glad you've run him off. I'm just afraid you'll leave and he'll be back."

"You got any idea who it might be?" I ask.

She glances back at the posters again, seems to consider something, but then looks back at me and shakes her head.

"You sure?" I ask. "You seem to—"

"There was a guy on *Campground Killer* who gave me the creeps. He was sad, really. He asked me out and I shot him down."

"He a little dude?" Merrill asks. "Fast as hell?"

"He's little, I guess. No idea how fast he is. You mean like in running?"

"What's his name?"

"*I* don't know," she says, as if she's offended by the suggestion that she would. "Maybe Jarred or Jacob or Justin. I really don't remember."

"Is his name not on the poster?" I ask.

"*No*," she says, outraged by the prospect. "God, no. He was just a PA. Oh, sorry, Rena. I didn't mean . . . You're great. And you do a lot of different things."

"It's okay, Hailee," Rena says, her voice soft, her mouth dry. "I knew what you meant."

Merrill says, "Is Simien makin' a porno too? Shootin' both movies at the same time?"

Hailee bursts into tears, jumps up, and rushes out of the room. After a moment, she peeks around the corner of the door. "I can't. I just can't. I'm going to bed. Y'all can answer the rest of their questions. Go ahead and tell them about the whole sordid affair. Whatta I care? The entire world will soon know."

She then slams the door shut so hard it rocks the trailer, rattling the pots and pans in the small kitchenette.

"So, I take it he is," Merrill says.

"Yeah," Alison says. "Poor girl. She's tryin' her best to be this like real and respected actress. Me, I could give a shit. I'm just happy not to be working at the Waffle House anymore, but Hailee . . . She thought even if it wasn't in the cards for her to be America's next sweetheart, she might at least be the next scream queen. And she was on a pretty good little run of decent B horror movies and a movie of the week thriller, and she thought this film might take her to the next rung of the ladder of her so-called career—'specially if Simien was going to make it as artistic as he claimed. He pitched it to her as a sort of arthouse indie thriller that might even be a darling for certain awards. She had no idea about how his slimy ass was financing it. Her mom, who's her manager, takes care of all her contracts and shit. Hailee didn't even read what she was signing—and apparently neither did her mom this time. At least not closely enough. She arrives and we start filming and everything's going okay. Script doesn't make sense but she figures we're shootin' out of sequence and Simien is giving himself the option of taking the story in different directions in editing so . . . And then comes the night of the sex scene. Poor thing still doesn't know she's making a porno. And the way Simien talks . . . she's thinking this is all about art and making the best, most realistic movie possible, so she goes along with actual penetration— several notable indie films have, and it gives them a certain caché, and she'll do anything for her art, for an artful film and then they get into the scene and— Well, I wasn't there. It was a closed set, but—"

"I was," Rena says. "It was awful. It's hard to imagine a worse experience. It started out okay enough, but the longer it went—and it went long—the more aggressive Logan became and the more Simien encouraged him to. It was the most humiliating and degrading thing I've ever seen. I tried to stop it, but Simien actually grabbed me and covered my mouth and held me still until he called cut. It was like being forced to watch a rape."

Alison says, "We can't decide who's worse—Logan or Simien."

"We figured one of them is now stalking her," Rena says.

Alison says, "Simien is so controlling, but that prick Logan actually asked her out after all he did to her."

"That's why she's so scared," Rena says. "Why she's such a mess. She has every right to be. I feel so bad for her. And so guilty that I couldn't stop it."

"No wonder she won't call her mama," Merrill says.

"She was praying Simien would take the buyout and we could all get out of this nightmare," Alison says. We all were. It's one thing for someone like her to have to endure what she's enduring, but to know that even when this is over there will always be a porn film out there, that she will never again be known as a straight actress. She'll forever be a porn star. She's devastated. Crushed. She's been biding her time, holding out hope that it would be bought by the girls' families and destroyed, but now that that's not going to happen . . . I'm not sure if she'll be able to go on."

"Simien has told her if she doesn't finish filming, he'll ruin her and that he'll still release the porn footage anyway," Rena says, "but that if she will finish the shoot, that he won't use her real name on the porno."

"It's in her best interest to finish filming," Alison says, "but I'm not sure if she can."

41

The next morning, I am sitting at the kitchen table reading through Meagan's and Dylan's posts about Naomi and Sasha as Johanna and Taylor eat their breakfast.

Ben is right. They are creepy and disturbing, but are they evidence of anything other than typical teenage overreaction?

Both my girls slept well and are in great spirits, but I can tell they miss Anna too, and I remind them she'll be home in just a few more days.

"And we've got the Wabi Sabis concert at the river this weekend," I say. "We'll pack a picnic and take a frisbee and some games and you can each take a friend if you want to."

They cheer and squeal with delight.

"Let me know who you want to take and I'll call their parents."

"I love you, Daddy," Johanna says. "Thank you."

"You're the best daddy in the whole wide world," Taylor says.

"You two are the best daughters," I say. "Hey, tell me what y'all think of this video."

I pull up the video of Dylan's *Song for Sasha* and hold my phone where all three of us can see it.

"Who is Sasha?" Taylor asks.

"A girl he's crazy about," Johanna says. "Right?"

I nod.

We watch in silence as Dylan softly sings about his loss, anguish, and pain to discordant chords that don't match the melody on a small, beat-up six-string.

"He's weird," Taylor says.

"Yeah," I say, "you girls always avoid boys like him."

"Did she break up with him?" Johanna says. "Or..."

"They were never together," I say. "He just had a crush on her."

"Wow," she says, and I can see her mind working.

I pause the video, not wanting to expose them to any more of it.

"That reminds me," I say. "Guess what I bought?"

"A puppy?" Taylor says.

"*Noooo* ... not a puppy."

"A motorcycle?" Johanna says.

"*Noooo* ... not a motorcycle."

"Then what?" Johanna says.

"What? What? What?" Taylor chants.

"A *guitar*."

"A guitar?" Taylor says. "That's silly."

"Yes, it is," I say. "I was thinking about trying to learn to play it and I wondered if either of you would like to learn too?"

"I would," Johanna says.

"Not me," Taylor says. "I want a puppy."

"Awesome," I say to Johanna. "I'll find us a teacher or an online course we can take together. It'll be fun. I'm so glad you want to."

"I hope y'all are better than him," Taylor says, nodding

toward the image of Dylan frozen on the small screen of my phone. "Oh, Sasha. Oh Sasha. Oh Sasha."

"Be hard to be worse," I say.

My phone begins to vibrate and the paused image of Dylan is replaced by a phone number and text that reads *Maybe Sasha's Mom.*

"Finish your breakfast and put everything up and your bowls in the dishwasher," I say. "Let me take this and then we'll go. Okay?"

I stand and walk into the living room.

I had left several messages for Sasha's mother, and had about given up on her ever returning any of my calls.

"Detective Jordan, this is Margo Grande, Sasha's mother, returning your call."

"Thank you so much for calling me back."

"I wasn't going to," she says. "But I could tell you weren't going to stop calling and leaving messages until I did."

"Sorry if I—"

"I'm calling to tell you that I have nothing to say about any of it," she says. "I want no part of the circus that Reese Newman and others seem to want to keep going indefinitely. My daughter's death was a tragic accident and I will mourn for her every single second of every day of the rest of my life. But I'm going to do that in private. And I'm asking you nicely to respect my privacy. *Please.* Good day, sir."

And with that she is gone.

42

"I just don't see how they're not connected," Dad is saying.

I nod.

The two of us are standing on his front porch. I am here to drop off Johanna for him and Verna to keep today. Johanna and Verna are inside. Taylor, who I still have to take to school, is waiting for me in the truck.

"That many dead girls in the same vicinity," he adds. "I realize Naomi and Sasha's bones were found miles away from where the girls in the boat were, but Naomi's and Sasha's were found miles apart from each other. And though we don't know for a fact that they went anywhere close to that boat, it's reasonable to assume they did. Especially since the candy wrappers in the picture match the ones found inside the boat."

The discovery of the boat and the bodies in it is the most significant potential development in the case in years, and Dad is not just excited about it, but encouraged by it. He's more hopeful he'll be able to solve the case now than ever before.

"But even if they are connected," he is saying, "we have no idea how or why. We don't know who they are or why they were there like that. It's . . . it's just bizarre. Raises as many questions as it answers. More."

As far as I can tell it doesn't answer any questions—at least not yet. But I know what he means, and I'm just so happy to see him this excited and engaged.

"How the hell did that big boat get that far back into the swamp?" he is saying. "Who does it belong to? Who were those girls in it? Why were they there?"

I hesitate to say anything at all, but before he goes too far down a path that might be filled with false hope, I say, "We're not even sure they were there at the same time Naomi and Sasha were. They could've come after."

"They were there," he says. "I know it. And it's connected. I know that too. I've lived with this thing long enough to have a feel for it."

I nod. "I don't doubt that," I say.

"What do you make of the girls inside the boat just being left in there to die?" he says.

I shrug. "Not sure what to think. It's—"

"You think the killer sat outside the boat and listened as they slowly dehydrated and died? Think he gets off on that? He could've killed Naomi and Sasha the same way. That would explain why there's no sign of violence on their bones either. Maybe he just did it in a different place—or even out in the open out in the swamp, which is why we discovered their remains so much sooner than the girls in the boat."

"It's possible."

"I want to look at all the evidence again," he says. "All the calls and pictures, the backpack and bones—in light of finding the boat. May cause things to make sense that haven't before."

"Sure could," I say. "I've got to get Taylor to school and take care of a few things, but I'll check back in with you a little later and we can go over it together if you want."

"Okay, sounds good," he says.

I start to step off the porch but stop, turning back toward him and locking my eyes onto his. "You seem very happy and hopeful," I say.

He nods vigorously. "I am."

"Have you considered starting your treatments again?" I say. "Getting back on the meds so you can—"

He smiles. "Actually, I was talking to Verna about that last night. I think I just might. Definitely considering it."

43

T aylor and I are rockin' out on vocals and air guitars to some CCR tunes on our way to school when Merrill calls.

I turn the music down some and turn off the front speakers, and Taylor continues to sing as I answer.

"I may not be cut out for security and investigative services," Merrill says.

"Oh, yeah? Why's that?"

"I may have just threatened and beaten the hell out of my client."

"Which one?"

"The one and only auteur extraordinaire."

"Not like he was a payin' client," I say. "Plus he's a pompous poser porn director who may have aided and abetted his leading man in rape."

"Sort of what I told him," he says. "Though I wasn't as nice about it. Tol' him whether he wants to take Reese Newman's money or not was up to him, but that there was no way I was letting him film any more of the porno or let any of the footage he has already shot see the light of a computer screen. He started up with his normal art talk bullshit, which I was able to control myself through, but when he said the bitch signed a contract and there was nothin' she nor I could do about it, I showed him a few of the things I could do about it. He probably won't have to go to the hospital but he'll be movin' awful slowly and peeing blood for a few days."

"Did you get the footage?"

"Gave him to end of business today—whatever the hell that is on a film shoot—to get it together for me. Said he would."

"The *end of business* was a nice touch," I say.

"Professional, right? That's what I thought."

"Let me know when you're going back and I'll go with you," I say.

"Long as you promise not to do anything rash or violent," he says. "That never solves anything."

I park at the school and walk Taylor to her classroom. We hold hands crossing the street, but she lets go as soon as we're on school grounds where one of her peers might see. When we get to her room, I whisper that I love her and tell her to have a great day, but don't dare hug her or kiss her.

Her teacher, a perky, sweet twenty-something young woman in her second year raises her eyebrows when she sees me and gives me a curious expression. "Heard y'all found something horrifying in the swamps over near Pottersville yesterday," she says.

I nod and give her an expression of my own that I hope conveys that I can't talk about it, and turn and head back toward my truck.

Before I'm halfway across campus, four other people—two teachers and two parents—ask me about what we found in the swamp yesterday.

I remove my phone from my pocket to fake a phone call to avoid other questions, and as I'm holding it up to my ear it begins to vibrate with an actual incoming call.

It's Sam.

"Great timing," I say. "Thanks for calling."

"What am I saving you from?"

"Just people curious about what we found yesterday," I say. "It's not a big deal, but these are my neighbors and friends and it's awkward to tell them I can't tell them anything."

"Just do what I do and make up the most outrageous shit you can think of and see how long it takes to get back around to you. Promise you it'll be a lot quicker than you think."

"I don't doubt that."

"So," she says, "I finally got some info back from one of the hookup sites Sasha was on—Intimate Experiences—"

"Exchanges," I say.

"Intimate Exchanges," she says. "You're not going to believe who else was on it."

"I might," I say.

"People are infinitely fascinating, aren't they?"

"But rarely surprising," I say.

"Too true. Too true."

"So who else was on it?" I ask.

"None other than the hostest mom with the mostest," she says. "Robbie Gaines."

44

"Do you like sex, John?" she asks.

This isn't about me and I'm not about to let her make it about it, but I figure answering her question honestly might go a long way in getting her to be open and honest with me.

"No," I say, shaking my head. "I love it."

Thinking of sex, saying out loud how much I love it, makes me ache for Anna, body and soul.

She nods. "I knew it. I can tell."

As if continuing the same conversation in the exact came circumstances as several days ago, Robbie Gaines and I are back on her front porch, Jay and the wild boys in the front yard.

"I do too," she says. "That's why I knew you did. I can tell sexual from asexual people. I'm a highly sexual human being. And though I love and appreciate my Jay, he is not. We only have sex when he wants to. When and *how* he wants to. That means about twice a week he rolls on top of me, kisses me a few times, maybe pinches my nipples or fondles my breasts, but not always, and thrusts a few times until he reaches climax and that's it. I tried for years to get him to do other things—to go down on me, to do things I like, to let me come too, but . . . it's like he's just . . . I don't know. Incapable or something. He's a good man and husband. A good partner. I have no complaints. Well, just the one. Eventually I gave up and started taking responsibility for my own sex life. I'm discreet and discerning and only my partners know anything about what I get up to."

"Was Sasha Grande one of those partners?" I ask.

She shakes her head. "She was supposed to be. I mean, we contacted each other on IE before she ever came here. That's the reason I volunteered us to be the host home. But . . . she got here . . . we just . . . weren't into each other. It happens some-times. You have these great conversations and interactions online or on your phone, but in person . . . I was too old or she was too young, though we both had been with older and younger. It was awkward with her staying here at the house and having a friend with her. It was doubly tricky because of the crush Dylan quickly developed for her. And a thousand other reasons I couldn't even begin to explain. Bottom line is it didn't happen."

"What *did* happen, exactly?" I ask.

"What do you mean?"

"How far did it go?" I ask. "How intimate were you two, exactly?"

"I'm a pretty open person," she says. "I've already told you a lot—far more than most people reveal about themselves. But I don't think it's necessary to get into graphic details. I will say it didn't go very far and that we didn't have sex."

"I'm sorry for being so invasive," I say. "But I have reasons for asking and they're all related to the investigation. I have no desire to know anything about your personal life otherwise. I'm not judging you or Sasha in any way. I'm just trying to get as clear a picture as I can."

She drops her head into her hands and shakes it slowly. When she looks up she says, "And if I refuse?"

"All this can be formalized," I say. "I'm trying to keep it from coming to that, but . . . the case is open and active again, and FDLE is involved. With what we discovered yesterday there will be a lot of intense attention on every aspect of the case again, so . . ."

"It's more humiliating than . . . than anything else," she says. "I could tell the moment she saw me that she thought she had been catfished or something. And yet . . . probably because they were staying with us . . . she . . . It was like she tried to play along a little, but I could tell it was out of obligation or to ingratiate herself to me. I don't know. We talked a little—about the lifestyle some. I don't have many people to talk to. We kissed and made out a little, but very little. I think she would've kept going, but I put a stop to it."

"Who else knew about it?"

"No one."

"She didn't tell Naomi?"

"She said one of the coolest things about Naomi was that she never asked any questions or wanted to know anything—just let Sasha be Sasha."

I nod and think about it.

"I swear to you I'm tellin' you the truth," she says. "And I had nothing to do with whatever happened to her. Do you believe me?"

"Even if I do," I say, "and there's no way for me to be sure, but even if I believe you . . . What if someone saw or overheard you? That gives powerful motives to both Jay and Dylan."

45

"Today, we're dealing with theories and unanswered questions in the case of Naomi Newman and Sasha Grande," Merrick is saying.

"So far we've covered who these two young women were," Daniel says. "Why they were here. We've gone over all the evidence that was found—including the cell phone data, the camera, the backpack, and the remains."

"Right," Merrick says. "And on today's episode we're going to just dive into the various theories out there and go over all the questions that haven't been answered."

As I drive away from the Gaineses', I put on Merrick McKnight and Daniel Davis's true crime podcast.

There's something comforting and reassuring about hearing them again. They stopped podcasting back when the Randa Raffield case went sideways on us and Daniel was abducted, so for Daniel to be back and for the two of them to be working together again is inspiring.

Daniel says, "I'll start by saying . . . as much as I love a good murder mystery . . . and as much as I wish there was some big mystery at the heart of this case . . . I just find it very, very hard to believe that foul play was involved. It's just a terrible, unfortunate accident. Do you know how unlikely it is that they were murdered? Who murders someone for days and lets them keep their phones and cameras?"

Merrick says, "Exactly. Can't murder someone for days. That's not a thing. I've heard some people say that the murderer made all the calls and took all the pictures trying to make it look like they were lost in the wilderness and still alive. To me that's the most farfetched theory being touted."

"Even more than alien abduction?" Daniel asks.

"Well . . . at least as much," Merrick says. "Why would an alien abduction take so long? Why would the aliens let them keep their phones and cameras and leave their bones behind?"

"Think about a murderer," Daniel says, "be he opportunist, serial killer, or someone known to the victim—why would he feel the need to go out into the swamp every day and make failed 911 calls?"

"I heard someone say that that's why the calls are at approximately the same time of day," Merrick says, "because the guy had to go to work and could only go out and make the calls at certain times."

"People like answers and when there are none, they fill the void with theories and speculation, which is a stimulating and enjoyable exercise—we do it on this show—but to be responsible we should all either stick to reasonable speculation or make sure there's at least some kind of evidence for every theory we come up with, particularly the outlandish ones."

"Totally agree," Merrick says.

"We'll get into arguments for foul play a little later," Daniel says, "but let's stick with it being an accident for now. I think it's far more likely that they got lost and hurt or injured or bitten or stung or sick than anything else. Snakes, spiders, gators, wasps, hornets . . . the list goes on and on. The swamp is full of things that can kill you. Then there's the possibility that after being lost for a while they ate something poisonous or drank dirty water that made them sick. They'd be vomiting and have diarrhea and be dehydrated in no time—and no matter how much they drank of the contaminated water, they'd get worse and worse. If they ate the wrong thing—mushrooms or something else—they'd be hallucinating and have no idea of what was real and what wasn't. Depending on what they thought they were seeing, they could've hurt or killed themselves or each other. And let me be clear about this—everything I've read and heard about these two young women is that they were smart and determined and capable. I do not believe they merely got lost. If that's all it was, they would've been able to make it out or stayed in a single location and been found by the searchers. What *I'm* saying is that I believe something happened to them —something that injured, compromised, or killed them. Otherwise they would've made it out of there alive."

"That's a good point," Merrick says. "We're not questioning the strength or intelligence or survival skills of either Naomi or Sasha."

"Exactly."

"So," Merrick continues, "you're saying you believe what happened to them was a tragic accident, which is reasonable and certainly fits a lot of the evidence, but do you want to explain how you deal with the evidence that seems to contradict it?"

"Sure, yes, that's good," Daniel says. "But let me say up front . . . I can't respond to . . . I don't have an answer for everything. But you're right, I should explain how I deal with things that seem to contradict it being a case of accidental death."

"Want to start with the backpack?" Merrick asks.

"Sure."

"If they had some sort of accident, why were all of their things in the backpack? Why was the backpack in such good shape? Why was it found where it was?"

"Okay . . . so, obviously, like everything else, I don't know. These are just some possible explanations. I'd say that the fact that everything was in the backpack and in good shape argues against their deaths being violent or sudden. So . . . I lean toward a scenario of one or both of them getting injured or hurt or even sick, but with enough time to realize what was going on and put everything in the backpack."

"But if they had time . . ." Merrick says. "If they saw their potential fate on the horizon . . . why wouldn't they record a message for their loved ones?"

"I don't understand that," he says. "To me the fact that they didn't is a mystery and something troubling no matter what you think happened—unless you believe someone killed or grabbed them and they didn't have access to their things. As far as their backpack being in good shape . . . all I can say is that I don't believe it ever went into the river. I don't know what happened to it—how it was so protected, but I don't think it ever went into the water."

"What about their bikini tops being in the backpack?"

"Again, not sure, but I'd guess either they had extra ones or they took them off to bathe or swim and whatever happened to them happened then."

My phone rings, pausing the podcast and blasting its factory-set jingly tone through the truck's speakers.

It's Merrill, and I take the call through the truck's built-in mic and speakers.

"I fucked up," Merrill says.

"How?"

"Hailee," he says. "She hadn't been followed since the night we chased his ass in the woods. Thought maybe it was over because Reese Newman or Thomas McCloud were behind it."

"Makes sense," I say.

"Well, I was wrong. She's been abducted."

46

When I arrive at Oak Grove Campground, Merrill and Simien are standing in front of Hailee's trailer, the cast and crew forming a wide, loose circle around them.

"Our poor, dear Hailee," Simien is saying to Merrill. "Instead of beating me up you should've been protecting her."

Merrill's glare at Simien causes him to shrink back some. "That's one," he says. "And *one* is all you get. Ordinarily, you wouldn't get even one, but under the circumstances I'm gonna give you a pass—but don't say shit like that again. And don't think this changes shit. You still only have until end of business today to hand over all the footage."

"How can you even think of that right now with Hailee missing?"

"It's what she would've wanted," Merrill says, only a glint in his eyes and a slight twitch of his upper lip giving away any hint of sarcasm.

"*What?*" Simien says. "You think she's already dead? Oh my God."

Merrill hands me a sheet of printer paper.

I take it and study it.

It's a full-color printout of an email sent to Simien a short while ago.

It includes a photograph, which looks to have been taken with a phone, that shows a naked Hailee, her body smeared with dirt, sweat, and blood, tied to a pine tree in the middle of the woods.

Beneath the photo it reads: Halt Production. Await Instructions.

I look back at the picture.

Something about the image brings to mind St. Sebastian, and I wonder if any nude figure tied to a tree would.

Hailee's hands are tied together above her head, elongating her torso and raising and flattening her small breasts. Her head droops down to the left, her hair hanging down around it.

The small pine tree she's tied to is narrow, its base charred, and it's surrounded by other pines, oaks, and cypresses.

"Very theatrical," I say.

"Is, ain't it?" Merrill says.

"Quality's not great, but a few things stand out," I say.

"Such as?"

"It's not a planted pine," I say. "Not part of a crop. It's surrounded by several different species. It wasn't taken over in Gulf, Bay, Calhoun, Franklin counties or anywhere where the hurricane hit—none of the trees are leaning. And it's in an area where there's been a recent forest fire, either natural or controlled."

"Narrows it down some," he says.

"Whoever has her wants her humiliated."

"You two," Merrill says to Alison and Rena. "Thought y'all were stayin' with her?"

"We did," Alison says. "Just like every night. Only went back to our trailers to get ready this morning."

"Did you actually see her this morning?" he says.

"Well, no. Her door was closed just like it always is."

"Did anyone see her this morning?" he asks, looking around at the cast and crew.

No one did.

"What about last night?" Merrill says.

"After she went to her room, she never came out again."

"Did anyone see her or anything or anyone suspicious last night or this morning?" he says.

No one had.

"Y'all can go back to your trailers," he says. "If you think of anything—anything at all—let me know as soon as possible."

"What're you gonna do?" Simien asks.

"Find her. And whoever's responsible for her disappearance."

"What about the police?"

"About to call them," Merrill says, nodding toward Simien, Alison, and Rena, "but you three come with us first."

As Merrill leads us into Hailee's trailer, I notice that neither woman will get anywhere close to Simien.

"Put your hands in your pockets," Merrill says. "Don't touch anything. Take a quick look around and let me know if anything is missing or out of place."

The two young women begin looking around.

Simien says, "It speaks well of my art that someone is going to such great lengths to stop it, but . . . I'm so weary of being buffeted on every side."

"Are you going to do as the note says and stop the production?" I ask.

"They've left me no choice," he says. "Can't very well make a film without a leading lady . . . *unless* . . . Wait a minute. That could work. Alison, how would you like to be a movie star?"

"Huh?"

"I can change the story. We can have Naomi die and Sasha survive—well, at least until the end of the picture. I can make you a star. I . . . I hadn't thought of this before, but . . . This could be . . . Yes, this might be exactly what we need to propel our film into another stratosphere. We need to write a media release and get it out there. Do some interviews. Can you imagine the publicity?" He sweeps his right hand across the air like he's highlighting an unseen banner. "Actress Abducted from Acclaimed Auteur's Film Set."

"You empty, arrogant, vile prick," Rena says.

Everyone turns to see the once quiet PA who has found her voice.

"Hailee is missing," she continues. "*Missing*. Someone has her. Finding her is all that matters. And none of us are going to do anything but try and find her. And we're certainly not going to exploit her abduction for publicity. What the *fuck* is wrong with you?"

47

"Again," Daniel is saying, "there's a lot I can't explain. The bikini tops in the backpack and the folded jeans shorts are among them. I have a harder time explaining them than I do the backpack itself, but I see them as unknowns more than evidence that foul play was involved."

When I turn my truck on, the podcast continues. And I let it —listening as I drive away from Oak Grove Campground.

While Merrill continues to question Alison, Rena, and Simien and wait for a Potter County sheriff's investigator to arrive, he has asked me to search the area for possible locations where the picture of Hailee could've been taken.

"What about all the failed attempts to get into Sasha's iPhone?" Merrick is asking. "How do you explain those if it wasn't a third-party abductor or killer?"

"Two possible ways," Daniel says. "Either Sasha was dead by then and Naomi was trying to access her phone but didn't know the code."

"Yeah, that makes sense," Merrick says. "If something happened to you right now, I wouldn't be able to get into your phone."

"Exactly," Daniel says. "To me that's the most likely scenario. And . . . I guess . . . the truth is Sasha doesn't have to be dead. They could've been separated and Naomi had her phone for some reason, but it's most likely she was dead. The second possibility is not as likely, but still possible—and that is that Sasha was still alive, but so sick or out of it—from dysentery, dehydration, venom, or some psychotropic trip from a hallucinogenic, like mushrooms."

Daniel sometimes sounds like the retired college professor he is. He is highly intelligent and his arguments are reasoned and sound. I can imagine he and Sam have some truly epic conversations and debates.

"And let me just add about Sasha being injured or sick or even dead at this point," Daniel says. "I read somewhere recently that during the initial analysis of Naomi's leg bones, they discovered evidence of a condition that causes your muscles to inflame. Evidently it leaves evidence in the bones as well. The condition is caused by overexertion. That suggests to me that it is at least possible that Naomi was carrying Sasha—or trying to—or at least helping her. And that's where the overexertion came from."

"That's interesting," Merrick says. "I hadn't heard that."

"It may not be true, but if it is . . ."

I try to think about the best possibilities for where the photo of Hailee might have been taken—undamaged trees and a recent forest fire. Most of the forest fires in the area are controlled burns conducted by the division of forestry instead of naturally occurring and necessary fires started by lightning strikes or the like.

I call a friend of mine with the division of forestry and while I'm waiting for him to call me back, I turn the podcast back on.

"Okay," Merrick says. "What about the image of what appears to be a man on Naomi's camera?"

"I just don't think that's what it is," Daniel says. "I think it's a trick of light, a reflection, a digital artifact or something else, but not a man."

"And the bones?"

"You mean the difference in decomposition?" Daniel says.

"Right," Merrick says. "How could Naomi's be bleached if not by a chemical agent used by her killer?"

"I think for whatever reason Sasha's remains were in one part of the swamp and Naomi's in another and that accounts for the differences in the condition of their bones. I think Naomi's were probably cleaned by scavengers sooner and remained out in the open, exposed to sunlight all day every day until they were found."

"But there were no scavenger marks on them and they weren't found in the sunlight."

"I'd say that so few were found that perhaps others do have scavenger marks on them. And as far as the bones not being found out in open direct sunlight—they could've been dragged by animals to a new location shortly before they were discovered."

"If a third party or parties weren't involved," Merrick says, "how do you explain the search teams never finding them? Not just not finding them, but not finding any evidence of them during the entire time they searched?"

"It's a . . . The swamp is so vast and dense and difficult to navigate . . . And the . . . the search teams were so few and so small . . . they just missed them."

"And while we're on the subject of the searches," Merrick says, "we should say thank you again to everyone who worked so tirelessly to find them. Starting with Sheriff Jack Jordan and his department, but also Search and Rescue and Fish and Game and every single volunteer. The host family Naomi and Sasha were staying with, the Gaineses—Jay and Dylan practically lived in the swamp during that time, looking for them, and Robbie and Meagan and the boys set up a staging area in their yard and fed all the volunteers."

"And Benjamin Brooks," Daniel says. "He was a vital part of the search efforts—and we should say again, I know we've mentioned it before, but we haven't said it lately—his book, *Lost Innocents*, is one of our resources for this series of shows. If you haven't read it, get yours today. It's a great read. There's a link on our site and if you order it from there, our podcast gets a small affiliate percentage back from Amazon, which helps pay the bills."

Hearing Ben's name reminds me that as a wildlife officer he probably knows of recent forest fires, so I pause the podcast again and give him a call.

He's not far from where I am, and so we decide to get together for him to see the picture and help me search for the location.

On my way to meet him, I turn the podcast back on.

"Yes, it does," Daniel is saying. "And there was also Horton Joshua, the head of the TDC and an ecotour guide who was scheduled to give the girls a tour on the next day after they disappeared and whose search efforts led to the discovery of the bones. And Naomi's family, putting up and raising reward money, particularly Reese Newman and . . . What's her attorney's name? McCloud, I believe. Tom McCloud."

"And finally, Maurice Marcus, the extension agent, 4-H leader, and the organizer of the wilderness camp Naomi and Sasha were here to volunteer at," Merrick says. "He was also instrumental in the searches, actually using the camp counselors and attendees to participate in the search once they arrived. I hope we're not leaving anyone out. Thank you all for all you did to try to find Naomi and Sasha. Your efforts were heroic."

"Absolutely," Daniel says.

"I'm sure there are others," Merrick says, "but for now the

final piece of evidence that many believe points to third-party foul play instead of death by misadventure that I want to ask you about is the missing photos—the deleted images 509, 510, and 511 from Naomi's camera, which experts say can't be done from a camera, can only be done by placing the memory card in a computer."

"I admit . . . for me . . . this is the single toughest piece of evidence to explain," Daniel says. "And the truth is . . . I can't. I can give you a few ideas, maybe, a theory or two, but they'd just be guesses. I have no underlying basis in fact for them."

"Such as?"

"Such as, it's at least possible that in addition to everything else in the backpack, the girls had a laptop too. They could've used it to delete the photos and then lost it in the swamp somehow, but there's nothing to suggest that. I'm just saying there could be an explanation—we just don't know it. There's just so many things that are inexplicable—or at least unexplainable given our limited knowledge. Give you an example . . . This morning while getting ready and eating breakfast and trying to rush out of the house, I somehow put my car keys in the dishwasher. Now, just think if something had happened to me right then—something natural like a heart attack or something unnatural like an abduction or even a home invasion robbery in which I was killed. Everyone would wonder what the hell my car keys were doing in the dishwasher and all the armchair detectives would venture theories—many of them wild and outlandish—all because they're unaware of the simple reality of what actually happened and how it had no bearing on anything else that happened."

"That's a good point," Merrick says. "You're right. I've investigated and reported on hundreds of accidental and suspicious deaths and they all have unanswered questions, little things that can't be explained."

"I'm not saying that's what this is," Daniel says. "As I say, to me this is the most convincing evidence of third-party involvement. I'm just saying it's at least possible that there is another explanation. Hell, maybe this camera actually did delete those photos even though it wasn't supposed to be able to. Tech often surprises us and does things it's not supposed to, and doesn't do things it *is* supposed to."

"Too true," Merrick says. "All too true."

"We just don't know and may never."

48

"Who in the *hell* would abduct *her*?" Ben is saying as he studies the photo. "And why? Just to shut down the production? Could it be McCloud? Buying Simien off didn't work, so he's resorting to kidnapping?"

"He and Reese have to be on our suspect list."

He has climbed into my truck, and we are talking through possible areas to search for recent forest fires.

Before leaving the campground, I had snapped a picture of the photo of Hailee with my phone, which I had texted to him when he got in the truck with me.

"Wonder if this has anything to do with what happened to Sasha and Naomi or us finding that boat with the remains in it —or both, maybe they're connected to each other too—or if it's completely separate and is just about shutting down the production?"

"Could be about Hailee or Simien for other reasons," I say. "Maybe telling him to stop the production was to divert suspicion away from the real reason."

"That's true," he says, still looking at the photo. "I can't be certain, but . . . the char marks look a little too high up on the tree to be a controlled burn. We usually don't let them get quite this high."

"It's possible that Simien himself has her," I say. "This happened after we found out he's financing his movie by making a porn film at the same time, and that it may have involved Hailee being raped."

"What?"

"Yeah, and this comes right on the heels of Merrill beating him up and telling him he had until this evening to turn over all the porn film footage to him. He could be trying to keep her quiet and cover up his crime or it could be part of some scheme relating to the film."

As he continues to study the picture and think of places it could have been taken, I call Merrill and share with him the thoughts we've had about Reese, Thomas McCloud, and Simien.

"Okay," Ben says as I end the call with Merrill. "I have some ideas about where to look. But there's quite a few spots and they're spread out. It's probably best if we split up since we have a ticking clock."

"Just tell me which ones you want me to check."

He does, then rushes back to his truck, and we speed away in different directions.

As I race down the rural highway toward Ward Ridge where a recent forest fire had occurred, I call and check in with Dad and let him know what's happening, talk to Johanna for a few minutes, see if Verna can pick up Taylor from school, then turn the podcast back on.

"So, I guess it's my turn," Merrick says. "I'll just start by saying I'm playing devil's advocate so we can cover as much as possible, but I don't necessarily disagree with what you've said."

"In the same way, I'm open to foul play being involved," Daniel says.

"I agree with you that the most compelling evidence of

third-party foul play is the missing photos, but there are other things too. I rarely hear anyone mention this, but I find it hard to believe their phones lasted as long as they did—even with powering them down for much of each day."

"You're right everyone seems to be impressed with the way they used them so sparingly and mostly kept them off, but I wonder if anyone's done an experiment to re-create what they did to see if it's even possible."

"And it's highly unlikely their phones were fully charged when they went into the swamp," Merrick says. "They were probably on them pretty much nonstop like most young people. They could've been down to fifty percent or even lower before they took a single step into the swamp, but even if they had a lot more charge than that, I don't see how any steps they could've taken would lead to the results they got. Then there's the backpack, of course. Not only does it have everything in it in great condition, but the backpack itself is dry and clean and in great condition. I think it had to have been stored some-where—by the killer, along with their bodies, which is why all the searchers never found them."

Daniel says, "Those are good points and some of them are quite compelling, but to me the biggest question is . . . If this is the work of a killer and he has both girls and all their things, why put them out there to be found at all? Why not dig a hole out there and bury them and all their belongings in it? Do it right—and nothing would ever be found."

"That's a good question," Merrick says, "and though there are a variety of answers and theories floating around out there, let me just deal with one that, though obscure, should be taken seriously. There's actually a serial killer being pursued by the FBI and other law enforcement agencies who makes his murders look like accidents. I don't care for the nickname some of the agencies have given him—the Angel of Accidental Death

—but the fact that he has a moniker lets you know just how legit this is. And the thing is . . . every death attributed to him has a lot of similarities to this one—namely, that he leaves just enough evidence to sow doubts and spark speculation but never enough to tip his hand."

"Fascinating," Daniel says. "I've never even heard of him."

"A lot of people haven't. He moves around a lot and is believed to be responsible for at least fourteen deaths in six different states. Our listeners can look him up if they want to. There's a lot of information online about him. But it doesn't have to be him for this to be murder. It could be another serial killer or predator. You could have a scenario like in national parks where predators lurk, waiting for unsuspecting young women."

"The problem I see with that," Daniel says, "is unlike parks or popular hiking spots, the swamp has no set or maintained trails and has very, very little traffic. A killer wouldn't know where to lurk and could be out there for months or more likely years before seeing anyone."

"That's certainly true," Merrick says. "But what if—instead of waiting in the woods for his victims, he follows them in?"

"I still see some logistics issues, but that's far more likely than the other way, waiting out there for them."

"But, as is true in most cases of murder," Merrick says, "it's far more likely to have been committed by someone known to them or an opportunistic killer than a serial killer. And it's entirely possible that whoever did it didn't intend to kill them. It could've started off as something else and turned into a momentary act of rage."

"But that's the thing," Daniel says. "It wasn't momentary. It went on for days—days in which they had their phones and cameras. Why didn't they take pictures of him or write a message about what was happening to them?"

"Maybe they did," Merrick says. "Maybe that's what the deleted photos were."

"He just happens to be the kind of stalker and killer who carries a laptop into the swamp with him."

49

"What's your ten-twenty?" Merrill asks, using the ten code for location.

Back when we both worked inside the prison —him as a CO, me as a chaplain—ten codes were part of our daily communication, and though the sheriff's department I work for uses them, it's mostly between dispatch and patrol, so I don't hear them nearly as much anymore.

"Ward Ridge," I say. "Just about to leave. There was a recent forest fire out here, but there's nothing that looks like the background of the photo. You?"

"Leaving the campground," he says. "Potter Sheriff's Department is on the scene. Trying to figure out what to do next. You need my help runnin' down the possible locations of the photo?"

"Ben and I split them up," I say. "Shouldn't take too long."

"Then I think I might go have a little chat with ol' Tom McCloud."

"Let me know if you need backup with ol' Thomas not Tom McCloud."

"Day I need backup with somebody like him, the day I gettin' out the game."

"Just don't challenge him to a foot race."

"You'd think I could best him," he says, "one of my strides equalin' about three of his."

"You would think."

He doesn't say anything right away and we are quiet a moment.

I'm in the relatively new position of helping Merrill with an investigation instead of the other way around. I'm following his direction and trying not to take the lead in any way, but with Hailee missing and the clock ticking I may have to offer a suggestion or two or give some unsolicited advice.

"What else?" Merrill says.

"Huh?"

"What else I need to be doin'?"

"What else you thinkin' about doing?" I ask.

"I's gonna let the sheriff's department do what I can't do," he says. "They got the manpower to knock on more doors and chase down more leads than I could ever get to—even with your help."

"True," I say. "And wise."

"They also got the authority to subpoena phone and bank records."

"Yes, they do," I say. "It'd be nice to know what they find."

"Chaquille gonna let me know as soon as they come through."

"Excellent. What did the search of her trailer turn up?"

"Not much. Alison and Rena said they couldn't tell that anythin' was missing. Her car's still parked out front and her keys were in her purse, which was turned over and sort of dumped out in her room. There was some cash and a credit card, but couldn't find her driver's license. Broken mirror and chair. Makeup slung all over the place, and there was blood splatter on one wall and some drops leading to the little back window, which looks like where he entered and removed her from."

"How much blood?"

"Not a whole lot. Crime Scene collecting it now and dusting for prints. About to process her car."

"Did y'all find her phone?"

"Yeah, but . . . Alison thinks she may have had two. Says she can't be sure, but . . ."

I think about it.

"So what else should I be doing?" he says.

"You're doing great," I say. "Have everything in hand . . ."

"Except?"

"Only one other thing I can think of right now," I say.

"Oh, shit," he says. "We need to track down the guy from *Campground Killer* who creeped her out."

"That's the only other thing I can think of right now," I say. "And you already thought of it."

"What'd she say his name was? Jarred or Jacob or Justin. Something like that."

50

B en and I spend most of the day searching every place on his list—and two more my friend at the division of forestry gives me—yet find none that could have been where the picture of Hailee was taken.

"There's got to be thousands of places around here where small fires occurred that we know nothing about," Ben is saying.

We are parked on the side of a flat, empty rural road, our trucks facing opposite directions, talking to each other through our open driver's side windows.

"I'll ask around and keep trying to come up with other places we can check," he adds, "but . . . it could've been just about anywhere."

"No matter where it was taken, it'll probably provide some clues as to who took it," I say, "but if its's on private property it'll probably tell us exactly who it is."

He nods. "True. Any word from Sam on the remains we found in the boat or updates on Sasha and Naomi's case?"

I shake my head. "Not yet."

"I just keep trying to figure out if this—Hailee's disappearance, but really so many things to do with the film—has anything at all to do with the original case."

"Hard to see how," I say, "but it could."

"Wonder if we'll ever know," he says. "And not just about the connection but about all of it—what really happened to Sasha and Naomi, who all's in that boat and why, who was following Simien or stalking Hailee, who took her."

I remember something I wanted to ask him.

"Did Naomi's or Sasha's family help with the search?" I ask. "I know Reese started raising awareness and reward money right away, but did she or any others actually get out and participate in the search?"

He shrugs. "Some, I guess. I mean, they definitely went out some, but not very far and not very often. And maybe I'm just comparing them to your dad and me and some of our amazing volunteers, especially some of the search-and-rescue people. Some of us—especially early on—would search all day and much of the night. The most committed would come in with the others at sundown, hose the mud and muck off, grab a bite to eat, rehydrate, and head back out after the others left for home. Wasn't many and it was far more dangerous, not only because of the darkness but because we were often on our own, but if that had been my daughters out there, nothin' could've kept me from going back out. I question his motives now, but even Horton Joshua did far more searching than the girls' families. What made you ask?"

"I was listening to Merrick and Daniel's podcast and they mentioned Reese putting up reward money but didn't say anything about her searching when they were acknowledging the searchers, and I just wondered."

"Sasha's mom came at first but didn't stay, but Reese . . . She got here quick and stayed a long time. Her husband came and went some, but Reese and her little minion McCloud never left, as far as I know. 'Course, I wasn't much more than a kid at the time, so I'm sure there's a lot I missed. But I'll tell you this . . . Your dad was impressive. He wasn't a young man and he ran circles around everybody else—'cept maybe Jay and Dylan. *Damn.* Now every time I think about them or Horton I wonder if something else was motivating them—like maybe instead of trying to find the girls, they were trying to keep their bodies from being found or something."

"Hopefully we'll find out for sure," I say. "And maybe we'll owe some apologies."

"I sure hope so," he says as he cranks his truck. "At least to Jay and Dylan. Hell'll freeze over before Horton ever gets one from me."

I crank my truck, roll up the window, and pull away after he does.

I'm about to call Merrill when my phone vibrates.

It's Sam.

"Things are moving fast," she says. "But I wanted to let you know . . . At least one of the girls is from Cuba and there's a good chance they all are."

"How do you know that?"

"One of them had somehow hidden a note inside her bra. Had her name and phone number and said to tell her parents she loves them."

That hurts my heart and I have to blink my stinging eyes several times.

"So we know for sure she was Cuban, but the rest of them were wearing clothes and shoes from there, so . . . we're thinking they all were."

I start to say something but she stops me.

"Sorry," she says. "I've got to take this. I'll let you know more when I can."

"Thank you," I say, but she is gone.

51

"These are extraordinary," I say. "So incredibly beautiful. And show so much talent. You've really got a gift."

I'm at Dad and Verna's place looking at artwork Taylor created at school, while eating chicken and dumplings Johanna helped Verna make for dinner.

"Wow," I say after another big bite, "these are the very best chicken and dumplings I've ever had. Truly. So good and so filling. Are the dumplings made from scratch?"

"They sure are," Johanna says, beaming like her little sister just has.

"Such talented girls you've got, John," Verna says. "No wonder you're so proud of them."

"They really are," I say. "And I really am. They take after their mothers."

We are sitting at their dining room table—a girl on either side of me and Dad and Verna across the table from us. Through the huge bay window, the moon can be seen rising over and on the lake.

I had called Merrill a few times this evening and left

messages for him, and will have to go out again to help him
once he calls back, which causes me to savor and enjoy these
moments around the table with my family all the more.

"Speaking of mothers," I say, "Anna will be home in just a
few more days."

"Can't wait," Johanna says.

"Me either," Taylor says. "I miss Mommy."

"Me three," I say. "She should be back in time for us to take
her to the Wabi Sabis concert and to play and have a picnic at
the landing."

"*Fuu—un*," Johnna says.

"*Fuu—un*," Taylor repeats.

"Yes, it will be," I say. "I may have to go back out tonight and
help Uncle Merrill with a case, but I'll come back and stay here
tonight so I can see you in the morning, okay?"

Dad says, "We put a rollaway bed in their room for you so
you don't have to keep sleeping on the floor."

"Thank you," I say, "but the Minnie Mouse doll and the
Moana bathrobe were just fine."

"I'm surprised you can walk the next morning after sleeping
like that," he says.

"Can we play hide and seek until Uncle Merrill calls?"
Johanna asks.

"Sure," I say. "Anything y'all want."

"Yeah, hidin' and seekin'," Taylor says. "Daddy, you count,
we'll hide."

"You got it," I say. "But be careful and take good care of Papa
Jack and Verna's house."

"They can't hurt anything," Dad says. "Let 'em have at it."

They squeal as they jump up and run to hide.

I count to twenty-five and then begin my search.

I take my time finding them, ignoring Taylor's laughter and
loud whispers.

Evidently they approve because they insist I be *it* for three more turns.

The call from Merrill comes as I'm halfway through my fourth count, and I solicit Papa Jack and Verna to take my place while I talk to him.

"Thought I'd be callin' you 'bout helpin' with the Hailee thing," he says.

"You're not?"

"Simien's body was just found," he says. "He was tortured and beaten to death."

52

"I've already called the sheriff's department," Merrill is saying, "so we don't have long."

He, Dad, and I are standing just outside Simien's Airstream, leaning in the open door, looking at the crime scene without touching anything.

The night is dark and cool, the woods around us echoing with the humming, buzzing, and power-saw sounds of crickets and frogs and birds.

About ten feet behind us, but creeping up slowly, the cast and crew of *Lost Innocents*, who have now lost their leader, strain to see what's inside the blood-splattered camper.

Inside the small living area of the Airstream, Simien Eggers's shirtless body is taped with gaffer tape to a plastic folding chair, his arms pulled back behind him, his head hanging forward.

The same black gaffer tape holding him to the chair is over his mouth.

Gaffer tape is used by film crews to tape down cables and other temporary setups on both soundstage and locations, and

I wonder if it belonged to Simien and was already in his trailer or if the killer brought it with him.

I glance around to see if there's any other production equipment. There is some. In one corner, a large role of gaffer tape lies on the floor next to a boom mic stand and an assortment of lights.

A drop of blood rolls out of Simien's hairline, down his forehead, and off the end of his nose to splat on the linoleum floor.

I look back at him.

Open cuts, smears of blood, and bruises cover much of his exposed body, while his hair and jeans are wet with blood, sweat, and other bodily fluids.

What happened to him didn't happen quick.

"This took a while," I say. "He had to be alive for that bruising to occur. Nobody saw or heard anything?"

"Say they didn't," Merrill says.

On the floor in front of him, smeared with his blood, the tools of his death are scattered about—a large kitchen knife, a simple black-handled ice pick, an empty syringe, and a blue-headed, wooden-handled ball pein hammer.

"Somebody knew what they were doing," I say. "And not just with the torture. If every killer left behind their weapons, we'd close a lot fewer cases."

"No question," Dad says.

Most law enforcement officers and forensic experts agree that if murderers would wipe down the weapons they use and drop them at the crime scene there would be far less to connect them to their crimes.

"What *is* a question," Merrill says, "is how the hell I can be so bad at this?"

"This didn't happen while you were guarding him," I say.

"Yeah, happened while I was looking for the *other* person I's supposed to be protectin'. I'm oh for two in this shit. I'd take early retirement but can't go out like this."

"You were a volunteer," I say. "You warned them you were just one man and there was a limit to what you could do. Told them to protect themselves. And no one has been watching or following or stalking them lately. None of us saw this coming."

"He's right," Dad says. "Don't blame yourself for this. You did all you could do to protect them and you're doing all you can do to find her. Now, let's find out who's behind all this."

"Thoughts?" Merrill says.

"I would think you only torture someone like that for punishment or to try to get information out of them," I say.

"Agree," Dad says.

"If the same person's behind both," I say, "why abduct Hailee and torture her in the woods and leave Simien in his trailer and torture him here?"

"Took a big risk to do it here," Dad says.

"It's possible this is the work of two different people with two different motives," I say, "but it's far more likely to be related."

"Simien's bigger than McCloud," Merrill says, "but seems weak and soft."

"If the syringe was used first," I say, "wouldn't matter what size the person was. Inject him with something to subdue him and . . ."

"That's the way I see it," Dad says. "You think Thomas McCloud's behind this?"

"Not necessarily," Merrill says. "Just sayin' a smaller person could've done it."

"The guy we caught creepin' Hailee's trailer was smallish," I say.

"Potter's finest be rollin' up here any minute," Merrill says. "Y'all seen enough, let's ask the thespians and artisans some questions before they do."

53

W e split up and begin questioning the cast and crew, but eventually wind up back together with Logan Taylor-Johnson, Alison Miller, and Rena Hanan.

"This film has been cursed from day one," Logan is saying. "And now it's over. All our work. All our effort and investment . . . for nothing."

"Who does something like that?" Alison asks. "Is that what happened to Hailee out in the woods? We're actors for fuck sake, not mobsters."

"Are we next?" Logan asks. "Are we in danger? Should we leave tonight? No reason for us to stay, is there? I mean, it's not like we'll be shooting anymore. This movie is as dead as its director."

"Is that why it was done?" Rena asks. "Tryin' to shut down the production?"

"We don't know," I say. "It's possible."

Dad looks at Logan. "Sheriff might have something to say about you leaving."

"Well, unless he's gonna provide me protection . . . And

even then, look what happened to them—and y'all were supposed to be protecting them. Nah, man. Fuck that. I'm out of here."

"We need to stay and help," Rena says. "Hailee could still be alive. We've got to find her."

"Y'all thought any more about who might have her?" Merrill asks.

They all shake their heads.

"Hell," Alison says, "I thought Simien may have had something to do with it. Shows how much I know."

"How so?" I ask.

"Because I was so wrong about him being—"

"No," I say. "How did you think he might have been involved?"

"Oh, well . . . You know how he is—was. I actually thought he might have borrowed money from the wrong people or Hailee finally had enough and tried to quit or was going to the police about what they did to her."

She tilts her head toward Logan as she says this.

"Don't say *they*," Logan says. "All I did was what I was directed to do. I've done hundreds of shoots like that. I thought it was all kosher and consensual. Hell, it was in front of several witnesses. If Simien tricked her or whatever that's on him, not me. I wouldn't've so much as laid a limp dick on her if I thought she didn't know what was going on. Ask around. I've got a great reputation in the industry."

"So you've done porn before?" Dad asks.

Alison says, "He's a straight-up porn star. That's why Simien cast him. They've worked together many times before."

"What happened here today?" Merrill asks. "When did y'all last see Simien?"

"It was such a cluster," Alison says. "That sociopathic bastard wanted to still shoot today. Wanted to write Hailee out and continue with me in the lead role."

"Even I thought that was too heartless," Logan says.

"We all stood together in protest," Rena says. "Everyone refused to work. For many of the cast and crew, they were too upset or thought it was insensitive to work today. They weren't actually quitting."

Alison says, "Simien threw one hell of a big titty baby fit and stormed into his trailer. That was—when, maybe sometime between two and three. We all sort of did our own thing, but most of us were here all day. As far as I know, no one saw Simien come out of his trailer again."

"I went to take him his dinner," Rena says. "Around seven— the usual time. Tapped on the door and called out for him. Opened it when I saw it was unlocked and . . . All that blood. It's the most horrific thing I've ever seen."

"And no one went into this trailer at any point after he did?"

"Not that anyone saw," Alison says. "We asked around."

"Does that mean the killer was in there already, waiting on him?" Logan asks. "'Cause if so . . . it means it wasn't anybody from the cast or crew."

54

As a Potter County sheriff's investigator takes over the crime scene, Dad, Ben, and I are standing about fifty feet away, not far from Hailee's trailer.

Ben had called after he had gotten home from work to see how else he could help with the search for Hailee and I let him know what's going on.

Merrill is a few feet away from us on the phone.

"I just don't see any way in which this isn't connected to what happened to Sasha and Naomi," Ben is saying. "It's like the houseboat we found. Just can't see any way in which it's not all related."

Dad nods his head. "It's possible it's not, but I'd say it's highly unlikely."

"I think whoever killed Sasha and Naomi also killed the women in the boat and Simien and took Hailee," Ben says. "But I have no idea why."

"Even money it's a cover-up," Dad says. "I bet he killed Naomi and Sasha to cover up the bodies in the boat and killed Simien and Hailee to cover that up."

I nod. "That makes the most sense with what we know so far, but . . . there's a lot we don't know."

Merrill walks over, returning his phone to his pocket.

"Did the picture of Hailee look sexual to y'all?" he asks. "I don't mean just 'cause she was naked, but the way he posed her?"

We all nod.

"*Posed* is the right word," I say. "It was as theatrical as it was sexual. Made me think of paintings of the martyrdom of Saint Sebastian. An image that has been highly sexualized over the years."

"That was Jodi Avenarius's roommate from Orlando," Merrill says. "Finally called me back."

"Who?" Ben asks.

"The PA on the *Killer Campground 3* shoot who creeped Hailee out," Merrill says. "He lives in Orlando and works when he can get it on small productions there. His soon-to-be ex-roommate Cliven says he has mental issues and is on medication for a variety of conditions—at least he was until about a week ago when he went off them and disappeared. Says ol' Jodi fancies himself a filmmaker and is the most obsessive little fucker he's ever seen. Feels slighted by the world, the film industry, and every woman he's ever been around for any length of time. Says he's obsessed with and or bears grudges against a world full of women, but he's actually heard him use the name Hailee Benson."

"Maybe this isn't connected to what happened to Sasha and Naomi," Ben says. "Maybe I was wrong about that. Avenarius could've abducted Hailee because of obsessive passion or to pay her back for rejecting him and he could've killed Simien because he thinks he's stolen his job or something."

"Or out of retribution," I say. "If he's been here for a week stalking Hailee he could've seen or heard about what Hailee went through in the porn scene."

Dad says, "As much as I don't want to, we've got to let Hugh Glenn know so he can get a BOLO out on him."

55

I know things aren't going to go well when Sheriff Hugh Glenn pulls up with Horton Joshua in his passenger seat. Dad steps over to Glenn. I follow.

"You can't be here," Joshua says. "I have a restraining order against you."

"I was here first," Dad says. "Plus, I've got vital information for the investigation."

Hugh Glenn in his most patronizing voice says, "Jack, I know you miss the job. I do. And I know you want to be involved, but you can't. Now, I just got here. I don't even know what we've got yet. Give me a chance to look things over and confer with my boys. Anything you think we need to know, tell the officer who interviews you."

"You're really that insecure and vindictive that you can't accept information from me?" Dad says.

"Jack, please don't make another scene," Glenn says. "I'd hate to have to arrest you in front of everyone. I understand you don't have long . . . And I'm sorry about that. I genuinely am. But don't waste what little time you have left playing pretend investigator. That's never what you were, even when you wore the badge. You were always more a politician than anything else."

"He was a great investigator," I say. "Still is. But even mediocre investigators have the intelligence and lack of ego to accept information and or help when it's offered to them."

"I'd say even a mediocre investigator would've solved the original case five years ago when it happened," he says. "And if one *had* . . . we wouldn't have a missing woman and a dead director."

Dad starts to say something, but Horton Joshua says, "Look, Jack, if you want to be involved either see if Hugh will hire you or run for sheriff again—if you're still with us then."

The two men then walk away, and I have to hold Dad back from going after them.

"Come on," I say. "I'll call Sam and let her know. And we can get Reggie to put out the BOLO."

Glenn yells at a nearby deputy as he's walking toward Simien's trailer, "Clear the area. Get these goddamn pedestrians out of my crime scene."

56

B ack at Dad's, after tucking the girls in, Merrill and I sit at the dining room table watching *Killer Campground 3* on my laptop while waiting for Sam to stop by when she leaves the crime scene.

Dad and Verna are in bed. Merrill and I are the only two people up in the dim, quiet house.

"You still blame yourself for Taylor's abduction, don't you?" Merrill says.

I start to respond, but he continues.

"Guilt must be eatin' your ass alive," he adds. "No other explanation for you punishing yourself like this." He nods at the screen. "What I want to know is what the hell I did? Why I gotta suffer too? Is it 'cause of the way I fucked up this case?"

The movie is even worse than I thought it would be—a low-budget B horror picture seemingly without a script and *with* bad acting and abysmal production value.

Fortunately we don't have to watch much of it.

Early in the movie, a masked killer ties a naked female victim to a tree in the woods and tortures her.

"So now we know it's Jodi's creepy little ass," Merrill says.

"And what art inspired his imitation. Now, we just got to find him. See if any of his social media shows a connection to the Panhandle?"

I check.

It doesn't take long to determine that Jodi Avenarius has no social media at all—at least not under his name.

"Big surprise," Merrill says.

A few minutes later Sam arrives, and we tell her about Avenarius and show her the clip from the movie.

"Well, hell, fellas," she says. "Y'all've done all the work for me. Thank you. I'll get a BOLO out on his creepy little ass tonight."

Merrill shakes his head. "*Fuck*, I hope she's still alive."

"Wonder if he plans to take her back to Orlando?" Sam says.

I nod. "We need to get his tag number and description of his vehicle out—especially to Highway Patrol on I-10 and 75."

"If he stuck around to kill Simien," she says, "he should still be on the road."

"*Fuck*, I hope he hasn't killed her," Merrill says again.

"Give me a minute to set this all in motion," she says, and steps out onto the front porch to make her calls.

"If she's dead," Merrill says, "I'm out. I'll go back to being a CO or sell insurance or some shit. May anyway, but if I let her get killed . . ."

"The hell you *will*," Dad says from the hallway.

He pads the rest of the way to the table and sits down across from us.

"Listen to me, Merrill. You're good at what you do, and you didn't *let* her get anything. You hadn't even been hired to protect her. You warned her. This is not on you, *but* . . . even if it was, even if you had been hired to protect someone and they got hurt or killed in spite of your efforts . . . You don't quit. You don't throw in the towel. You keep going. You keep protecting and helping and you do so knowing that you can't help or protect everyone. That's the job. You do what you can and that's all you can do. You have any idea how many people John and I have failed to protect, failed to save? Think about this case alone. If Naomi and Sasha were murdered, then I'm responsible for letting their killer go free for another five years so far. Think about that. No telling what kind of damage he's done in the time. No telling how many more people he's killed. That's on me. And I'm tough enough to handle it because that's the job. And I know you're a hell of a lot tougher than I am."

"Nobody that tough," Merrill says.

"Martin Fisher's murder still haunts me," I say, "and that's the first one I was responsible for. Think about how many there have been in the decades since then."

"Okay, *shit*," he says. "I won't quit. I'll hang around at least 'til I fuck up as many cases as y'all have."

"That's the spirit," Dad says.

Sam walks in. "Sheriff," she says, nodding toward Dad.

He hasn't been in office for a few years now, but he will forever be known as *Sheriff*—as he should be.

"Okay," Sam says, "everything is in play. Hopefully we'll have his ass in custody and Hailee Benson back making bad movies in no time."

"Good," Dad says. "Now, what can you tell us about the victims in the boat?"

57

"Those bodies have been in that boat a very long time," Sam says. "Years. The pathologist says that the rate of decay varies greatly from situation to situation—it would've been drastically different if they were on the ground out in the swamp instead of in that houseboat—but in general, heat and humidity accelerate the process dramatically. She says that in three or four weeks the bodies could be completely skeletonized. There might be some tendons left but for the most part their bodies would likely be destroyed. Says even inside an enclosed boat like that flies would still get in and reach the bodies—and we found evidence of dead flies and larva around the remains."

"Do we have an estimate of how long they have been in there?" Dad asks.

"She says she'll have a more accurate estimate eventually, but her exact words were, 'the bodies were skeletonized in three or four weeks and those skeletons have been in that boat for three or four years.'"

"So," he says, "it's possible they were there when Naomi and Sasha went missing."

She nods. "Definitely possible. She says the bones should be able to be used to determine the sex, size, weight, and maybe even general racial makeup. And with dental records and any DNA, they'll help with identification. Things like previous bone injuries or devices implanted in the victims can also help lead to the right medical records. A forensic anthropologist has been called in and we should know a lot more soon, but . . . thanks to the note hidden in the bra of one of the victims and where it has led us, at this point all we expect the autopsy info to do is confirm most of what we already know. And this is what we know . . ."

She shuffles a few folders around, opens one, and glances inside.

"We know that all the girls were from Cuba," she says. "We know that they were between the ages of twelve and twenty-two. We've been working with the Cuban Ministry of the Interior and the Policía Nacional Revolucionaria. They were aware of these girls being missing—them and many more like them. They were believed to have been kidnapped, abducted, even sold in some cases to a sex traffic ring bringing Cuban girls by boat to different parts of Florida. They were mostly taken to Miami and the Keys, but now it looks like some of them came a lot farther north, entering various rivers and taken inland to small, rural landings that nobody pays much attention to, then from there transported by vans to various places all over the country. Several agencies were aware of this happening and had actually apprehended some of the traffickers as close to us as St. Marks —and returned some of the young girls to Cuba— but this is the first known case of them using the Apalachicola. I seriously doubt it's the first, but . . ."

"Any idea how they got in that boat or that boat got so far inland?" Dad asks.

She shakes her head. "Nor who it belongs to. Nothing in it to tell us and no registration or any identifying documentation anywhere. Obviously they weren't being transported in that boat, so probably one boat brought them up through the Gulf and then another through the bay and up the river. Our best guess is they were put in that houseboat where it sits now. We may never know who it belongs to or how it got where it did."

"I have a good idea," Dad says. "Answer me this— Who is often seen in the company of very young, attractive women more than half his age and way out of his league? Who creeped out Naomi and Sasha and found their remains and told his worker where to find their backpack? Who showed up at the crime scene tonight to keep any eye on things?"

"Horton fuckin' Joshua," Merrill says.

"Horton fuckin' Joshua," Dad says.

"Well," Sam says, "looks like I need to take a closer look at Horton fuckin' Joshua."

58

I 'm dreaming of kayaking with Anna and the girls in the Dead Lakes when Merrill wakes me up.

"John," he whispers as he shakes my arm.

I blink open my eyes to see him standing over me in the dim room, and am disoriented and don't know where I am.

I look around and realize I'm on the rollaway bed in Johanna and Taylor's room at Dad and Verna's.

"Huh?" I say. "What is it?"

"Get dressed," he says. "Come with me."

He eases out of the room and I quickly get dressed and follow him.

"Come on," he says. "I'll explain on the way."

I follow him out to his car and get in.

"Have you slept any?"

"Nah," he says as he pulls away from Dad and Verna's house and down their long drive. "My mind's been spinning. I . . . I've been thinking—something kept bugging me. I was like, I know where that picture of Hailee was taken, but I couldn't come up with it. Until . . . I went out driving and thinking. Cranked up some Kid Cudi and sped around thinking about everything and nothing and . . . I think I came up with it. Least I came up with what had been just outside of my conscious. Had some other thoughts too but . . . we'll get to those directly."

He drives toward Oak Grove Campground but turns on a side road just before it.

"I saw something similar to that and smelled the char of the forest fire when I was walking to the tree stand that night we saw Hailee's stalker."

He pulls up and parks where he had before, and we get out and follow his path toward the tree stand.

We don't have to go far.

Within fifty feet or so we not only find the spot where the photo of Hailee was taken but some discarded rope, some of which still dangles from the back of the small pine where she had been tied.

"Look at the rope," Merrill says.

I do.

"It's not cut or bloody or— You know how the film shows ol' Jodi's inspiration for the staging of this scene?"

"Yeah?"

"The same could be said of Hailee," he says.

"She staged it herself?" I ask.

"The rope is not cut or dirty or bloody," he says. "Hell, it looks like it's never even been tied. She probably just held it back behind the tree in her hands."

I think about it.

"I tell her nobody is following her anymore and that night she disappears and Simien gets the email with the photo telling him to stop the production. Who wanted the production stopped more than she did? I bet not even Reese did."

"I bet you're right."

As he pulls out his phone and makes a call, I realize that I don't even know what time it is.

I consult my own phone. It's 2:32 a.m.

"Chaquille," Merrill is saying into his phone, "I wake you up?"

It's obvious the Potter County deputy was sleeping and just as obvious that Merrill didn't care.

"Wouldn't'a had to, your ass woulda called me earlier like you said you would."

He's quiet for a moment, then says, "You sure? . . . Well, okay, then, my bad. Go back to sleep."

After he ends the call and returns the phone to his pocket, he looks at me. "Says he never called me with the results of Hailee's credit cards usage because there hadn't been any."

"Disappearing on your own is very difficult to do," I say. "Unless you have really good fake IDs and lots of cash."

"Guess my black ass was wrong," he says. "Thought for sure she did it herself. Was the thing that made the most sense to me."

"She could've had help," I say. "Or . . . Come on."

59

We drive over to the front of the campground, park, and sneak in.

We check Hailee's trailer first.

On the way over, I had told Merrill how I thought it was possible that Hailee had hidden in the woods after taking the photo and sending the email to Simien from her burner phone. Then snuck back into her trailer after it had been searched and everything died back down.

We search Hailee's trailer thoroughly. She is not here. However, it appears that more of her things are missing now, so unless they were taken by the crime scene techs—and they didn't look to be items that would have been—then she had come back at some point and gotten them.

"*Unless*," Merrill says, "somebody stole them."

"True," I say.

We determine that if Hailee is here the most likely places for her to be hiding are either with Alison or Rena.

"*Unless*," Merrill says, "she killed Simien for his Airstream and she don't mind a little blood on the linoleum."

"Will check it if we strike out at Alison's and Rena's."

Our search begins and ends in Alison's trailer.

There we find Alison, Rena, and Hailee.

"I was going to the police in the morning," Hailee says. "I was just so scared."

We are in the tiny living area of Alison's camper trailer, the three pajama-clad women on the small couch made for two.

"I knew everyone would think I killed Simien," she continues, "but I swear on my life and that of my mother that I didn't. I wouldn't. I couldn't. I couldn't kill anyone. I just wanted to put an end to this nightmare. That's all. I thought if he lost his leading lady, he'd have to pull the plug on the production, which would be a win for everyone. That's it. That's the extent of what I wanted. All I did was make my room look like a struggle had happened there, crawled out the window, took a pic out in the woods, and emailed it to Simien. That's it. I swear it. I snuck back into my trailer and have been hiding until what happened to Simien and then I was too scared to stay alone, so I came over here tonight."

"She's telling the truth," Alison says. "We didn't see her or know anything about it until tonight."

"They had nothing to do with it," Hailee says.

Merrill's eyes grow big and I can tell something has just occurred to him. "I believe you," he says. "*Shee-it*, I might be better at this PI shit than I thought."

"Oh yeah?" I say.

"Either that or the Holy Ghost just whispered in my ear who did it."

"As long as you figure it out," I say, "doesn't matter how."

"You know who was the most upset about the rape in the porn scene?" he asks. "I mean after Hailee herself. Wasn't Alison, who said it comes with the territory and is better than working at a gas station. It was Rena, the sensitive, compassionate, quiet PA. It was her small ass that was watching your trailer that night, not McCloud. And not as a stalker but as a protector, to make sure nothing else bad would happen to you."

Hailee looks over at Rena. "Really? You did that for me?"

"And her ass ain't all that fast," Merrill says. "She didn't run into the woods. She hit the branches so they'd be rustling when we got back there and snuck back into her trailer, which is how she was able to come out with everybody else when we walked around front and asked them to. Since she was the one watching you . . . you stopped being stalked when she started staying with you at night. She was now watching from the inside."

"It fits," I say.

"What they did to her," Rena says. "The vile, filthy animals. Degrading her and . . . and no one was going to do anything about it. Well, I would at least try to stop anything like it from happening again."

"And you did," Merrill says. "Or thought you did. But then she disappeared. And you became more and more convinced that Simien was behind it or knew something about it—after all, the email went to him. So you shot him up with some kind of drug to make him compliant, taped him to that chair, and tortured him until he told you where she was . . . Except he didn't know."

"Nobody was doing anything to find her," Rena says. "The cops around here are a joke . . . and you two . . . you're the bastards that let her get taken."

"Except she didn't get taken," Merrill says. "She did all this shit herself, which means you killed an innocent man. Well, innocent of Hailee's abduction. He's guilty of a lot of other shit —that scene where Hailee was raped, bad movies, general fuckin' pompous assery. But only you, little girl, are guilty of murder."

60

Driving away from the Potter County Sheriff's Department, after we had given our statements and where Rena Hanan is now being interviewed and arrested, I say to Merrill, "That was impressive."

"What's that?"

"The way you solved that case," I say.

"Nah," he says. "Tol' you. All I do is ask WWJJD?"

"You were way ahead of me the whole way," I say.

"Only 'cause you weren't workin' the case. I'm serious—when it comes to detecting, I always ask what would you do or try to remember what you've done in other cases. Now, when it comes to tough-guy work, I don't ask WWJJD. That's more a What Would Bad Ass Merrill Monroe Do?'"

"It certainly is," I say, "but once again you proved you can do both security and investigating."

"Still don't know who was stalking Simien to begin with," he says.

"Yes you do," I say. "If you think about it. Nobody was following him—stalking him in the classic sense. Hailee, who blamed him for what had happened to her, was harassing him."

"So the stalker became the stalkee," he says.

"Until she became the abductor and abductee," I say.

My phone vibrates in my pocket and I pull it out. It's a text from Sam.

"Jodi was found in Orlando," I say. "Hasn't left town in months. Has witnesses to prove it, so it wasn't him."

"Good to know," Merrill says. "We'll mark him off the list."

I text her back and let her know Merrill solved the case and that the killer is in custody. Without going into great detail, I give her a brief overview of both Hailee's abduction and Simien's murder, and let her know that at the time we left the sheriff's department, Hugh Glenn hadn't decided if he was going to charge Hailee yet or what he would charge her with if he decides to.

When I don't hear back from her I assume she's already fallen back asleep.

"So," Merrill says, as the first soft glow of false dawn appears on the eastern horizon, "if what happened to Hailee and Simien has nothing to do with the original case, it gets us no closer to solving it."

"Not only that, but now we won't have Simien's film to tell us who did it. But one silver lining of you solving this is that we can now focus on the other exclusively, which I think we should do after a few minutes of sleep."

"You go ahead and sleep in," he says, "'cause I can tell you who did it—that big blob of a bastard Horton fuckin' Joshua."

"You're probably right," I say. "Wouldn't bet against you tonight. But even if you are, we still have to figure out a way to prove it and charge him with it."

"I'm sure that'll come to me in my sleep," he says. "I'll let you know in the morning."

61

"Miss Thelma," Dad is saying. "I just need a little more information from you and I'll go away for good. You have my word on that."

It's the next morning, the day before the concert and fundraiser for Naomi and Sasha at Gaines Landing.

Dad, Ben, and I are back on Thelma Washington's porch in White City.

I'm running on two hours of sleep, morning hugs from my daughters, and two cups of coffee.

"Ask what you want, Sheriff," she says. "Done went all-in when I talk to you before."

"Won't take but a minute," he says. "We just need to know if any of the young women Horton went out with were Cuban."

"Cuban?"

"Yes, ma'am."

She shakes her head. "No. No, sir. They weren't."

"Okay," Dad says, the disappointment apparent in his voice, "well, thank you any—"

"Never took them out," she says. "Always kept them in."

"He had girls from Cuba come to his home?" Dad asks, his voice rising in pitch and volume.

"Yes, sir, he did. That's a fact. And ain't a one of 'em acted like they really wanted to be there. They'd sometimes get there before I left of an evening . . . but they's never there the next morning when I got back. And *girls* is right. Some of 'em look so very young. Hard to tell sometimes these days. Some youngins looks older than they are and some older ones looks younger, so . . . can't be sure, but some look awful young to me."

"Do you have any idea how they got there?" Dad asks. "Would Horton go somewhere to get them? Would someone bring them?"

She nods. "Mr. Victor and some other dark Spanish-looking young man would always show up with them—him, two or three young Hispanic girls, and a box of them stinky cigars. Took me days to get the smell out of the house."

"Victor Pérez?" Dad asks.

"Yes, sir."

Victor Pérez is a wealthy and well-respected developer, an older Cuban man with a young wife and small children, known for seaside subdivisions with a distinctly Spanish colonial style.

"Thank you," Dad says. "Thank you so much, Miss Thelma. We won't bother you again."

62

"We got 'em," Sam is saying.

She has joined me, Dad, Ben, and Merrill at the dining room table in Dad and Verna's farmhouse, which has become our de facto war room.

We have just told her what Thelma Washington has told us.

"We can't use Miss Thelma as a witness," Dad says.

"Won't need to," she says. "They'll roll over on each other. Men like them always do. They're so self-centered, egotistical, and narcissistic they'll only look out for themselves. And I guarantee you we will find connections between Pérez and those running the operation in Cuba. They'll roll over on him. He'll roll over on them. He and Joshua will roll over on each other."

"So," Ben says, "are we saying that Sasha and Naomi stumbled on their sex trafficking operation and they or someone who worked for them killed them?"

"I'd say that's most likely," Sam says, "but we won't know for sure until we interview them."

Through the huge bay window on the back wall I can see

Verna and Johanna peddling a paddle boat on the smooth surface of the small lake, the morning sun causing them to glow and gently refracting off the water, and I long to be out there with my little girl rather than in here talking about the horrors that had happened to other fathers' little girls.

"Both men are extremely wealthy and very connected," I say. "They will have the best attorneys that dirty money can buy and will be able to call in all kinds of favors from powerful people who will protect them out of their own self-interest."

She nods. "No doubt, but those are the very rats that jump the ship at the first sign it's starting to sink."

"I hope you're right," I say, "but in my experience these are the very people who rarely face any form of justice from our legal system."

"I would agree if they had just stuck with the sleazy, greedy white-collar crime that made them their filthy lucre, but we're talking about the kidnapping, enslaving, rape, and murder of tens if not hundreds of women."

Merrill says, "Does my heart good you can still harbor such hope with all you've seen and been subjected to."

"Think about the justice you brought about last night," she says to Merrill. "That was amazing by the way, and think about how much more these bastards have done compared to those misguided young girls."

"Misguided young girls often get punished by our *in*justice system," he says, "even when they white—'cause woman is the nigger of the world—but rich old white men rarely ever do."

"I don't disagree that the justice is disproportionate, Yoko," she says. "Hell, I'm a woman—I used to have the tits to prove it —but this isn't backroom bribes, insider trading, and tax shelter schemes. We're talking about human fuckin' trafficking. Some of the little girls on that boat were twelve years old. Children kidnapped from their parents, raped, beaten, drugged, enslaved, and left to die slowly of starvation and dehydration on a dirty old houseboat in our swamp. Just picture Horton Joshua's fat, nasty blob of a body on top of a child like that and tell me I'm not going to put them down hard."

"I won't tell you that," he says. "But I'll tell you this—if you won't, I will."

63

While Sam sets up interviews with Joshua and Pérez and the others do what they can to help, the girls and I drive to Tallahassee and pick up Anna, who arrives earlier than expected.

"It was a truly transformative experience," she says, "and I'm glad I did it, but . . . I couldn't bear to be away from y'all another minute and I was able to get an earlier flight."

"We're so glad you did, aren't we girls?" I say.

They squeal and cheer from the back seat.

"I think that's the most words I've said in a week," she says.

"Glad you saved 'em for us. We've missed you so much."

"Not as much as I've missed y'all."

Our hands are touching on the seat between us and she squeezes mine as she says this.

"So how was it?" I ask. "Did you find it difficult?"

"Was just like you said. Such a struggle to begin with, then I thought I was losing all grip on reality, then something shifted inside me, and it became this transcendent . . . I'm not sure what. I started to say *experience*, but it wasn't like something I was experiencing as much as something I was being, something I became."

I nod and smile.

A few years back I had participated in a silent meditation retreat, but the one I went to was less than half the length of the one she had just completed—or almost completed.

"It was one of the most unique and life-changing processes I've ever been through," she says, "and I wouldn't change having done it, and I don't think it's something I'll ever need to do again. So, tell me what you guys have been up to."

She turns in her seat and listens intently as Taylor and Johanna excitedly recount their week—epic games of hide and seek with Dad, cooking with Verna, playing at the park, boating on the lake, slumber parties at Papa Jack and Verna's, making arts and crafts and dinner, and mostly missing Mom.

"Oh, I could just eat y'all up," she says. "So very precious. I can't believe how much y'all've grown since I've been gone."

"They have been so sweet and helpful and flexible and fun," I say. "Just the biggest, best girls in the world."

"What about you?" she says, turning back to face me. "What've you been up to? Have you and Papa Jack made any headway on the case?"

I turn up the radio, lower my voice, and tell her some of what has happened.

"*Wow*," she says. "I mean . . . That's . . . *Wow*. And Merrill . . . How about him? Those were some great deductions."

"Really were," I say.

"And earlier that night he was talkin' about quitting?"

"Yeah," I say. "Now he's talking about franchising."

She laughs and I realize just how much I've missed her laugh.

"I missed everything about you," I say, "but maybe your laugh the most."

"The way I've been lately I would've thought you'd be grateful for the break."

"No more than I would a break from water."

She smiles and her face lights up, and apart from the two radiant little angels in the back seat, the rest of the world dims.

"I feel the same way," she says. "Only more so. We'll have to see what we can do about quenching this thirst we have."

I reach over and touch her face with the back of my hand and she takes my hand in hers and kisses my fingertips.

"God, I've missed your hands," she says.

"Geez, people," Johanna says, "get a room."

"Yeah," Taylor says, "get some rooms."

The three of us laugh, which so pleases Taylor that she says it over and over again.

She keeps repeating it and we keep laughing for several miles until our cheeks hurt and our eyes burn and we slip into silence.

"Geez, people," Taylor says again, "get some rooms."

And we all start laughing again.

By the time we exit I-10 in Greensboro, both girls are softly snoring, and Anna has unbuckled and slid over in the seat beside me as if we were in high school.

"Wonder if the young people still ride around like this?" I whisper to her.

"Missin' out if they don't."

She lays her head on my shoulder, her soft hair caressing my neck, the sweet scent of her perfume wafting over to further intoxicate me.

I say, "I wish we could *geez people get some rooms* right now."

"Me too," she says, placing her hand on my chest. "If we didn't have the kiddos I'd say fuck a bunch of rooms and find a dirt road to pull down."

That makes me want her even more, and I say, "Did I mention how glad I am to have you back?"

We drive down the straight, flat, empty rural road in silence for a long while, and eventually I can feel her twitching and hear her breathing deepen and know she is falling asleep.

Later, as we're nearing the Bristol bridge, she wakes and says, "I keep thinking about those poor girls. Naomi and Sasha, the ones in the houseboat, and the ones not in it, and as usual I can't help but think about our girls and what if it was them."

"I know," I say. "Me too."

"What y'all are doing . . ." she says. "All of you together—you, your dad, Merrill, Ben, Sam, Chaquille and all the others—you're taking some truly evil and powerful sadists and sociopaths off the board. Think about the little girls just a few years older than Johanna and the fate you're saving them from."

"Wish there was a way to save them all," I say. "And to do so retroactively."

"It's not that kind of world," she says. "I wish it were, but it's just not."

"No," I say. "No, it's not. And never will be."

64

"Well," Sam is saying, "they were ready for that."

"Seem to recall someone tellin' you they would be," Merrill says.

"So someone did," she says. "So someone did. But I'm not giving up."

It's later that night, and Sam, Ben, Merrill, Anna, and I are in our kitchen. I had called everyone when Sam said she was stopping by, but Dad said he wasn't feeling up to it and asked me to call him afterward to let him know what was said. I had offered for all of us to come to his place, but he said he was in bed and needed to stay there.

"What happened?" Ben asks.

"Today was just the preliminary interviews to get them on record," she says. "The plan was to tap their phones after talking to them to see if they'd call each other or anyone else who was involved. But they were so prepared for the interviews, so careful with every word they said, that there's no way they're going to call anyone or say anything incriminating on the phone."

Unlike at Dad's, we are spread throughout our galley

kitchen instead of all at the table. Merrill is sitting on the far counter in front of the microwave. Ben is leaning against the framed opening separating the living room, dining room, and kitchen, and Sam, Anna, and I are at the table.

"You mind taking us through exactly what happened and what was said?" I ask.

As we begin talking, Anna stands and quietly serves drinks and snacks.

Merrill says, "Didn't get beverages or refreshments while you's away."

"Nice to be missed," she says.

"I started with Horton," Sam says. "He's more accessible, not as polished or powerful as Pérez. Of course, by the time I got to Pérez his attorney was waiting with him. They're guilty as sin but have an answer for everything. I'm talkin' about credible, documented answers for everything I asked them. Either they or their attorney were handing me documentation before I had finished the question."

Ben starts to say something but Merrill interrupts.

"If anyone acts surprised, I'm gonna lose my shit," Merrill says.

"Both men say the exact same thing about the young women," Sam says. "Occasionally, Victor's nephew would stop in when he was passing through and he always brought cigars and girls who liked to party. Both men admit there was some drug use and that they even suspected the girls may have been prostitutes, but they didn't ask and they never paid them. Victor says his nephew's father died when he was young and so he supported him and his mom while he was growing up, then paid for his college and set him up in business. Says the nephew is grateful and knows his uncle likes fine Cuban cigars and tight young Cuban women—his actual words—and if he paid the girls he never mentioned it to either his uncle or Horton."

"What's the nephew's name?" Ben asks.

"Sammy Pérez. We'll get to him in a minute. So, right there . . . They both admit to contact with the girls or young women, whichever the case may be, without admitting any wrongdoing, and they do it in such a way that we can't disprove it."

She pauses and takes a sip from the bottle of water Anna had placed on the table in front of her.

"For his part, Horton claims he couldn't have killed Naomi and Sasha because from the time they went into the swamp until well after the last time they took photos or tried to use their phones someone was with him, and that he never went out into the swamp searching alone—only always part of a group. And his biggest alibi witness . . . deputy at the time, now sheriff, his close pal Hugh Glenn. There are others, of course, but the sheriff was with him the most. And get this . . . he has sworn affidavits from all of them."

"Like any innocent person would," Anna says.

"Exactly."

"That sleazy . . ." Ben says.

"Wealthy, well-connected, well-represented white man?" Merrill asks.

"He says he found the backpack out in the swamp inside a hollowed-out cypress trunk, and since he had already discovered some of Naomi and Sasha's remains wanted someone else to find it, so he enlisted the help of his maid. And then with condescending, fake humility adds that if I feel the need to reprimand him for tampering with evidence, he guesses his otherwise stellar record of public service can take it. As far as being the one to find everything, he says it's because he worked harder, knows the swamps better, and spent more time searching than anyone else."

"That's such bullshit," Ben says.

"For his part, Pérez, or rather his attorney, said that he was out of the country during the time that Naomi and Sasha went missing. Gave me copies of receipts and even a thumb drive with video footage on it of a conference he spoke at. Says he hasn't seen the houseboat in question, but it's actually possible that it's his—or rather one that was owned by one of his companies—but if it is he reported it stolen back on October 1, 2014."

"A few days after Sasha and Naomi went missing," Ben says.

"Exactly," Sam says. "They even produced a police report and insurance claim to prove it. And, tragically, it was around this same time that his beloved Cuban cigar and tight young women–-supplying nephew was killed in a home invasion is Cuba—for which he also produced a police report."

"The motherfuckers are gonna get away with it," Ben says. "With all of it. I . . . I can't . . . I'm just so damn . . . I'm so sick of the sickest, most sadistic bastards among us bein' untouchable. I've got to go."

"Before he does," Merrill says to Sam, "will you paint that picture for us again of Horton's untouchable big blob ass on top of a twelve-year-old?"

"*Merrill*," Anna says, her voice rising in surprise and rebuke. "That's not fair."

"No, it's not," he says, walking out behind Ben, "but not feeling very fair right now."

65

Anna and I are in bed together for the first time in a week and I'm more content than I can say just to be holding her.

I'm lying on my back, my arm around her, and she is draped across me, her fingers caressing the hair on my chest.

I'm exhausted and sleepy but fighting to stay awake a little longer.

"I'm so sorry about the outcome of Sam's interviews," she says.

"I had so hoped to help Dad clear it before . . . but it's not looking like that's going to happen."

"It's still possible, isn't it?"

"I don't see how."

As usual, our dim bedroom sanctuary is a cool swirl of window unit, even though we have the central unit on, a box fan, and the sweet sounds of Johanna's and Taylor's sleep-breathing coming through the monitor on Anna's bedside table.

Though the girls are just across the hallway and old enough not to need a monitor, it makes us both feel better to have it on.

"Are you sure Horton and or Victor killed Naomi and Sasha?" she asks.

"I'm not sure of anything."

"Is it possible—I know they're guilty of participating in the sex trafficking—but is it possible they didn't kill Naomi and Sasha?"

"That's what I'm saying. I have no idea. It's possible. Anything's possible. I can't even be certain it wasn't just a tragic accident like so many believe. It's possible they died of—that the swamp killed them, and Horton just found them or their remains and their things and moved them away from where the houseboat was. But even that . . . I have a hard time believing Victor and Horton knew the houseboat with the remains of the six girls was out there—especially given that it could be linked to Victor. I think if they had known, they'd have burned it or moved it or at least removed the remains from it. They're way too careful to just leave it out there like that waiting to be found. They had to know it'd be found one day. It makes far more sense to me that they didn't know, that something happened to whoever did know they were there and he wasn't able to come back for them—the nephew or someone who worked for him."

"Say that's the case," she says. "Then who killed Naomi and Sasha?"

"I don't know," I say.

"You always know—or have some sense of who it might be."

"Not this time," I say. "Not with this case. I'm lost. Like I said, I don't even know if they *were* killed by someone. I've gone over and over the evidence and no matter how many different ways I look at it I just can't come to a definitive conclusion."

"You don't have a theory?" she asks. "You always have theories."

"Not this time," I say. "I don't have anything coherent enough to be a theory, and as soon as I begin to formulate one, the elements shift and I start on another one that's in direct opposition to the one I was just working on. It's . . . it's maddening. I just keep thinking I'm letting Dad down. He's gonna die without me helping him close this case."

"You're such a great and gifted detective," she says. "It's one of your many gifts—just behind fatherhood and husbandhood. If that amazing mind of yours can't deduce the truth from the evidence you have, it's because you don't have enough evidence. I've seen you solve too many cases that no one else could. Maybe with this one you're going to have to take a different approach. Maybe with what is known it's not solvable. If so, so be it. You've done your best by your dad. But if it is solvable, maybe it will have to be done in a totally different way this time. I don't know. I'm not sure what I'm saying or what it means, but I know that right now what you need is sleep. Go to sleep now. Let me hold you while you sleep and let's talk about it some more in the morning."

I close my eyes, attempting to quiet my mind, and drift into dreams.

A moment later, my eyes pop open and I reach for my phone.

"That was quick," she says.

"Just remembered I haven't looked at what Meagan and Dylan posted about Naomi and Sasha."

It takes a few minutes for me to find, during which time Anna's breathing changes and I assume she's asleep, but when Dylan's first video begins to play she stirs.

"He wrote a song about them?" she asks.

"Several," I say.

We watch a few of the melodramatic and angst-ridden teenage tributes to what are clearly idealized versions of Naomi and Sasha, fantasies of young women he clearly didn't know well.

After we've endured as much as we can of Dylan's songs, we

turn to Meagan's posts, which consists mostly of bad, simplistic, overly rhyming poems and incoherent essays.

"I'm not sure which is worse," Anna says. "Or more disturbing."

"It's a close call."

"Is it just typical teenage theatricality," she says, "or something else? There's loss aplenty, sure, but is there guilt and regret too? Are they confessions?"

I succumb to sleep with those questions swirling around my mind with the texts of Meagan's poems to the soundtrack of Dylan's songs.

66

"Remington James," I say when I wake up.

"Huh?" Anna says.

"Camera traps," I say.

"Yeah?"

"I'm gonna set a trap," I say. "A camera trap to lure the killer —if there is one—out into the light."

"How?" she says, sitting up in bed and turning toward me. "Tell me. I knew you'd figure something out. You just needed me back in our bed and a good night's sleep so your subconscious could work."

I sit up, prop my pillows on the wall behind me, and lean back on them.

"You remember Remington James," I say.

"Of course. That reminds me we need to go check on his memorial garden when we can. See what the hurricane did to it and what we've got to do to rebuild."

"Yes we do. Some aspects of this case have reminded me of his—the swamp, the photos, the camera evidence—and his camera traps were in my dreams again last night."

"Makes sense," she says, nodding vigorously. "I definitely see the similarities and connections."

"I can't remember much of my dreams, but I woke up thinking I needed to set a trap—one that will reveal whether there is a killer or not and who he or she is. Like you said, if I can't figure it out through the evidence we have and normal deductive reasoning and putting puzzle pieces together, come up with another way. So really this is your idea."

"Well, you're welcome," she says. "Now tell me all about my brilliant plan."

"If someone killed Naomi and Sasha then obviously that someone doesn't want to be identified and arrested, which is why, if they exist, they probably erased the three photos from Naomi's camera."

She nods.

"What if at the fundraiser today I announce that based on multiple witness statements and other evidence, including some of the photographs from Naomi's camera, we now know that Sasha also had a camera that we believe has evidence of their killer's identity on it? I could say that the girls hid it away from their other things and left clues as to how to find it—clues that have gone unrecognized until now. I could announce that we now believe, based on the picture from Naomi's phone with the candy wrappers and red ribbons on the tree stump and the candy wrapper Ben and I discovered near the houseboat, we know where the camera is. I could say that in the morning Ben and I are going to lead the original investigators of the case, including the previous sheriff of Potter County as well as current law enforcement working the case, to retrieve the camera and the evidence that it contains. Don't you think the killer, if there is one, will try to go out there today or tonight and find and destroy that evidence?"

"I do."

"So the first thing we'll do this morning is go out there and set up the trap," I say. "We'll plant some of the wrappers and other markings that make it pretty evident where the camera is and we'll cover the entire area around it with camera traps that will capture photos and video of the killer when he or she comes to take it."

"A camera trap," she says appreciatively. "Damn, I came up with a brilliant plan."

"Think it could work?"

"I think it could," she says. "But, of course, I would. I came up with it."

67

By the time Ben and I get back to Gaines Landing from setting the trap in the swamp, the concert fundraiser is in full swing.

The large sand lot of the landing is filled with people in lawn chairs, on blankets, and on the open tailgates of trucks, their legs dangling, kicking back and forth to the beat of the music.

The Wabi Sabis have already taken the stage and are playing a kind of folk-pop Americana version of Queen's "Fat Bottom Girls."

People mill about and move around, greeting each other and visiting in a typical small-town manner, while young kids chase each other around yelling and squealing things that only make sense to them.

To the right, backdropped by a wide slough coming off the river, a long row of school-carnival-type booths constructed of random, scrap, and mismatched wood, house homemade games, arts and crafts, and lots and lots of food—fried fish, grilled hamburgers and hotdogs, funnel cakes, snow cones, smoked pulled pork sandwiches, and stir fry.

An all-female Americana folk-pop band of middle-aged white women doing an acoustic version of "Fat Bottom Girls" is unexpected, intriguing, irresistible—and the crowd responds well to the way the delightful ladies rock the flatbed stage.

The sounds of the band, of acoustic guitar, ukulele, upright bass, and washboard percussion, mix with the conversation and laughter of adults, the shrieks and squeals of children, the pounds and pops of the festival games, and the swish and sizzle of open-flame outdoor cooking to join the river landing sounds of birds and breeze and flowing and splashing water to create a kind of rural-life soundtrack I find familiar and comforting.

"We're the Wabi Sabis," Jennifer Rollins is saying, "and we're very happy to be here with you today to support this good cause. Our hope is that the money we raise here today can bring about more tips and a break in the case, so we can find out once and for all what really happened to Naomi and Sasha and get the answers and the justice their families deserve. Wabi sabi is an ancient Japanese art form which embraces imperfection. Sort of perfectly imperfect just like all of us. We're from just down the road in Panama City. I'm Jennifer Rollins and I play guitar and provide some vocals. To my right is Val Woods on vocals, ukulele, and mandolin. To her right is Julie Bullock, our fabulous upright bass player."

"She's fabulous *and* upright?" Denise asks.

"She's fabulous, her bass is upright. And to my left, on corny jokes, washboard, percussions, banjolele, and vocals is Denise Denaro. Thank y'all for having us."

I look around, searching for Anna, Dad, Verna, Merrill, Zaire, Sam, and the girls, and see that all the major players in this current crime drama are present. Jay and Robbie Gaines, Dylan, Meagan, and the wild boys sit in Saturday morning soccer chairs directly in front of center stage. Horton Joshua stands near Hugh Glenn's reelection campaign booth. Victor Pérez, in clothes far too formal for an outdoor riverside fundraiser, sits cross-legged in a cushioned springer rocker in the back, his young family in smaller, less comfortable and substantial chairs around him. Various members of the cast and crew of the now canceled *Lost Innocents* movie mill about. While in the back, mixed in among the old pickups with their tailgates down, is an idling SUV with, unlike the other vehicles facing forward, windows up and air-conditioning running. Reese Newman and Thomas McCloud sit separated from everyone else by glass and steel.

"This next song is an original we all wrote together in a treehouse Airbnb in Montgomery, Alabama," Val is saying. "It's called 'Low-key Crush.'"

"You okay?" I ask Ben.

He's staring into the distance, a distressed look on his face. I follow his gaze over toward Horton Joshua and Victor Pérez, who are now standing next to each other not from where Potter High cheerleaders operate a dunking booth.

"All they've done," he says, "and they just walk around like they're normal human beings. Who does that?"

"Most monsters don't look like what they are," I say. "And almost none of them think they are."

His lips twist into a frown and he begins to nod slowly. "Scary thought. Anyway . . . My blood sugar must be out of whack. I'm'a grab something to eat. Want anything?"

"I'll take a bottle of water or a diet anything-but-Pepsi if you come in close proximity to drinks."

He nods. "Go ahead and get with your family. I'll find y'all."

"Not sure *I* can find them."

I continue searching the crowd as the Wabi Sabis transition from a Taylor Swift song I'm not sure the name of to a cover of the Dixie Chicks "Long Time Gone."

By the time I locate Anna, who is standing with Sam over in the back corner between the last row of people seated and the booths, the Wabi Sabis are playing "Walking After Midnight."

"They're great," Sam says, nodding toward the stage as I walk up to them. "Not sure I've ever seen so much fun, positive energy in one place before. And their song selections!"

"Told you," I say, and I hug them both and kiss Anna.

Anna whispers in my ear, "I've got a crush on you and there's nothing low-key about it."

I kiss her again. "Did I mention how glad I am to have you back? And how much I wish we could *geez people get some rooms*."

"Not enough," she says.

Anna is really back, and not just from her week away, and though I know it's not likely, I say a prayer she will never go away like she did again.

"Where're the girls?" I ask.

"Where else? Playing games with Papa Jack and Verna."

I look over toward the booths to see if I can spot them.

"Everything all set?" Anna asks.

I nod. "Think so, but I'm doubting doing it now. Suddenly seems stupid and doomed to fail."

"Well, it's not," she says.

Sam says, "I think it's a great idea. And, truly, what do we have to lose?"

"If I get up there and just thank the Sabis, you'll know I lost my nerve."

"Not sure I've ever seen that happen," Anna says.

"It's not pretty," I say.

"Look," Sam says, "if I can have my tits cut off and get shot in the fuckin' face and survive, you can get up there and lie with certainty and conviction."

Merrill walks up and looks down at Sam, locking eyes with her. "Sorry to have takin' my frustration out on you last night."

"A few comments doesn't constitute *taking it out* on me. And you were right."

"I was wrong to say so."

"Forget about it," she says. "I have."

He looks at me. "We gonna sneak out into the swamp and set up on the trap after you make your little announcement?"

I nod.

"We're gonna take a short break," Denise Denaro is saying from the stage. "And while we do there's going to be some announcements and drawings for prizes, and then we'll be back with lots more music, so stick around. First up is someone we worked with on Hurricane Michael relief and think a lot of, Pottersville's most famous son . . . John Jordan."

"She'd'a said most *infamous* son," Merrill says, "she'd'a been callin' my black ass up there."

"Y'all watch how people react to the news," I say, "and see if anyone leaves abruptly."

"Just quit delaying and get your ass up there," Sam says.

As I make my way up to the stage, Meagan Gaines appears beside me, matching my pace.

"I know who killed her," she says.

"*Her?*"

"*Them.* I mean them. I have proof. It was Dylan. He was so obsessed and jealous and . . . he caught Mom and Sasha together—they weren't doing anything, but he flipped out. He . . . stalked her like prey out there in those woods and butchered her like an animal. You should hear the songs he's written about her."

"I have."

"You have?"

"I've seen your posts too," I say. "Dylan wasn't the only one obsessed with Sasha, was he?"

"Hold on, now," she says. "Wait just a—"

"We know who did it," I say. "We've uncovered new evidence. Just make sure your entire family listens to the announcement I'm about to make."

"Dylan has a gun," she says. "On him right now."

I look back over my shoulder at Dylan, who is hovering just behind the lawn chair Robbie is sitting in.

He gives me a cold, wicked grin.

Pulling out my phone, I text Merrill to move over closer to Dylan and keep an eye on him.

"Don't say I didn't warn you," Meagan says. "And if that sick bastard kills my mom I'm gonna burn this town to the ground."

68

"How about the Wabi Sabis?" I say a little too loud into the mic. Backing up a bit, I add, "Give them another round of applause."

The crowd gives another roaring round of applause.

"I know others will, but I wanted to thank you all for being here and supporting the efforts of finding out what really happened to Naomi and Sasha. I've worked with the families of a lot of victims over the years and I can tell you that not knowing adds an additional almost unbearable amount of suffering to an already insurmountable grief. So thank you. I also wanted to beg you—if you or anyone you know has any information about Naomi and Sasha, please come forward with it. The reward amount is huge and growing, but the freedom and release that comes from unburdening yourself is priceless."

I regret using that term because it makes what I said sound like a credit card commercial and I pause for a moment.

"As many of you know, Simien Eggers, the director of the movie being made about Naomi and Sasha, had promised to reveal their killer here today, but sadly, he was killed a couple of days ago. But even though he won't be here today and we have no idea what he was going to say—it could've just been a publicity stunt—we believe we have new evidence that has the potential to lead us directly to the person responsible for Naomi and Sasha's untimely deaths."

I can feel myself stalling. It's part of the reason I'm adding in words like *untimely*.

"Based on witness statements and—"

Out of the corner of my eye, I catch a glimpse of two figures walking onto the stage. When I glance over and see that it is Horton Joshua and Victor Pérez I stop speaking and turn toward them, my hand instinctively dropping to the gun on my hip.

They are walking tentatively, their hands up in a placating gesture—and then I see why.

The gesture isn't placating and they're not walking tentatively.

They're walking on stage against their will, their hands held up as if they are under arrest.

Rising behind them and towering over them as he steps up onto the stage is Ben, who has his gun out and pointed at the back of their heads.

Gasps erupt from those in the crowd still watching the stage, but many, especially those over by the booths, aren't aware of what's going on.

"Ben, what're you—"

"Change of plans, John," he says. "These two have something they want to confess. Slide over and let them have the mic."

"This isn't the—"

"Now, John," he says. "Don't have long before somebody tries to take me out."

I slide over and Ben shoves the two men up to the mic.

"Tell the truth," Ben says. "Tell nothing but the truth and you live."

Pérez clears his throat and says, "I—*we*—used the services of . . . of underage . . . sex slaves from Cuba. My nephew used to bring them to this country. I knew what he was doing. We knew that these girls had been kidnapped from their homes."

My guess is that he is so forthcoming because Ben had convinced them he would kill them before they ever reached the stage and he knows that no forced confession under such duress would ever stand up in court.

"Me too," Horton says. "I knew too. We shouldn't have. We were wrong to turn a blind eye to what was happening to these girls and for having sex with them, but I had nothing to do with what happened to Naomi and Sasha. I swear. I've never killed anyone. I was wrong to do the sex stuff but that's all I did. I found their remains and that backpack. That's all. I did not kill them."

"I did not kill them or anyone else either," Pérez says.

Ben slides them to the side with one of his massive arms while continuing to hold the gun on them with the other, then steps to the microphone.

"These are evil, sociopathic men who rob little girls of their lives," he says. "But . . . so am I. I helped John here set a trap for Sasha and Naomi's killer this morning—and I am that killer."

I find his admission startling but not all that surprising. It's as if hearing him say it instantly causes several other observations to fall into place.

I think about all the clues I had ignored or explained away —Ben's involvement in the case to begin with, how he was present at all the places Naomi and Sasha were while they were here, the bar, the bonfire, etc. I think about how active in the search he was and how unlike most of the others involved, he was one of the few to ever go out searching alone. I think about how obsessed he has always been with the case—so much so that he felt a compulsion to write a book about it. But he felt so guilty that he donated away all the proceeds from that book. I think about how uncomfortable he seemed when we complimented him for his generosity. I think about how his rage and hostility at Joshua and Pérez was really an expression of his anger at himself. I think about how in conversation and in his book he's the only person I ever knew to refer to the victims as Sasha and Naomi instead of Naomi and Sasha like everyone else. I think it's not only because of his preference for and obsession with Sasha but his knowledge of the order they died in. Now I see that in many ways his book had been a confession —one I failed to hear.

"Well," Ben continues, "I should say, I killed Naomi. Sasha was already dead. I didn't intend to do it, didn't know I was going to do it the moment before it happened, and I'm so, so very sorry. It's the only thing like that I've ever done, the only violent, evil act—except for keeping it a secret all this time. I'm so sorry for that too. I thought if I could just do good, just . . . be a good man and . . . I wrote the book as a way of processing and confessing and trying to comfort the families . . . and I donated all the money from it and the sale of the movie rights to them. And I was . . . I was doing okay with it. Had buried it in a box deep, deep down inside of me and just didn't think of it very often, but then . . . seeing these two evil bastards and how they . . . I loathed them. And then I saw I *was* them. And I knew I couldn't live with this any longer. I'm sorry for what I did. If I could take it back I would—would have right after I did it. The only thing I could do now is . . . John, there's a full confession in your truck. I'm not asking for anyone's forgiveness, but I am sorry. I'm so, *so* sorry."

As he is speaking, Pérez and Joshua have been slinking away and are near the far edge of the stage.

"Ben," I say. "Give me the gun and let's talk about this, okay?"

"Okay," he says. He then lifts his head up and makes a wide-eyed expression toward the back parking lot. "OH MY GOD, WHAT IS THAT?" he yells, then, as everyone turns to look, he quickly lifts the gun to his temple and squeezes the trigger.

69

The confession letter left in my truck is handwritten in blue ink on college rule notebook paper that has been tri-folded. It appears to have been written hastily with no preparation or forethought and no editing or revising.

I didn't intend for any of this to happen. I was a kid, an impulsive, stupid kid. And one impetuous act led to everything else. It was like at every juncture when I could've stopped or turned back I . . . I just couldn't. I wasn't thinking straight. I was caught up in a way that I can't even explain—partly because I don't fully understand it myself. All I know is that when I think back to what happened, when I look at that kid who did it, I know it's not me. It can't be. I'm nothing like him. I could never do what he did. And yet it is. It's me.

Like nearly every other young person in town I was intrigued by the two young women who came to volunteer at Mr. Maurice's wilderness camp. I was smitten with Sasha like everybody else was, but I thought Naomi was attractive too—alluring in her own way that was just as seductive, only in a different way.

When they went missing I was like this is my chance to be a hero, to finally show a girl that Big Ben isn't just a big awkward goof.

I had nothing to do with their disappearance, nothing to do with what initially happened.

I was eager to help find them, wanted to be the one who did it, so I volunteered to help and I was allowed to work closely with Sheriff Jordan and some of the search-and-rescue teams.

The only thing less than honorable about my motive was that I wanted to be seen as a hero—and not just to the two lost girls, though especially to them, but to everyone.

I searched day and night. And that's probably part of why I did what I did. I was sleep-deprived and running on caffeine, crappy food, NoDoz, and raging teenage-boy hormones.

I would go out with big groups during the day and smaller groups at night. And sometimes, when there wasn't a group, I'd go out by myself.

And that's when it happened. It was a dream come true—the kind of stuff that happens in movies, not in real life. Not in my life. I found them. By. My. Self. I'd be a hero for sure.

But I was wrong. About everything. I didn't find them. I found Sasha. And she was already dead. I don't know how she died. I'm guessing snake bite.

She was lying there. Looked like she was sleeping. She was so beautiful, so peaceful and pure. She looked like this beautiful angel that had crash-landed on earth and was sleeping it off.

And I was . . . I was overcome. Overwhelmed. I had to . . . I wanted to . . . No, I had to touch her.

I knelt down beside her and . . . caressed her cold hard cheek. She felt so different than she looked. But I didn't care.

I touched her lips with my fingertips. And then . . . my heart was beating so fast . . . and then I leaned down and kissed her.

I was always this big awkward boy. Never had a girlfriend. Never touched a girl before.

I don't know what I was thinking. I wasn't thinking. I was . . . I don't know what I was doing. She was wearing this thin cotton tank top and I . . . I touched it. Then I just felt it for a moment. Then I pulled it up.

And suddenly I was seeing the beautiful bare breasts of this excruciatingly beautiful creature and I just stared at them for a long, long moment. But then I had to touch them. I had to.

I cupped my hand—my fingers are so big and fat, my hand so huge—and I gently placed it over her breast and just held it. It was cold and kind of flat and hard and I didn't care.

And I felt so guilty. So turned-on and happy and so guilty and ashamed.

And at that moment Naomi walked up and caught me.

"What the fuck are you doing?" she said.

I jumped. I was startled. I reacted. I didn't know what I was doing. And yet I did. I spun around and hit her—hard. A hammer fist to the face with my huge hand. And she was stunned and staggered and fell down.

I tried to help her, but she screamed at me. She just went crazy. She was probably crazed anyway from being lost in the swamp and her best friend dying and then she catches me doing what I'm doing and then I hit her and . . . It's no wonder she was crazed. Anyone would be But I was trying to calm her down and she wouldn't calm down.

"Get the fuck away from me you sick fuckin' freak," she screamed.

Then she started kicking and spitting and she got up and tried to run away and I panicked.

I told myself I had to calm her down to save her but when I hit her again I knew what I was doing. I knew I could never let her tell anyone what she caught me doing. She had caught me being a sick pervert and without admitting it to my conscious mind I knew I'd rather kill her than be known as that. She was the only other person on the planet who knew what I had done. I couldn't let her live.

Think about that. I would rather be a killer than have anyone think I was a sick twisted pervert. I'm telling you I wasn't thinking straight. I was in a nightmare and I couldn't get out no matter what I did.

I didn't kill her right then. And I told myself I wasn't going to. I subdued her and I took her and all their things with me, back to my boat and up the river to an old houseboat my family owned. Nobody but me ever went to it and it was far enough away that no one would be searching there.

I left Sasha where she was and figured she'd be found, but she never was.

I kept Naomi alive for a long time. Kept warring within myself not to kill her. Every day I'd go out searching and every night I'd go give her food and water. And then the tropical storm hit and then she escaped on me.

While I was away she was able to untie herself and break out of the houseboat. She took the backpack with all their things in it. Her phone was dead by then, but Sasha's was still working and she tried and tried to access it, but it didn't matter. Wasn't any signal anyway.

She took a bunch of pictures with the camera the night I finally found her, but none of me. The one that looks like a man screaming is just some sort of—the truth is I don't know what it is, but it's not me.

I've thought many times that if she hadn't escaped I wasn't going to kill her, that I was going to eventually win the war inside me and let her go, but while trying to get her back I killed her. The details of how don't matter much now, do they? Anyway, I don't want to talk about them.

I bleached her bones to try to destroy any evidence and I put them out back over closer to where they went into the swamp. Scavengers must have scattered them after that.

I put all their things in the backpack and left it in the swamp inside a hollowed-out tree base. I did it hoping it would give some comfort to their parents. Didn't even think about it being kept from them as evidence and I couldn't have fathomed all the wild theories the phone data and photos would lead to. Horton Joshua must have erased three of the images from the camera when he first *found it. Guess they showed something he didn't want seen. I don't know.*

What I do know is that I'm sorry as hell about everything and I can't live with it anymore. I should have killed myself a long time ago. I'm finally ready now.

Please make sure the families know their girls didn't suffer much and they were good, fine girls until they breathed their last breath.

I'm sorry. I really and truly am.

70

"Guess anybody's capable of anything," Dad says.

"Most people are capable of more than they think—good and bad," I say. "But I don't believe we're all capable of what he did."

"Hope not," he says. "Hard to believe *he* was capable of that. And what he did... I just... I really can't."

Dad and I are on his back porch later that evening, the soft pink glow of sunset fading fast.

"Glad the families finally know," he says. "That's something. And in a way, we were both right. I mean Ben and me. It *was* an accident *and* a murder."

"That's true," I say, "but he had an unfair advantage. He knew what happened."

"Feel a little relieved," he says, "and in some small way . . . somewhat vindicated. But at this point I'm mostly just glad to have the truth out there and have this case over and done with. Thank you for all your help."

"I didn't do much on this one," I say.

"The hell you didn't," he says. "You're just used to solving them while the rest of us are still wondering what's going on."

"Certainly didn't solve it."

"You know as well as I do that many times the act of investigating is itself all it takes to get things moving on a cold case," he says. "Stir things up, get people to come forward with new information or to cause the killer to confess, which is what happened. And it wouldn't have if we hadn't done what we did. Everything that you did, everything we all did, led to what happened. It led to us exposing Horton and Victor and a sex trafficking ring as well as all three confessions. We got the family the information they needed and we took three bad guys off the board—and all of that is thanks to you and Merrill and Sam."

"Oh I'm glad for the result," I say. "I just didn't contribute much."

"You contributed far more than you're giving yourself credit for and I'm all kinds of grateful to you."

"Doubt Horton and Victor will do any time or face much in the way of consequences," I say.

"Probably right. Though they may be looked upon and treated differently now. Everyone could tell their confessions were real. And they may have more trouble headed their way. I've decided to start treatment and run for sheriff again."

"That's . . . ah, Dad, that's great. You're obviously needed here."

"Actually, I'm just doing it to give Jake a job," he says of my younger brother who had been unemployed since working as a deputy in Dad's department.

"Nepotism I can get behind," I say.

71

When I get home, I find Anna and the girls drawing on the back patio with pretty pastel sidewalk chalk.

"Daddy," the girls squeal.

"Wanna color with us?" Taylor asks.

"More than anything," I say.

I sit down on the concrete with them, take the chalk I am handed, and join the artistic project already in process.

"How are you?" Anna asks.

I nod. "I'm okay."

"You want blue or purple?" Taylor asks, holding out two chunks of well-worn chalk.

"Blue, please."

"There you go," she says.

"You girls are so talented," I say. "I'm afraid my mess is going to ruin your beautiful drawings."

"That's okay, Daddy," Taylor says.

"Yours are great, Dad," Johanna says. "Really."

"And we'd want them with ours even if they weren't," Anna says.

"That's right," Johanna says. "It's a family portrait."

"What can I do for you?" Anna asks. "What do you need?"

"This," I say. "Just this."

"Have I mentioned how glad I am that you're home?" she asks.

I smile.

"Geez, people," Taylor says without looking up from her drawing, "get some rooms."

PLEASE POST A REVIEW

Please take a moment and post a review of this and other books my Michael Lister. It really helps and is greatly appreciated.

GET BLOOD PATHOGEN NOW!

Get the latest John Jordan Mystery Thriller, BLOOD PATHOGEN, now by going to www.MichaelLister.com

GET THE LATEST NEWS

Sign up for Michael's Readers' Group at www. MichaelLister.com and receive the latest news and reviews of the best in mystery, thriller, and crime fiction.

ALSO BY MICHAEL LISTER

Books by Michael Lister

(John Jordan Novels)

Power in the Blood

Blood of the Lamb

Flesh and Blood

(Special Introduction by Margaret Coel)

The Body and the Blood

Double Exposure

Blood Sacrifice

Rivers to Blood

Burnt Offerings

Innocent Blood

(Special Introduction by Michael Connelly)

Separation Anxiety

Blood Money

Blood Moon

Thunder Beach

Blood Cries

A Certain Retribution

Blood Oath

Blood Work

Cold Blood

Blood Betrayal

Blood Shot

Blood Ties

Blood Stone

Blood Trail

Bloodshed

Blue Blood

And the Sea Became Blood

The Blood-Dimmed Tide

Blood and Sand

A John Jordan Christmas

(Jimmy Riley Novels)

The Girl Who Said Goodbye

The Girl in the Grave

The Girl at the End of the Long Dark Night

The Girl Who Cried Blood Tears

The Girl Who Blew Up the World

(Merrick McKnight / Reggie Summers Novels)

Thunder Beach

A Certain Retribution

Blood Oath

Blood Shot

(Remington James Novels)

Double Exposure

(includes intro by Michael Connelly)

Separation Anxiety

Blood Shot

(Sam Michaels / Daniel Davis Novels)

Burnt Offerings

Blood Oath

Cold Blood

Blood Shot

(Love Stories)

Carrie's Gift

(Short Story Collections)

North Florida Noir

Florida Heat Wave

Delta Blues

Another Quiet Night in Desperation

(The Meaning Series)

Meaning Every Moment

The Meaning of Life in Movies

Don't miss the newly revised edition of the book that started
it all!

A missing mom and a suspicious death force a reluctant
detective out of self-imposed exile in this fast-paced mystery
thriller.

Special Newly Revised Anniversary Edition!

Detective John Jordan thought he had put murder investigation
behind him for good—his own good. Leaving Atlanta, he
returns to Florida in search of the serenity that has so long
eluded him.

Until he witnesses the shocking and bizarre death of an inmate
in state prison custody and is asked to find a missing mom by
her young children. John realizes he can't run from his true
calling any longer. Now he must determine if the suspicious
death he witnessed is murder, accident, or suicide and what

really happened to Candace Miles on the night she vanished off the face of the earth—even if it costs him his life to do so.

Start reading this exciting, stand-alone whodunit today and see why millions of readers adore John Jordan.

"Crackles with tension and authenticity." — Michael Connelly

Includes a Special Introduction by Michael Connelly.

MICHAEL CONNELLY INTRODUCTION

It's hard to write a book. You have to keep so many plates spinning on sticks. You've got the plot. You've got the place you are writing about. You've got the what-happens-next plate that can never wobble. You've got the momentum plate. You've got the humor plate. And the compassion plate. And I could go on and on. You've got the need to blend all of these things together into one act and keep them spinning, always spinning. Oh, and did I mention that you are holding all of these sticks up and spinning all of these plates while walking on a tight rope? No, wait, walking would be too easy. Change that. You are actually riding a tricycle on a tight rope.

Yes, it's a major high wire act, fraught with danger and failure, and that wire is the most important part of the whole thing. That high wire is character, and the whole thing comes crashing down plates and all if you don't have it right. If that wire is not taut and reliable and secure. If that character is not one for the ages.

Now with all of that, think about getting back on that high wire with the same character time and time again. Six shows a week and two on Sunday. It is not for the faint of heart, I can tell you that. It is hard to do it once. It is harder to do it time and time again. And that's what writing a book series is like.

And that is what Michael Lister has done for 20 years with the character of John Jordan and what he has been able to do for 20 years with his own muse. Not just sustain. Not just keep his balance on the wire. Not just go back to the well again and again. He has filled the well, he has expanded the boundaries of what he does with character. He has gotten better. He has somehow been able to find within him the inspiration to get back on the wire and do it again, only better.

It may be that the challenge and accomplishment of this can only be fully known and understood by the one who does it. No matter. Take my word for it. Michael Lister has become a master storyteller in his first 20 years and he's only getting started.

Michael Connelly
January 2017

AUTHOR'S NOTE

I became a writer in the summer of 1994.

Three years and three months later, in the fall of 1997, I became a published author.

During this time, two true crime cases dominated our culture, the public national trial that was the O. J. Simpson case and the horrific, tragic death of JonBenét Ramsey—both of which are experiencing renewed interest as I write this, because they too are marking their twentieth anniversary.

Power in the Blood was my very first attempt at writing a novel—not just my first novel to be published, but the first I ever wrote.

Writing is like anything else—you learn by doing, by practice. I've been practicing the craft of writing for nearly twenty-three years now. In that time I've gotten better at it, grown and evolved, discovered my voice, honed my style.

After twenty-plus years of writing, the *Power in the Blood* I would write today is not the *Power in the Blood* that was published twenty years ago. Of course, if I hadn't written that *Power in the Blood* back then, I wouldn't be able to write *Cold Blood*, the novel I'm working on as I write this. Way leads to way.

Book leads to book. Everything builds on that which comes before.

The writer I am today is only because of the writers I was before.

How did I become that first fledgling writer?

I was probably born with a love of story. I can certainly remember craving story as a child. Being moved by story are among my earliest memories.

As a teenager who was reading mostly nonfiction, I was led to detective fiction by, of all things, a TV show. *Spenser for Hire* led me to the books by Robert B. Parker the show was based on, and I fell in love with character, prose, and dialog.

After high school, I moved from my small Florida Panhandle town of Wewahitchka to Atlanta—not unlike John Jordan—and though I was there for theological training, it was a lit class taught by Tricia Weeks that was to be among the most inspirational and influential of my undergraduate degree program.

Then I happened upon the 1990 Avenel edition of G. K. Chesterton's *Father Brown Crime Stories* in a dusty old bookstore in Atlanta the year I graduated from theology college and was ordained, and it was nothing less than serendipitous. During that momentous year of transition, as I was being born into my adult life, Chesterton in many ways became my literary father, and Brown the fictional father to my ecclesiastical sleuth, John Jordan.

Between 1988 and 1994, I attempted on and off to write short stories and screenplays, but it wouldn't be until the summer of '94, as I was finishing my graduate degree in theology and about to enter into full-time prison chaplaincy, that I became a writer. That summer, in an upstairs room at my parents' house I converted into my library and study because my small home didn't have room for them, in the semi-coolness provided by the inefficient window unit, after a long and drawn-out delivery, a writer was born. John Jordan was born. This book was born.

It was during this time that I discovered other crime writers who have had a profound influence on my work, like James Lee Burke and Michael Connelly (who has contributed an essay for this book). It was also during this time that I attended my first novel-writing workshop taught by Lynn Wallace (who has also contributed an essay for this book).

And because way leads to way and book leads to book, I began a kind of self-designed curriculum for my education as a new writer, which included Shakespeare, Hemingway, Dostoevsky, Tolstoy, Melville, Chandler, Faulkner, Flannery O'Connor, Updike, Roth, Irving, DeLillo, Fitzgerald, and Cormac McCarthy.

Over the next twenty-plus years, I continued my education and training, and after some thirty books, thirteen of which are John Jordan novels, here I am.

I feel like somewhere along the way I learned to write some, and I hope twenty years from now I'll have learned a lot more.

At some point during the past twenty years since *Power in the Blood* was first published, probably back around the time I learned a little about writing, I began wanting to rewrite it. I've thought about it for years, but was uncertain as to how to approach it or when to take the time away from current and future books to do it. And then a couple of years back it occurred to me that the twentieth anniversary of the book would be the perfect time.

The moment I decided to rewrite *Power in the Blood* for this special edition, I had to decide exactly what that meant. Was I going to toss out the original and start over? Was I going to keep the original and just tweak and lightly edit? Was I going to change the story? The plot? The style?

Ultimately, I chose to keep the original book, but do heavy

revision without changing the essential plot and characters in any fundamental way.

This new, revised version of *Power in the Blood* more closely matches my style, my voice, my approach to the novel today than the original version from twenty years ago. However, since I kept the characters, plot, and structure of the original, this new version is a hybrid—neither completely the novel I would have written back then, nor the one I would write today.

This is a remodel instead of new construction. I kept the bones of the original book, the foundation, some of the wiring, walls, and plumbing, but rebuilt and repurposed and redid most everything else. This new version is not a completely new house, but neither is it an old one either. In that way, I believe it shows the first-time novelist I was *and* the twenty-sixth-time novelist I've become.

The writer I've become has increasingly been about what I leave out as much as what I put in. Saying more, evoking more, discovering more with less—fewer words, less exposition, less explanation—has been the biggest part of my particular evolution. And this new version of *Power in the Blood* reflects that. Whatever else it is, it's cleaner, leaner prose, and closer to my authentic style, my true voice.

I hope you enjoy this version of *Power in the Blood*, that it serves as a good introduction to John Jordan. And, most importantly of all, I hope you see in it the seeds of what the series will become and want to journey with John throughout the entirety of the books featuring him, however many books that ultimately turns out to be.

Michael Lister

January 2017

VISIT WWW.MICHAELLISTER.COM

CPSIA information can be obtained
at www.ICGtesting.com
Printed in the USA
BVHW031005200420
577957BV00006B/47/J

9 781947 606555